Praise for

LEGACY OF THE GRAY GHOST

"To totally enjoy this delightful novel it pays: First, to know your history of the Civil War; Second, to know your football and enjoy author Gerry Zimmerman's detailed play by play summaries as he brings Coach Willie Hairston's Raiders through an exciting season; and Third, to appreciate university life in the gentlemanly late 1950's in beautiful Virginia. I really recommend this book to the reader who loves good fiction."

- Bill Baker
Former President of the Motion Picture Association
Former Assistant Director & Chief Spokesperson of the F.B.I.
Former Director of Public Affairs, C.I.A.

"Being a Virginia native, and an avid horseman, who lives in the area where *Legacy* takes place, I am very familiar with the legendary Gray Ghost. I always love rehearing the tales of his exploits. I also found myself laughing and cheering for the Mosby football team and it's coach, Willie Hairston, as they faced many obstacles to their success. As a criminal attorney who often represents the underdog seeking justice, I could relate to the team's satisfaction of achievement from hard work and determination. This is a must read for those who refuse to surrender."

- Blair D. Howard
Attorney at Law, Warrenton, VA
Virginia's famous and highly regarded trial attorney who has handled numerous high profile cases over the last 40 years

"Deep in enemy territory with no easy way to escape is just how a lot of people like it. *Legacy of the Gray Ghost* tells the story of John Mosby and his band of raiders who dared to go deep into Union territory... A fun and exciting read of adventure... Legacy of the Gray Ghost is a CHOICE PICK."

- The Midwest Book Review

LEGACY OF THE GRAY GHOST was awarded:

The GOLD MEDAL WINNER as BEST SOUTHERN FICTION BOOK of 2011

Legacy of the Gray Ghost is Historical Fiction. A rather large prologue tells the true story of the legendary John Mosby, leader of a band of Confederate cavalrymen on daring raids deep behind Union lines during the Civil War. His fame came from his ability to strike quickly and then seemingly disappear, earning him the name of the Gray Ghost.

The book turns to the story of how one of Mosby's Raiders, at the end of the Civil War, goes on to found a family that becomes very successful and then establishes Mosby University in Virginia in 1908 in honor of the old Gray Ghost.

Much of the story takes place in 1958, the 50th anniversary of Mosby University's founding, and features the very funny behavior of the students and the football team, which had been floundering and was on the verge of being canceled.

Readers of historical fiction, humor and football will enjoy reading this story and will cheer the Mosby Raider football team during the historic 1958 season.

As a lover of history, I was pleased to read the opening of this story. I was then pleasantly surprised when the story turned to more modern days with an excellent look at university life in the 50's. The setting for the story is quite memorable; the characterization is first rate and the dialog spot on. I particularly appreciated the humor as I read through the exploits of the football team. The author managed to capture the essence of college life in the middle of the century. Well done.

READER'S FAVORITE.COM

. . . .

LEGACY OF THE GRAY GHOST was also named as the BEST HISTORICAL FICTION BOOK of 2011 by www.BooksandAuthors.net

THE SPECTER OF RACISM REARS ITS UGLY HEAD WHEN

Mosby's Raiders Return

GERRY A. ZIMMERMAN

Mosby's Raiders Return
©2013 Gerry A. Zimmerman
All rights reserved. No part of this book may be reproduced, stored in or introduced into a retrieval system, or transmitted, in any form, or by any means (electronic, mechanical, photocopying, recording or otherwise), without the prior written permission of the copyright owner, except in the case of brief quotations embodied in critical articles or reviews.

Disclaimer:
The facts surrounding the actions and life of Colonel John S. Mosby in the prologue of this book are a part of the history of America. These facts set the stage for the work of fiction that follows it and were the inspiration for the author's creation of the fictional Mosby University. Many of the places named in the book are actual places, but the rest of the names, characters, institutions, places, and incidents are the product of the author's imagination or are used fictitiously. The only exception to the use of fictional names in the book is that of the artist JR Eason and Dr. Homer Rice and some additional references contained in the notes at the end of the book.

Any other resemblance to actual events, places, persons, living or dead is entirely coincidental and has no basis in reality.

Address All Inquiries to:
La Casa Z Publishing Group
39081 N. 102nd Way
Scottsdale, AZ 85262
lacasaz@cox.net
www.GerryAZimmerman.com

Zimmerman, Gerry A.
Mosby's Raiders Return / Gerry A. Zimmerman. — 1st ed.
p. cm.   Includes bibliographical references.

ISBN-13: 978-1-62620-481-2

Published by
La Casa Z Publishing Group
Scottsdale, Arizona USA

Editor: Barbara Crane
Cover Design: Dream Graffx, www.dreamgraffx.com
Interior Layout: Fusion Creative Works, www.fusioncw.com
Printing Services: Country Press of Lakeville, MA
For additional copies, visit: www.gerryazimmerman.com

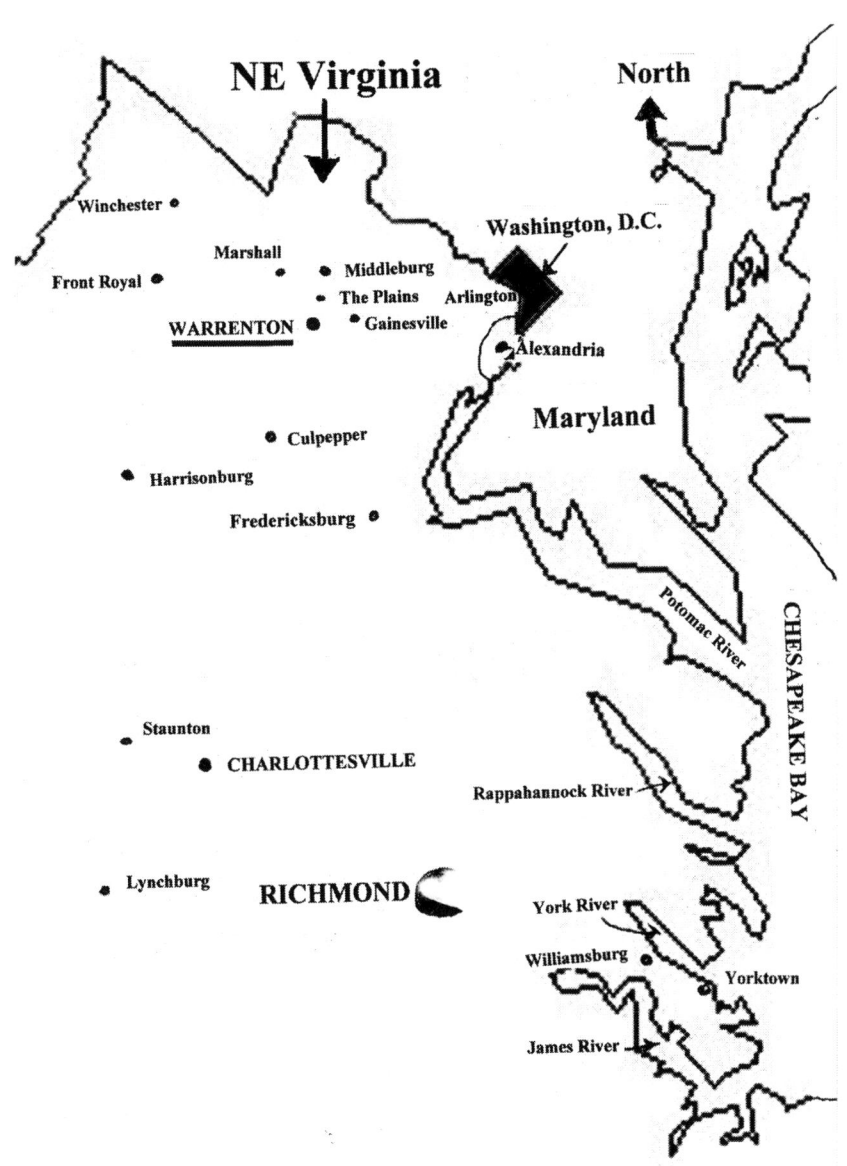

Colonel John Singleton Mosby
The Gray Ghost

IN MEMORY OF

Fred Carey

Fred was a good man, and much more than just a "Houseboy" to the Beta brothers of Sigma Nu at the University of Virginia. His dedication, loyalty, kindness, and tireless service was truly appreciated by all of the many generations of fine young men who had the privilege of knowing him.

PRAISE FOR

Mosby's Raiders Return

Another winner for Gerry Zimmerman. What a great story! Old familiar characters and new exciting ones keep the reader waiting to see what happens next. This is not your typical football story, but a story of life, the beginning of a new age in sports and education. The writer has captured life on an all-male university as it should have been, funny and entertaining. Very nicely done.

Rating 5.0 stars   READERS' FAVORITE

Acknowledgments

I'm most appreciative of the advice offered by my friend Fritz Stobl MD. This brilliant Neurologist is also a successful author who has now written three books. He encouraged me to continue my writing and to proceed with my ideas for a sequel to my original work, **Legacy of the Gray Ghost.** Fritz pointed out that, there are many well-known and successful authors, who weren't really discovered or recognized until after they had written multiple books.

Special thanks to the amazing creative talents and vision of Amanda Graff of Dream Graffx. She did a superb job of capturing the essence of **Mosby's Raiders Return** in her design of the book's front and back covers. This was the second time we worked together, and after being very pleased with the fine work she did on the book design for **Legacy of the Gray Ghost**, there was no question that I wanted to retain her superb services again. Amanda truly makes words and images become reality.

Marcus Esmay created my original website, and after this book was written, John Hogie did a great job of expanding the website to include information about this book.

Barbara Crane served as my editor. She offered many helpful suggestions on how to make the final product more readable,and minus the various grammatical errors that I had made. She also offered many positive suggestions which were incorporated into the manuscript.

Michael Dowell of ISBN Agency.Com and MooDoo Productions provided valuable assistance by expediting the acquisition of the ISBN number from the Library of Congress.

Shiloh Schroeder of Fusion Creative Works was responsible for formatting the manuscript into book form prior to printing and getting the manuscript ready for printing.

Mike Pinto and Dave Brooks at the Country Press have always done a first class job on printing jobs and are great to work with. They do quality work and stand behind it. They are the best.

I would be remiss if I didn't express my appreciation to my long suffering wife, Lucy, for her unending encouragement to me in all things, over the years. Although she might have sometimes wondered if my authorship efforts were worth the investment of my time and energies, she stood behind my decision to proceed. That wasn't really surprising since she has always supported whatever ventures I have undertaken, and I am forever in her debt.

Finally, I am grateful, that I had the honor of attending and graduating from Mr. Jefferson's University of Virginia. The exposure to the principles, that this great man espoused, was one of the greatest privileges that any young man could ever hope to experience.

Foreword

The book you are about to read takes place in Virginia in 1959. It's in the middle of the Civil Rights Movement, and a time when people used different language than they do today. The words "black" or "African American" hadn't entered the vocabulary of either blacks or whites. The issue of the day was desegregation, not diversity. To be accurate in terms of the period, I've had to use the word "colored" when referring to blacks, occasionally using "Negro" when the subject is a college or when the omniscient narrator is "speaking." I personally feel that the use of the word "colored" is objectionable, and "Negro" is a term that many others may think is outdated. Please be advised that I have used these words for accuracy, and not because I endorse the use of them.

You may be interested in the reason why I wrote this book. It's the second of two books set at a fictional college in Virginia—Mosby University—in 1959. The hero is Willie Hairston, a black man and the head football coach at Mosby, who guides his team to a championship season in the first book, ***Legacy of the Gray Ghost.***

I wrote these books, because I grew up in the D.C. and Northern Virginia area during a time when segregation was a way of life in America. It has always stuck in my craw that black athletes didn't get the respect they deserved—from white players and white coaches, but particularly from white sports writers who represented established and otherwise respectable newspapers. I well remember when Elgin Baylor—the great Hall of Fame basketball star—started his playing career in Washington, D.C. at Spingarn High School. Sportswriters in D.C. minimized his amazing ability, saying that he was *only* playing against others of his race. In doing so, they implied that the black teams were not as skilled as white players. History would ultimately prove these sportswriters wrong.

The two books I've written are fictional. They represent how I wish it had been, not exactly how it was. The "colored" young men of my day didn't become football players or coaches in Southern universities until a few years later. But it did happen, after blood had been shed in the Civil Rights Movement, and after southern football coaches realized they had to use black players to compete against the West, the Big Ten, and the Northeast. To these outstanding athletes, I offer my appreciation and the desire that all humans should be judged by the quality of their character as an individual and not the color of their skin.

Prologue

Virginia's legendary Confederate cavalryman **Colonel John Mosby,** also known as the **Gray Ghost,** led his band of mounted raiders and fearlessly penetrated deep behind Union lines. His legacy became the inspiration for the founding of Mosby University in the beautiful Northern Virginia horse country.

Although he had spoken out against slavery and succession prior to the Civil War, **John Singleton Mosby,** a native Virginian, enlisted in the Confederate Virginia Volunteers as a private once hostilities began. He fought in the First Battle of Manassas and served under General J.E. B. Stuart, who was impressed by Mosby's innate ability to gather intelligence by using disguises and penetrate the Union lines. This led to his receiving a number of rapid promotions. He eventually rose to the rank of Colonel.

In 1863, General Stuart, with General Robert E. Lee's approval, gave Mosby the command of a new regimental size unit of mounted soldiers called the 43rd Battalion, Virginia Calvary, Partisan Rangers. Mosby and his men soon became famous for their guerilla-like quick strikes and equally fast, daring escapes from deep behind Union lines. These actions wreaked havoc on the Union's supply lines and communications. Out of frustration, Union commanders had to deploy large numbers of troops to prevent future attacks. The stealth, precision, and the success of his raids were almost like those enjoyed by U.S. Navy S.E.A.L.S in the present day age. Mosby and his men would strike quickly and then, like unearthly spirits, be able to seemingly vanish into thin air. This ability led to his acquiring the nickname of the **GRAY GHOST**. Mosby became famous all over the country, since the news of his amazing exploits was even reported by the northern press in cities as far away as Boston.

In the spring of 1865, when it became apparent that the Confederate cause was doomed to failure, General Robert E. Lee made the decision to surrender his Army of Northern Virginia. A select band of Mosby's most trusted raiders were designated to become the carriers of the surrender orders and documents to Appomattox Court House, Virginia. General Lee's subsequent surrender on April 9, 1965, for all intents and purposes, ended the Civil War. Colonel Mosby then disbanded his troops but, finding it hard to accept defeat, he never offered up his personal surrender.

Oddly enough, following the war, Mosby later developed a close personal relationship with General Grant. In a strange twist of fate, he became his campaign manager in Virginia when Grant ran for president. Mosby worked as a lawyer for many years, both in private practice, and later as an Assistant Attorney General. He died on May 16th, 1916 and was buried in his beloved Virginia at Warrenton, in the heart of the beautiful horse country from which he launched many of his raids. His grave site is at the historic Brentmore Estate, where Mosby actually lived from 1975 to 1877. To this day, Mosby, the *Gray Ghost*, remains a legend to many residents in the lovely equestrian area in and around Warrenton and Fauquier County as well as in neighboring Loudon County and its town of Middleburg.

MOSBY'S RAIDERS RETURN is the sequel of the author's highly acclaimed novel, ***LEGACY of the GRAY GHOST.*** The book was named as the Gold Medal Winner of the Best Southern Novel in America in 2011 by ReadersFavorite.com and also selected as the Best Historical Fiction Book in 2011 by the highly respected BooksandAuthors.net.

Readers of that novel will recall that, at the conclusion of the Civil War, one of Mosby's young raiders, Robert Hamilton Howard Jr., who brought the surrender documents to Appomattox, went off to college to study engineering at the University of Virginia. Following his graduation, he later became a successful inventor and businessman, making him one of the wealthiest men in America. In 1908, he established a fine men's university named after the old Gray Ghost in Warrenton, Virginia. He was assisted in that task by his son Robert Hamilton Howard III, who became Mosby University's first president. The president's son, Robert Hamilton Howard IV, who preferred to be called Bob, had been the first member of their family to graduate from Mosby University. Bob had gone on to great success on Wall Street. Later he returned to Virginia and became president of the school when his father retired in 1944.

LEGACY of the GRAY GHOST tells the story of all the events leading up to 1958, the 50th anniversary year of the school's founding. It explains how their struggling football program, which was handicapped by a lack of athletic scholarships, was on the verge of being cancelled. Then, following the illness of the team's old coach, Willie Hairston, persuaded the Board to let him try to save the program. Mr. Hairston, the only colored student at the school, was a retired professional football player. Although he had never coached, he knew a lot about the game. The book also described the lifestyles and events in the beautiful horse country: fox hunting, polo playing, and steeple chase racing. Also featured is university life in the late 1950's in Virginia and the antics of the students. **LEGACY of the GRAY GHOST** centered around the events that occurred during that 50th anniversary season, which came to a conclusion when the undermanned Mosby Raider team went up against the powerful, unbeaten Oakmont University team, led by their irascible coach, Irv Swindle. When the Mosby Raider team, in a surprising upset, captured the prestigious Piedmont Pinnacle Trophy, the stage was set for ***MOSBY'S RAIDERS RETURN*** and the saga of how the team would attempt to overcome graduation losses and injuries in an effort to repeat its success the next season.

1

The prestigious academic institution for men known as Mosby University was located in the picturesque town of Warrenton in the heart of the beautiful Northern Virginia horse country, about sixty miles southwest of Washington, D.C. It was founded in 1908 by Robert Hamilton Howard, Jr., a wealthy former scientist and engineering entrepreneur, who had been one of Colonel John Mosby's Raiders during the Civil War. He was assisted in that task by his son Robbie (Robert Hamilton Howard III), who had enjoyed a very successful career on Wall Street and, like his father, had graduated from the University of Virginia.

Mosby University was designed by the nation's top architects and landscape designers, and the construction of the campus began in 1905. When it was completed three years later, it was not only beautiful, it was spectacular and featured rolling expanses of grass that were bordered by majestic trees and gardens. The campus was referred to as the *Estate,* since the land upon which it was located had once been the estate of one of the area's pioneering families. The buildings at the *Estate* were all of brick construction in the classic Georgian style, and the gardens behind them were separated by the same kind of curving brick serpentine walls that both Howards had admired at the

University of Virginia. In addition, formal gardens that featured boxwoods and fountains and flowerbeds filled with seasonal blooms were scattered around the *Estate.*

The three main classroom buildings were named after the three leading generals that former Raider Robert Hamilton Howard, Jr. had known as a young cavalryman during the Civil War; Robert E. Lee, J.E.B. Stuart and Stonewall Jackson. The Robert E. Lee Hall was the largest of the three and was located at the end of a spacious lawn common area. The J.E.B. Stuart Hall and the Stonewall Jackson Hall flanked the Robert E. Lee Hall and faced each other. Mosby Manor, the school's administrative offices, was located at the other end of the commons area. The school curriculum featured studies in liberal arts, science, engineering, and business. President Howard had wanted to expand the curriculum and previously announced plans to expand into law, architecture, and medicine in the future.

The first Board of Visitors was comprised of Robert H. Howard, Jr., the governor of Virginia at that time, and the legendary Gray Ghost, John Mosby. Mosby had retired from practicing law in the area and was 75 years old in 1908.

The first president of the school was Robert H. Howard III. In 1922, his son, Robert H. Howard IV became the first member of the family to graduate from the school with a degree in commerce. He followed his father's footsteps and went on to a successful career on Wall Street. His fortuitous advice, just prior to the stock market crash in 1929, had saved both the school, and the family fortune from financial ruin. When Robert H. Howard III retired at age 70 in 1944, his son returned to Warrenton and became the president of Mosby University.

Bob Howard, as Robert H. Howard IV preferred to be called, did an outstanding job in that role. The enrollment at the prestigious academic institution grew to about 3,000 students by the fall of 1958, when Mosby University celebrated its 50th anniversary. There had been a lot of excitement at Mosby University that year due to the success of its football team. Prior to its capturing the Piedmont Pinnacle Trophy, the program had been failing and was on the verge of being terminated. The anniversary celebration also featured the unveiling of a beautiful bronze statue of John Mosby on horseback.

Following the birth of young Robert William Hairston on June 29, 1959 at Warrenton General Hospital, it didn't take long, for new papa Willie, Mosby University's football coach, to realize his life had changed dramatically. The excitement that he and his family experienced as a result of his becoming the first Negro graduate of the highly respected Mosby University paled in comparison to the excitement surrounding the birth of their son. Now that he and his wife Sally had a child, Willie's whole world seemed very different. For one thing, sound sleep became a thing of the past. A small howl would frequently interrupt his formerly peaceful dreams when little Bobby would loudly demand that his diaper be changed or that he be fed. Sally carried the bulk of the load of taking care of things, but he did his best to help out and be a good husband and proud new father.

Given a nice bonus in appreciation for the coaching job he had done the previous football season, Willie was ready to buy a home for his family in the town of Warrenton. That town was home to Mosby University and Sally and Willie had been living in a small three bedroom house that they had been renting in nearby Gainesville, Virginia. However, now that he had some cash and a new five year coaching contract, owning a home seemed like the smart thing for them to do. Willie put in a call to Mosby University President Bob Howard's office right after Sally had come home from the hospital with their new child. President Howard was a nice, down to earth man. Anyone meeting him for the first time would have never guessed that he had been a successful Wall Street investor prior to becoming the president at Mosby. He had also been the owner of the pro football team that Willie once played for. Following Willie's retirement from football, Bob Howard had made it possible for Willie to go to Mosby, finish his schooling, and become Mosby's first Negro graduate. Another fact that not many people knew was that Bob Howard was the heir to one of the greatest fortunes in America. Willie was happy when president Howard's secretary put him right through.

"It's nice to hear from you Willie. How are Sally and your new son doing?"

Willie smiled and replied, "They are doing great, and I'm real glad that they are now home from the hospital. Speaking of a home, that's the reason I called you today. Rather than stay in that little house we've been renting down in Gainesville, I was thinking that maybe we ought to consider buying a home in Warrenton and wanted to ask your advice to see if you felt that might be a smart thing to do?"

"Willie, that sure makes a lot of sense to me. Your desire to put down some roots here in Warrenton makes me very happy as well. I know a good real estate agent and I will have him get in touch with you right away if that's okay?"

Willie replied, "Thanks Mr. Howard, but I wondered if you thought Sally and me being colored might be a problem in finding a place to buy in Warrenton. We have been going to church at the Second Baptist Church there, which I understand, has been around for over a hundred years. We have met a lot of nice people there in the Negro community, but I don't know how many of them own their homes or just rent houses or live in apartments."

"Willie, I can guarantee that won't be a problem, so don't worry about it. Warrenton may be a southern town, but most of the people here are very accepting of all their neighbors here, no matter what their race or religion might be, "Bob Howard said.

Concerns about how they might be accepted by any of their potential new neighbors in Warrenton quickly disappeared after they met their real estate agent, Bill Farnham. He allayed any fears they might have had, saying "Willie, the great coaching job you did at Mosby last year has made you a hero around these parts. Warrenton may seem like kind of conservative town to you and have a predominately white population, but you and your family would be more than welcomed by nearly everyone here. The Negro community here is very much a part of the town. The church you told me that you already attend is an important focal point for the people here and is well respected. Bob Howard told me of your concerns, but trust me, you've got nothing to worry about. Everyone around here loves and respects you."

After looking at several places, they soon found a beautiful four bedroom place in Warrenton. It had a den and a lovely recreation room and was located on a tree lined street in a nice neighborhood only a mile from the university. They submitted an offer and were delighted when it was accepted. Willie and Sally were also excited that they were able to close around the first of August, after Bob Howard made a call to Troy Barksdale II. He was the president of the big Tidewater National Bank in Richmond and was also a Mosby alumnus. President Howard persuaded him to give the Hairstons, a quick and favorable deal. Little did Willie and Sally know that getting a mortgage loan wasn't as easy as it turned out to be.

When President Howard called Mr. Barksdale, the initial response had been negative. Barksdale said, "Bob, I'm sorry, but I have to tell you that Tidewater National doesn't make mortgage loans to coloreds. We just don't feel they are good risks." Bob Howard replied, "I can understand how you feel Troy, but Coach Hairston and his wife are not run of the mill applicants. They are both college graduates, and he was the first colored graduate of our alma mater. He has an excellent five year contract which will give him more than an adequate amount of monthly income to be able to make his payments. He is also willing to put twenty percent down on the purchase. The bank has very little risk in this transaction.

Giving Barksdale no chance to argue, Bob Howard continued, "Since you are a graduate of Mosby University yourself, I assume you are interested in seeing that our football program continues to be successful? If Willie can't get a loan, he might just consider resigning and going to another school. Based upon the success he enjoyed last year,

I bet there would be a lot of schools who would love to have him as their coach. Think about the bad publicity and ill will that would be generated if he was denied a loan and went elsewhere. Imagine what would happen if he informed our local paper, *The Fauquier Times-Democrat,* that your bank didn't think he was good enough to qualify for a loan? There might be a backlash against the bank in the community. I don't know if you know it or not, but he has become quite a hero around here."

Troy Barksdale said, "I never thought about those possibilities. I'll tell you what, Bob. As a personal favor to you, I will see to it that Coach Hairston gets that loan, but it's going to be a hard sell to our board."

"I really appreciate that Troy, and if any member of your board wants to talk to me about the loan or Willie's character, just have them give me a call," said a smiling Bob Howard as he hung up the phone.

For Willie and Sally, 1959 had been a great year so far, highlighted by Willie getting a five year coaching contract, Willie's graduation from Mosby University, the birth of young Bobby, and now being able to buy a home. However, Willie knew that the upcoming 1959 football season would be there before he knew it, and he feared that it would be very hard to duplicate the success he and the team had enjoyed the previous year.

On August 3rd, Willie was ready to move his family into their new home. His assistant coaches from the previous season, Jack Johnson, Bobby Freeman and Rod Horne, were kind enough to help Willie make the move. His two new assistant coaches, Ray Crocker and Dan Benson, whom Willie had hired away from Oakmont University, showed up to help as well. It didn't take the gang very long to load up everything from the rental place into a U-Haul. After driving the short distance from Gainesville to Willie's new home in Warrenton, it also didn't take them long to get everything unloaded. Of course, having a case of beer on hand and some sandwiches that Sally that had prepared made it more like a fun get together than work. After he got moved in, Willie began focusing his thoughts and energies on his job. He was excited about the pending arrival of the players and practices which were scheduled to begin on August 17th.

As the men were sitting around relaxing and enjoying some beers after finishing the move, Jack Johnson spoke up. He said, "We are going to be hard pressed to make up for the loss of Hank Warwick this season. He was the anchor in our defensive line last year. Let's hope some new talent shows up to try and fill that void now that he has graduated."

Willie replied, "Hank did a great job for us, and you're right. I'm really grateful that Al Nelson is coming back at quarterback, but since Laurence Williams, our backup quarterback last year, has also graduated, we will be pretty thin at that position. However, we still have George Maizley, who played fullback and was our backup disaster quarterback last year. He may have to spend more time working on his throwing this year, unless we find someone else."

Rod Horne then spoke up. "Willie, you mentioned that President Howard had promised to consider admitting some qualified young men of color. Your graduation this past June really paved the way for the possibility of desegregation at Mosby University. Do you think we might get some young colored students to transfer here and help us out? Freshmen aren't eligible to play, so they would have to at least be sophomores. However, if they played elsewhere last season, we all know that they would have to sit out a year."

Willie replied, "I guess we will find out soon enough won't we? Our biggest problem here at Mosby is not being able to give out athletic scholarships, and then trying to compete against bigger schools like Oakmont, who give out a ton of them each year."

Ray Crocker and Dan Benson laughed. Ray said, "Considering the fact that you smashed Oakmont last year, I don't think you should worry about trying to compete."

Willie smiled and said, "I'm not sure whether Oakmont's Head Coach Irv Swindle is madder about losing that game or losing you and Dan to us. In any event, you can bet he will be gunning for us this season."

Dan spoke up, "Speaking of Oakmont, there was a colored starting sophomore basketball player there last season named Reggie King. He was a three sport star in high school, not only in basketball, but also in track, where he had the top time in the 440 yard dash in Pennsylvania as a junior. In football, he was an outstanding player, and he excelled on the gridiron as well. He was a star defensive cornerback and was also the starting quarterback at his Pittsburgh high school his senior year. He was looking like an All-Stater until he pulled his hamstring midway through the season and missed the rest of the games. Swindle told me to forget about him. Reggie recovered in time to be a star in basketball, make All State, and then get a basketball scholarship to Oakmont. I saw him play some basketball games last season as a sophomore starter, and he was a fantastic point guard and ball handler. He was very fast, and had an uncanny ability to find the open man and pass the ball to him for an open shot. I was astounded when he got benched toward the end of the season, since he was clearly one of the best players on the team.

Willie replied, "If he is still an Oakmont basketball player now, why are you telling me about him?"

Dan went on, "I knew him because I considered recruiting him for the Oakmont football team. I thought he was a nice kid, but after he got in Swindle's dog house last season, he confided to me that he might leave school. He also wished me good luck when he heard I was heading here to Mosby. He told me that he had heard that Mosby University was a good school. I told him it was indeed a fine school, and if he ever wanted to leave Oakmont, he ought to consider going to Mosby. However, I informed him that Mosby University didn't give out athletic scholarships, but did award academic ones. Also, I let him know that he would have to sit out a year to be eligible to play on the basketball team here, but if his grades were good enough he might qualify for an academic scholarship."

Willie asked, "How in the world did he get in Swindle's dog house being a basketball player?

Benson went on to say, "Swindle is not only the Head Football Coach, he's also the Athletic Director at Oakmont. His brother's son was the center on the university's basketball team. Swindle was pressuring the coach and this King kid, who was the main ball handler, to feed the ball to his nephew more often. Swindle threatened to revoke his scholarship if he didn't do it. He finally pressured the coach to bench Reggie and put in a less skilled player who would slow things down and try to get the ball to his nephew. I think Reggie was pretty frustrated. He was even thinking about quitting after Swindle threatened to take his scholarship away, in spite of his outstanding season."

Willie then said, "That sure sounds like Swindle. Did you ever find out what happened to him?"

"No," said Dan, "but I heard the kid made good grades and was a solid citizen. I bet the basketball coach there would hate to lose him because of Swindle, but he couldn't complain too much because Swindle was his boss."

Willie thought about what Dan had said. "You said he was quite an athlete in high school. I think we ought to try and find out if he did leave Oakmont and check with our admissions director to see if he applied to Mosby. He sounds like the kind of young man who might be able to help us out, if not in football, maybe on our basketball team after sitting out a year."

It had been a long day and a lot of work. The men finally decided that it was time to leave and let Willie and Sally get settled into their new home. Willie thanked all of them and reminded them that practice for the new season would begin on Monday August 17th.

2

The next morning, Willie and Sally were enjoying their first breakfast in their new home. Sally said, "That was nice of your assistant coaches to help us get moved. I hope they know how much we appreciate what they did. I bet all of you were worn out afterwards. How did you sleep last night, honey?"

Willie replied, "I flipped and flopped all night long, but it wasn't just because little Bobby cried any more than usual. I have a lot of things on my mind now that the new season will be here before we know it. Since the school and President Howard had enough confidence in me to give me a five year contract, I want to show everyone that they didn't make a mistake. However, I know it's going to be tough to do since we have lost some key players to graduation."

Sally smiled and said, "Willie, when you took over last year, you didn't know anything about any of the players, but you took the ones you had and did a great job of coaching them. I know my man can do it again. I'm not worried and you shouldn't be worried either." Then she went over and kissed him. The worried look on his face magically disappeared.

After breakfast, Willie went into little Bobby's room and looked at his beautiful young son sleeping peacefully in his crib. He reflected on how blessed he had been in his life, and it caused him to offer up a silent prayer of thanks. Then he went into his new den and put in a call to Frances Bidwell, the Director of Admissions at Mosby University.

When Frances picked up her phone, Willie said, "Good morning Mrs. Bidwell. This is Willie Hairston, the football coach here at Mosby."

She laughed as she replied, "Good morning to you too Willie. Like all of us here, I know who you are and please call me Frances."

Willie chuckled and said, "I look forward to meeting you in person Frances. The reason I'm calling you today is that I need your help."

"What can I do for you today?" Frances said.

Willie replied, "You are probably well aware that President Howard was a guest speaker at the N.A.A.C.P. annual convention in June this year. He told the attendees of the decision by many quality colleges to increase the opportunities for Negro students to attend many of the nation's finest colleges and universities. He went on to tell them that, Mosby University had just seen its first Negro student graduate this past year." He laughed and said, "I bet you know who that was. President Howard went on to say that he hoped to enable other qualified men of color would have the chance to come to the school. In his closing remarks, he told all the attendees to encourage bright and outstanding young men in their community to apply. I was wondering how that turned out?"

"Willie, I am well aware of that announcement by President Howard, and I can tell you that, as a result, we have received about 500 applications for admissions. Some came from graduating colored high school seniors as well as a number of students who would like to transfer from traditional Negro colleges to Mosby. Unfortunately, many of them didn't have the academic records that would meet our strict admission standards. However, about a hundred of them appear to be qualified and about twenty five of those may be offered academic scholarships." Frances replied.

Willie said, "That's great news, Frances. I was wondering if you might check out a student's name for me today and see if he has applied."

"I'd be happy to do that, Willie."

Willie went on, "The person I was looking for would be a possible transfer student by the name of Reggie, or maybe Reginald King. Has he applied?"

Frances told him it might take a few minutes before she ended the call. About ten minutes later she called back. "No, I'm sorry Willie. There's no one by that name on my list." Willie thanked her and then asked for one more favor.

"Could you advise any and all transfers that, while we don't give out athletic scholarships, if they are interested in trying out for any of our teams, they should do so? Also, let them know that if their grades are good enough, they might qualify for an academic scholarship at some point in time."

"Sure Willie, that would be no problem," said Frances.

After hanging up the phone, Willie came up with another idea, and called his assistant coach, Dan Benson. Willie told him about his conversation with Frances at the Admissions Office. He then said, "Dan, I know school is out now, but I was wondering if you might have any idea how to find out what that young man named Reggie King is planning to do this fall? If you learn that he is staying at Oakmont, just wish him the best. We don't want to give Swindle any cause to charge us with tampering and file a complaint with the NCAA."

Dan thought about it for a second and then said, "I know that he went to a tough inner city school in Pittsburgh called the 5th Avenue High School. When I was coaching at Oakmont, I had several occasions to call on their football coach there, since I handled the recruiting in the Pittsburgh area. He was a good guy and I got to know the coach there pretty well. I already told you that I looked at Reggie. The following year, I recruited one of his players named Horsie Dann, who was an outstanding running back and linebacker. Dann had a fabulous freshman year for Oakmont last season and is a sure fire starter as a sophomore this year. I would bet the coach there could tell me how to get in touch with Reggie."

Willie said, "Get on it Dan and let me know what you find out."

Dan called back about an hour later. "I just spoke to Coach Joe Hightower in Pittsburgh and told him I was now at Mosby University, he said. I asked him to keep an eye out for any scholar athletes that we might have a future interest in talking to. He told me that he would be happy to do that and wished me good luck. I also asked him if he knew how I could get in touch with Reggie King. He said, "No problem. I have his number around here somewhere. I also see him and him mama almost every Sunday at church so I know he's around. Let me find that number for you. Hold on for a minute, okay?"

Dan then said, "He gave me Reggie's telephone number. I tried to call, but no one answered."

"Great job Dan, keep trying and call me if you finally get in touch. Find out what he's planning to do this fall." Willie hung up and then wondered if he might be getting too excited about a kid who wasn't even playing football anymore. He had a lot more positions to worry about filling, and he really needed to concentrate on taking care of business. August 17th wasn't too far away and he knew that he had a lot of work to do to be ready. He got out his list of last year's roster and went over it to figure out who would be returning. He also noted who would no longer be available, because they had graduated.

On offense, Willie was very pleased that, Al Nelson, his star quarterback, would be returning for his senior year. After getting fitted for contact lenses the previous fall by Dr. Chattman, the Chief Ophthalmologist at Warrenton General Hospital, Al's accuracy improved dramatically. He went on to have an outstanding season. One of Willie's main concerns for the team was a lack of depth at that position. Laurence Williams, who was a very capable back up at quarterback, and a starting safety on defense, wouldn't be returning since he had graduated. As for running backs, the fact that fast Eddie "Ironhead" Ferrous, and hard running Fred Lammhandler would be returning was good news, but losing speedy Butch DeRose to graduation meant they were pretty thin at that position.

Fortunately, both Johnny Baugh and George Maizley were both returning at fullback. Maizley had also been the back-up disaster quarterback, but Willie really preferred to him to play fullback. That meant he needed to find someone else be the main quarterback reserve behind Al Nelson.

As for the team's receivers, losing star tight end Robbie Gunderson to graduation was another real blow to the team. Gunderson had also starred at defensive end, so that made the pain of not having him back even greater. Fortunately, big Parker Boardman would be back at tight end on offense. He might even be able to play defensive end if needed, and he figured to be an impact player. The best news for Willie was that all three of his top receivers would be returning: seniors Ronnie Wall and Garrett Gassman, and last year's sophomore sensation deep threat, Kenny Lynx, would be coming back for his junior year.

The offensive line would not have Frank Fanelli and Jim "The Bear" Duke out there playing guard, since Fanelli graduated, and Duke had flunked out academically. However, offensive guards Jack Delaney and Charlie "Radar" Giordano, who both had strong performances last season, would be coming back for their senior years. The team's starting center, big Dan Kojak, who missed his sophomore year due to a preseason injury, had one more year of eligibility and would be returning and graduating at the end of the first semester. Also, both of last year's big starting tackles, CC "Rider" Snyder and Henry Frumzeist, would be returning, so the offensive line should be one of the team's strengths during the upcoming season. Hopefully, they could find some quality backups to give the team some much needed depth.

The biggest loss on Defense was the graduation of star defensive tackle and team captain, Hank Warwick. Ashton Fincie, although a little light at the position, was quick and tough and did a great job playing the other defensive tackle position. He would be returning, but finding a replacement for Warwick was going to be difficult. Luckily both Billy Vorache and Baldwin Tucker would be coming back to play defensive end positions while Mac Gordon and Garrett Gassman, who also played receiver on offense, would be out there on defense at outside linebacker. As for the other linebacker position, George Maizley and Fred Lammhandler could rotate and handle the middle linebacker position.

Speedy Kenny Lynx had been an outstanding sophomore find last season both as a receiver and a cornerback. He would be returning, but losing Butch DeRose to graduation would mean that Willie would have to find another good cornerback. As for the safety positions, only Johnny Baugh would be coming back. Since Laurence Williams and Mac Goodrich had graduated, depth at safety was going to be another major concern for Willie. The lack of depth and experience in the Raiders' defensive backfield might encourage most teams they played to pass the ball frequently, until the team proved they could stop them.

Willie knew that the Mosby Raider special teams should be in good shape, even though kicker Ted "The Toe" Thompson had graduated. Little Manny Morales, who was from Argentina, had kicked off and tried long field goals. He had proved that he was a quality kicker last year. The team's outstanding punter, Dick "Cadillac" deVille was only a junior and would be returning.

Despite the number of quality returning players, Willie knew that the team's depth was very thin. He hoped that some new players would show up, and he could fill the obvious voids. Not being able to offer scholarships and trying to compete with powerhouse teams like the Oakmont Outlaws would always be a challenge, so the Raiders had to be quicker and smarter to survive. Colonel Mosby was always quicker and smarter than his opponents, so why shouldn't the team from a university that bore his name try to emulate his successful techniques?

3

Reggie King returned home to Pittsburgh at the end of the second semester of his sophomore year at Oakmont, wondering what the future would hold for him. His two years at Oakmont had seen him experience a variety of both the good and the bad. He knew now that he would not be going back there, despite having made good grades and starting on their basketball team. His mind wandered back to the events which had brought about his life's change in direction. He even began to wonder if he should have tried harder to comply with what his coach had demanded of him, rather than play the game the way he thought it ought to be played.

The skills that had made him successful on the basketball court, where his speed and lightning fast decisions had enabled him to pass the ball to whoever was open for an open shot or an easy basket, had led to his downfall. Rather than race up and down the court, his coach wanted him to slow it down and work the ball around in a more structured manner. He also wanted him to do his best to get the ball to Sheldon Swindle, Oakmont's lumbering 6'10" center, who also just happened to be the nephew of Oakmont's Athletic Director. Sheldon, had been the leading scorer the year before. His success was mainly due to his size and ability to make a lay in from close in, but the big senior was not very athletic or quick on the court.

Reggie recalled that the big game against the Frostburg Panthers was what had led to his benching. Subsequently, it also caused him to lose his scholarship. Oakmont was down by one point and there were only six seconds left to play. His coach had called a time-out. He told Reggie to bring the ball down court and either take the last shot or find someone open for an easy basket. The ball was thrown to Reggie, and as he raced down court, he beat the man guarding him and drove hard to the basket. Then he made a split second decision. He saw Swindle's man, the opposing center, leave Sheldon open as he moved over to try and block a possible shot by Reggie. Instead, as Reggie went airborne, he flipped the ball behind his back with a no-look pass, to set up an easy basket for his center. Unfortunately, Sheldon, whose reflexes were slow, was unprepared to receive the pass. It hit him in the face and bounced out of bounds as the game ended, and Oakmont lost. The stands erupted in both shock and laughter at Swindle's failure to catch the ball. However, Irv Swindle, the school's Athletic Director, was seated directly behind the Oakmont bench, and he was furious. He began to yell loudly at the coach and Reggie, too, as the game ended.

At the next practice, Reggie's coach informed him that he was no longer a starter, confiding to him that it was his boss's idea. The school's Athletic Director had demanded that Reggie be put on the bench following the embarrassing loss to Frostburg. He told the coach that Reggie's run and gun, "fancy schmancy" style on the court was the reason the team wasn't doing as well as they should. He went on to tell the basketball coach that they ought to be playing a structured, no-nonsense kind of offense, instead of this inner city, hot dog, race up and down the court, playground stuff.

For the few remaining games that season, the coach, who was probably fearful for his own job, refused to put Reggie in the games. Reggie became discouraged, so he didn't come to practice the final week of the season. Then, after the coach told Swindle about Reggie not showing up, Swindle canceled his scholarship. Knowing that he didn't have the money to continue his schooling, Reggie was wondering what the future would hold for him. In spite of the uncertainty, he was able to keep a positive attitude after talking to his mama who reminded him to have the faith that God was in control and had a plan for him.

Reggie had just come home from his summer job as an athletic and guidance counselor at the inner city Y.M.C.A. not far from his 5th Avenue High School in Pittsburgh. Being a local hero around there, he was able to help the kids hone their athletic skills. He also tried to encourage them to be good citizens and not be tempted to get into gangs or into other trouble. Several of them would meet up with him and his mama on Sundays and go to church with them. He was very proud of them when they did that.

Reggie heard the phone ring while he was in the shower. His mother was still at her job, and being her youngest child, there was no one else to pick up the phone since his brothers and sisters had already left the household. He stepped out of the shower, grabbed a towel, and answered it.

The voice on the other end said, "May I speak to Reggie King please?"

Reggie didn't recognize the voice. He asked, "Who's calling?"

"Reggie, this is Dan Benson. I met you a couple a years ago when I was a football coach at Oakmont University and was recruiting in the Pittsburgh area. You and I also had a chance to talk this past spring around the time you decided to quit the basketball team."

"I remember you, coach, and I also recall that you left Oakmont, too," replied Reggie.

"Yes I did," replied Coach Benson. "Frankly, I got tired of Coach Swindle's tirades and the shabby way he treated people. After I had an opportunity to coach at Mosby University and work with a quality head coach, I decided to leave Oakmont and move on."

Reggie laughed, "Now, I bet you can understand why I quit the basketball team. I'm curious, why are you calling me today, coach?"

Dan said, "Good question Reggie, and I want to be up front with you. But first, if you wouldn't mind, could you tell me about your plans for this coming year?"

"Mr. Swindle cancelled my scholarship after I quit the basketball team, so I'm kind of undecided where to go from here, but I was thinking about possibly applying to Tidewater State down in Richmond. However, they told me that I would have to sit out a year to be able to play basketball for them. They can't give me a scholarship this year, but they told me that I could work out with the team and possibly get one next year. Money's a little tight around here now, so I don't think I can afford to do that. I might have to work for a semester and then decide what I want to do."

The coach then said, "Reggie, would you mind telling me what kind of grades you got during your two years at Oakmont?"

Reggie laughed and said, "That was the best part of my experience at Oakmont. I was able to make Dean's List all four semesters; that made my mama very proud."

Coach Benson then said, "Tidewater State might be a good fit for you someday, but as you probably know, it's a small, predominately Negro school, and doesn't have the academic reputation and prestige of a school like Mosby University. Mosby doesn't give out athletic scholarships, but does award academic scholarships to worthy students. Also, the president of Mosby University has made a commitment this year to offer young colored men the opportunity to attend the university. The only colored graduate they have ever had there at Mosby is my boss, the head football coach, Willie Hairston."

Reggie replied, "I know. He's a great coach. I was in the stands last year and saw him on the field when Mosby came to Oakmont and kicked the Outlaw's butts."

Dan Benson laughed and said, "Since I was on the losing sideline, I saw it first-hand. It was an ugly game for the Oakmont Outlaws. Reggie, I have a question for you. If you could get an academic scholarship to Mosby, would you consider coming out for the football team? I know you didn't play football after high school, but I remember that you were a hell of a player prior to your injury back then."

Reggie said, "I have to tell you that I miss playing football, and if I was lucky enough to get any kind of scholarship to Mosby, I would definitely come out. It sounds great, but I think it is probably too late. I'm sure your practices begin pretty soon don't they?

"Yes! We start practice on the 17th of this month, so you might be late, but if I were to get you an application for admission right away, could you fill it out and get it back to me?"

"Yes sir, coach!"

Dan thought for a moment and said "Reggie, I just had an idea. It's about a four-hour drive from Warrenton to Pittsburgh. If you give me your address, I'd be willing to drive up there tomorrow and bring an application to you. How does that sound?"

"Wow, coach that would be great. I get off work at 4PM and will be home soon after."

Dan replied, "I'll try to arrive between 4:30 and 5PM. We will complete the application, and then I would like to take you and your parents to dinner."

"I only have my mom with me at home now, but I'm sure she would love to meet you. I know that she would be excited about my having a chance to continue my education at a fine school like Mosby University. My dad was a Tuskegee Airman back in World War II. He was killed in 1945 while flying his P-51 Mustang fighter plane and escorting some B-17 bombers during a bombing raid over Germany. Everyone in my family still misses him a lot."

Upon hearing what Reggie told him Dan said, "I'm sorry to hear of your loss. I've heard about the legendary all colored Tuskegee Airmen. I understand that they were also known as the Red Tails, because the tails on their planes were distinctively painted red. From what I've heard about them, they were highly decorated and had an outstanding record of service to the country. I know you must be really proud of your dad.

Reggie smiled and said, "I sure am coach, and all of us miss him, but we are a very strong Christian family. We know that he's in a better place now."

Just before he concluded the call, Dan took down the address. Shortly after he hung up, he called Willie Hairston.

"Willie, I wanted to get back to you about that young man, Reggie King that I told you about. I've got some really good news."

"I'm listening. I always like to hear good news," said Willie. Dan then told him about his conversation with Reggie and his plans to go there the next day and return with Reggie's application for admission to Mosby.

Willie said, "Great job, Dan. Your actions have only reaffirmed my decision to hire you this year. From what you tell me about Reggie, he seems like an outstanding young man, and he's apparently an outstanding athlete as well. Go see Frances Bidwell, the Director of Admissions. Get an application for admission and also one for an academic scholarship. Tell her I sent you, and ask her to give me a call to discuss something important.

Willie's phone rang a short time later. "Hi Willie! Frances Bidwell calling! Dan Benson just came by and picked up some applications. He asked me to give you a call. How can I help you?"

"Thanks for calling, Frances," said Willie. "I just heard about an outstanding young man, who has a Dean's List academic record over the past two years at Oakmont University. He may apply to Tidewater State, but he would love to come here if he could qualify for an academic scholarship. Frankly, the reason I am interested in him is that I think he might be able to help my football team. Dan Benson is going to drive up to Pittsburgh and get those applications signed and back to you in a couple of days."

Frances laughed and said, "Willie, you are a real go getter aren't you? But I have to tell you that, if he played football for Oakmont last year, he wouldn't be eligible to play for Mosby this year without a release from them. You and I both know that's not going to happen.

Willie responded and said, "I know, Frances. But he didn't play football for Oakmont last season, he played basketball, and he lost his scholarship for this year."

Frances said, "Well, I'm not sure I understand how a basketball player, who would have to sit out a year before playing on our basketball team would help you."

"I can understand why you might think that," said Willie, "but this young man was a star high school football player as well. He would probably have gotten a football scholarship somewhere after high school if he hadn't suffered an injury during his senior year. Fortunately, that injury healed a long time ago."

"Ah, now I understand. We will review his application when we get it and get back to you."

"Thanks, Frances."

4

Dan Benson came into his office briefly the next morning before hitting the road to make the four hour drive to Pittsburgh. When he was a coach at Oakmont, he had always liked his recruiting trips. They enabled him to get away from the never ending demands of Irv Swindle. Dan stopped and filled up his gas tank in Front Royal before continuing on north to Winchester. He noticed that gas had gone up some since the last time he refilled his tank. At almost 25 cents a gallon, it was getting pretty expensive. He hoped there might be some "gas wars" before long, to bring the price back down to a reasonable amount. His radio station was playing **Forty Miles of Bad Road** by Duane Eddy and his twangy guitar on the way to Winchester. Dan was smiling as he drove along because he really liked the song.

After grabbing a quick sandwich at a drive-in joint with roller skating waitresses in Winchester, he was back on the road heading north to Breezewood, Pennsylvania. From there he headed northwest towards Pittsburgh. Once he arrived, Dan went directly to the Edison Hotel on 9th Street, where he had stayed many times in the past. He checked in, showered up, and after relaxing a little while, headed to Reggie's place on 3rd Ave. around 4:30PM. The apartment building where Reggie and his mother lived was fairly old, but it looked like it had been maintained pretty well in comparison to many of the other places in the neighborhood. Reggie was expecting him and had a smile on his face when he opened the door.

"Hi, coach…good to see you again," said Reggie.

"Good to see you, too, Reggie. Is your mother home?"

"No, coach, she won't get home until about 5:30, but I have to tell you that she was pretty excited about meeting you and hearing about the chance for me to go to Mosby."

"I'm looking forward to meeting her, too, Reggie. I have an idea. I brought an application for admission to Mosby, as well as one for an academic scholarship. Why don't we get started on filling them out so that we can have more time for socializing when your mama gets here and we go out to dinner?"

"That sounds great coach," replied Reggie.

It didn't take long to fill out the papers. Dan could tell that Reggie was excited about the prospects of having an opportunity to go to Mosby. Dan also noticed that Reggie was looking like he had been working out so he said, "Reggie, you look like you have been keeping in shape. What have you been doing this summer?"

Reggie grinned and told him about his job at the nearby Y.M.C.A. He also told him that he had been working out a lot and running all summer. About ten minutes after they had finished all the paperwork, the door opened, and Reggie's mama came in. Dan stood up and introduced himself, and they made small talk for a little while. He told her about his leaving Oakmont and going to Mosby earlier that year. She smiled and said, "I'm glad Reggie isn't there anymore. Those folks didn't treat him right at that school."

Dan smiled, looked at her, and said, "Mosby is a fine university, and I am going to do my best to help him not only get in, but also get an academic scholarship if he can qualify. He's the kind of young man we'd like to see there." That statement brought tears of joy to her eyes.

She said, "He'd be a little closer to home than if he went to Tidewater State, and that would make me happy too."

Dan said, "I can understand that Mrs. King."

She said, "Don't call me Mrs. King, call me Florence just like all my friends do."

"Sounds great Florence, but you have to call me Dan, okay?"

"It's a deal," she replied.

It wasn't long before he took them down to his car and said, "What kind of food would you folks enjoy eating tonight."

Florence said, "Reggie and I like most any kind of good food, so we are open to whatever you might decide."

Reggie piped up and said, "Well, wherever we go, you can bet it sure won't be as good as your cookin', Mama."

Reggie's mother laughed and said, "Don't go giving me that jive talk boy. I'm sure you'll like whatever we eat tonight just fine."

Dan asked them, "Have you ever eaten German food? I know a place on Liberty Avenue called the Atlantic Grill that has fabulous German food. I bet a hungry young man would really enjoy it there, and maybe even his mama, too."

Florence smiled, "I've heard of it and have always wanted to go there."

"Great, then let's do it. I bet you folks will love it," replied Dan.

Later, after enjoying delicious wiener schnitzels, sauerbraten and German potato pancakes, both Florence and Reggie proclaimed the dinner that night as being one of the best they had ever eaten.

On the way back to their apartment Reggie said, "Wow, Coach! That was some meal tonight. Thanks! Is the food that good at Mosby?"

Dan laughed and said, "I'd be lying to you if I said it was, but the food at the university is good old down home kind of cooking, and your mama won't have to worry about you going hungry."

Prior to dropping them off at their place, Dan told them that Reggie's applications would be expedited, and he would be in touch as soon as he could. He said goodbye and headed back to the Edison Hotel for a good night's rest in preparation for the drive back to Warrenton the next morning.

Dan got up early the next morning, grabbed a quick breakfast and hit the road. Upon arriving back in Warrenton in the early afternoon, he went straight to the athletic offices in the hopes of finding Willie there. Only coaches Johnson and Horne were there. They told him that Willie was at his new house helping Sally empty some of the boxes from his recent move. Dan picked up the phone and called. "Hi, Willie, it's Dan. I'm back after a great meeting and dinner with Reggie King and his mother last night, and I have the applications."

"Way to go, Dan! Take them right over to Frances. She is expecting the applications and will begin reviewing them immediately."

"Will do, boss. I'm on my way."

After Dan dropped off the applications, he reminded Frances that Willie was anxious to hear if Reggie would be accepted and also if he qualified for an academic scholarship. He asked her if she would be kind enough to call him and let him know.

"Frances laughed and said, "Why do I get the impression that Willie really wants this young man to be here at Mosby?"

"Well Frances, I would think it is because Willie thinks Reggie might really help us out both this year and maybe next year too. "

"Tell Willie that I will review the applications and will be back to him shortly." Dan said thanks and was on his way, after she promised him she would look at them right away.

5

Morning had dawned in Honolulu. It looked like it was going to be another great day to go surfing at Waikiki. Twenty year old Kevin Kahana could smell the sweet aroma of plumeria blossoms wafting in though his window as he laid stretching and yawning after waking up. He had heard on the news the night before that the surf would be up, and he was feeling fired up about hitting the beach and catching some good waves. This former Hawaiian paniolo cowboy knew that the fun times on the beach and his summer vacation would soon be over. He would be heading back to the mainland to return to Mosby University in Virginia for his junior year. In the meantime, why not have a great time, before settling back into the tough academic regime that he had somehow managed to survive during the past couple of years.

The waves at Waikiki were usually pretty gentle compared with the ones Kevin loved to ride at Makaha up on the northwest side of Oahu, but at least they rolled a long way. Makaha was the place where big wave surfing was pioneered. Even though it was a long drive, Kevin also occasionally even liked to go up to the north shore of the island to the exciting Banzai Pipeline in the winter months when the surf was high. However, now that he was going to school at Mosby, he hadn't been back up there for a while. He wouldn't go all the way up there these days, since the ocean was pretty calm during the summer months when he was home.

Having grown up working on a ranch on the Big Island while in junior high and the first year of high school, he had felt very fortunate to have had the chance to go to the prestigious Punahou School in Honolulu after his parents moved to Oahu. He had never surfed until they moved there, since horseback riding had always been his main love. He still loved horses and enjoyed playing on a polo team at the park in Waikiki near the base of Diamond Head. Kevin's outstanding academic performance at Mosby led to an academic scholarship at Mosby University. Once he got there, he hooked up with a couple of his old paniolo buddies who were already enrolled. He was invited to join the Stallion Stable Lodge, which was one of the many organizations at Mosby that were similar to Greek fraternities at other schools. Kevin was looking forward to the return of the football season, too. He wasn't on the team, but he had the honor of dressing up in a Confederate uniform and riding around the field prior to games. He waived his sword, as he rode around the field while playing the part of the old Gray Ghost. It was a lot of fun, and he got a rush of adrenalin every time he performed. The girls seemed to think his role during the games was pretty cool, too, and it helped him meet a lot of pretty wahines. Life at Colonel Mosby's University had really been great!

Kevin had another reason to be looking forward to going back to Mosby University that fall. Tane Maaka, his best buddy from high school, who had gone to a community college in Honolulu for the past two years, had applied to Mosby, been accepted, and would be joining him there this year. Tane had been the Hawaiian state high school heavyweight wrestling champion when they were at Punahou. He was pretty big and strong. He had intimidated most of his opponents, not only with his size and strength, but also his fierce demeanor. In reality, he was like a big teddy bear off the mat and a lot of fun to hang around with. Tane and his parents had moved to Hawaii from New Zealand when he was two years old; they were of Maori descent. The Maoris were the native people in those islands and many people felt that they were originally from some islands in Polynesia. Tane's grades at Punahou had only been average, but he grew up following his graduation. He applied himself and got good grades at a local community college while working at night as a bouncer at a teen night club in Waikiki. Tane's father had become a very successful businessman in Honolulu. He had plenty of money to send Tane away to school. However, he had encouraged Tane to go to a local community college after high school. His father wanted to see if he would apply himself to his studies, before he spent money to send him off to a university on the mainland.

After breakfast, Kevin called Tane and said, "Hey bruddah, you wanna catch some waves today at Waikiki wid da King Kahuna?

Tane replied, "No bruddah, I got no time for dat kine of thing today. Gotta do some stuff to get ready to go over to the mainland for the new student orientation before classes start at Mosby."

"I'll be living at the Stallion Stable Lodge again this year and will look you up when I arrive," said Kevin. "I'll tell all my bruddahs there at the Stable about you, and maybe you will be invited to join so we can room together next year."

"Sounds great, Kahuna! Have a great day on the beach. I'll see you in Warrenton."

"One other thing Tane, before I hang up," said Kevin. "I know you haven't played any football since high school, and you didn't come out until your senior year since you were concentrating on your wrestling, but Mosby had a great football team last year and I bet they would have a spot for you on their squad."

Tane replied, "I don't know about that. I think I want to concentrate on my studies once I get there, but might wrestle if they have a team."

"I don't know if they do," said Kevin, but you ought to at least go by the practice field and watch the football team practice during orientation week."

Tane laughed. "You sure are persistent little bruddah. Maybe I will. See you there."

6

A week later, Mosby Head Football Coach Willie Hairston had just gone into his office at the athletic office building on August 8th to meet with his assistant coaches and review plans for the start of practice when the phone rang. It was Frances Bidwell calling.

"I've got some good news for you this morning, Willie," said Frances. "The admissions committee reviewed Reggie King's records; he has been approved for admission to Mosby. Due to his excellent grades while attending Oakmont, we are offering him an academic scholarship as well."

"Frances, bless you. You just made my day. Thanks for expediting this. I'll have Dan Benson get in touch with Reggie and give him the good news."

Willie went to the conference room and saw Dan sitting there enjoying a cup of coffee with the other assistants. He said, "Hey Dan, I just got a call from Frances Bidwell. Reggie King has not only been accepted, they are offering him an academic scholarship, too. Get on the phone and tell him to come on down and be here prior to practice starting next week. I think we found ourselves a cornerback, and hopefully he can be our back-up to Al Nelson at quarterback this year.

Who knows? He might even learn enough to become our starter at quarterback next year."

Dan Benson smiled and gave him a thumbs up as he replied, "I bet Reggie and his mama are going to be real excited when they hear the news. He's a good kid, and I think you are going to like him. He's quite an athlete and even a better person. With his speed, he should be a great cornerback. I'll give him a call this afternoon after he gets off work. I'll tell him to get here in time for the new student orientation and the start of practice."

Willie said, "Having him tryout for more than one position makes a lot of sense since we sure have some holes to fill at the skill positions." The meeting then began as the coaches reviewed the plan for the start of the pre-season training and practices. Willie could sense a feeling of excitement, even though he wondered if they could possibly enjoy the kind of success on the gridiron that they did during the '58 season. It wouldn't be long before all of them found out.

The weather in Warrenton was still hot and humid. Willie hoped that the team had been doing some running and working prior to their arrival in Warrenton. Once the players arrived, and practices began, they would discover that the running and the hitting could be pretty tough in the heat. Rod Horne, Willie's offensive assistant coach was in charge of physical conditioning. He had sent a letter to all of the returning members from last year's team in July and reminded them to get in shape, but he would find out soon enough who had taken his advice seriously.

The 1959 football schedule was out and Mosby would be playing the same teams they had played the previous year. They would have a bye once again, prior to the big final game against the Oakmont Outlaws at home. Willie posted the schedule up on the bulletin board outside the conference room at the Mosby athletic headquarters.

MOSBY UNIVERSITY 1959 FOOTBALL SCHEDULE

September 12th	PIKETOWN COLLEGE – Away
September 19th	LOCKRIDGE COLLEGE – Home
September 26th	GREENVILLE UNIVERSITY – Away
October 3rd	RED ROCKS COLLEGE – Home
October 9th	FROSTBURG COLLEGE – Away
October 17th	RADFORD COLLEGE – Homecoming
October 24th	CEDAREDGE COLLEGE – Away
October 31st	KLUTZTOWN COLLEGE – Home
November 7th	BLOOMSBURG COLLEGE – Away
November 14th	BYE
November 21st	OAKMONT UNIVERSITY – Home

Willie was happy they had the bye on November 14th since it would give him an extra week to prepare for the mighty Oakmont team. The winner of that game would get the Piedmont Pinnacle Trophy, which was now proudly displayed in the Mosby University trophy case. Everyone at Mosby, including President Bob Howard, wanted to keep it there. Winning the game against Oakmont last year was a key factor in Willie's getting his five year coaching contract, and he didn't want to let the school down.

When the meeting ended, the coaches all went to the University Diner in town to have some lunch. It was the only desegregated restaurant in Warrenton. The owner was a big Mosby football fan. He had put a notice in the *Fauquier Times Democrat* following the team's victory over Oakmont last season. The announcement stated that any and all coaches, players and fans of the Mosby Raiders were always welcome at the Diner regardless of their color. He lost some customers, but gained a lot more and, as a result, his business was booming.

Willie asked his Defensive Coordinator, Jack Johnson, how he thought the team could fill the void left by losing their star defensive tackle to graduation. Unless they came up with some new players, it looked like they might be thin on the defensive line.

Jack said, "One solution might be to go from a four man line with three linebackers to a three man line with four linebackers."

Willie thought about that for a minute and then said, "That might work, and would give us some flexibility, but I still think you have to have a real stud in there at nose tackle. Ashton Fincie is strong and tough, but I'm not sure he is heavy enough to handle that job. Fincie might be better as a defensive end in a three man line. We could always alternate our big offensive tackles in at nose tackle, but I would prefer to keep Snyder and Frumzeist fresh for offense."

"I guess we will figure something out once practices begin," replied Jack.

Ray Crocker, was the new linebacker coach. Like Dan Benson he had been hired away from Oakmont earlier that year. Ray spoke up, "I like that four linebackers, three defensive linemen scheme a lot. It gives you the potential of rushing either of the outside linebackers and putting pressure on quarterbacks, or having them drop back into coverage." Willie listened and nodded his head in agreement.

After lunch, everyone took off, knowing that once practices began, their chance for any free time was going to be pretty limited. Willie headed home to see Sally and little Bobby. He was proud of the little guy and couldn't get enough of seeing and holding him. He was thinking of Bobby, grinning from ear to ear as he heard the Drifters singing their hit single, ***There Goes My Baby***, on the car radio as he headed through town to his new home.

When Willie got there, Sally was surprised to see him. "I didn't know you would be home so early. It's a good thing my boyfriend got out of here just in time."

Willie laughed and said, "You mean that you were kidding me when we danced to that new smash hit 45 record you recently got by the Flamingos, ***I Only Have Eyes for You?*** Sally shook her head side to side, came over, and gave him a big kiss. They both laughed as she said, "Come on Willie. You know that the only other man in my life is sleeping in his crib right now, but he sure is good looking." Willie gave her a big hug.

After they sat down on the sofa together, Sally asked, "How do you think the team will do this year?"

Willie said, "I think we should be in pretty good shape, even though we have some holes to fill, but I got good news today when I heard that an outstanding young athlete from Pittsburgh has received an academic scholarship and will be joining us. As for the rest of the team and how it will go, I guess we will find out soon enough since practice starts next week."

7

Saturday August 15th was a busy day at Mosby University. It was the day that new students were supposed to show up for orientation. Over five hundred new students had come into town. Many had been brought by their parents the afternoon before, and all of the hotels and motels within about a fifty mile radius were booked solid. After checking in, the majority of the students were assigned to rooms in the dorms. After getting their keys and room numbers, most of them headed over to the dorms with their gear. The main student orientation was scheduled to be held on the morning of August 17th in the gymnasium. Following that, the new arrivals would schedule their classes for the first semester. Classes were not scheduled to begin until August 24th, and that would give plenty of time for late arrivals to come into town and be there prior to the beginning of the fall semester.

Reggie King was able to catch a ride from Pittsburg down to Warrenton from his older brother James, who had a night job as a security guard for a company in Pittsburgh. They took off early in the morning, right after James got off work. Reggie was assigned a room in the dorm with Clyde Langston, who was a second year transfer from a small Negro college in North Carolina and was from the Greensboro area. He weighed about 225 pounds and had played offensive line in high school. The two of them were a good pair. Reggie asked Clyde if he was going to be playing football for Mosby that season. Clyde said, "I didn't know they even had a football team here."

Reggie laughed and said, "Well, I don't think they had much of a team at Mosby until last year, but I plan to try and play this year. Practices start in a couple of days. Why don't you come with me and try out, too?"

Clyde replied, "I missed not playing last year, so maybe I will. Thanks for telling me about it. You said they had a pretty good team last year. Do you think I might have a chance to make the team?"

"They don't give out athletic scholarships here at Mosby, and all of their players are walk-ons. I would think you would have as good a chance as anyone if you showed the coaches that you could play," said Reggie.

Clyde then said, "When I was checking in, I met a couple of other coloreds who were being assigned as roommates to a room here in our dorm on the first floor. They looked fairly athletic, although not as big as me."

"Do you have any idea if they've ever played football?" Reggie asked.

"No, but we could go downstairs, find their rooms, introduce ourselves, and then ask them?" Clyde replied. "I understand that Mosby has always been known as a school for smart white guys, and there aren't many coloreds here. Having some others like us on the team would be fun."

On the way downstairs, Reggie said, "Do you remember their names?"

"I didn't catch their last names, but remember that one of them said his name was Ted, and the other said his name was LeRoyce," Clyde said.

Most of the doors to the rooms in the dorm were open, as the students were busy hauling stuff into them and socializing with others nearby. It was an exciting time for all of these young men, and spirits were high. Music was playing, and laughter abounded. After wandering around for a little while, Clyde spotted Ted coming out of his room.

"Hey Ted, Whaz-up? How do you and LeRoyce like your room?" Upon hearing his name, LeRoyce stuck his head out of the door and said, "Hey Clyde, who's your friend?"

"This is my new roommate, Reggie King," replied Clyde. "He's from Pittsburgh and tells me he's going out for the football team. He encouraged me to give it a shot myself. Have either of you guys played any ball in school?"

LeRoyce laughed and said, "Ted and I go back a long way. We both played together on the same high school team in Norfolk before heading off to school at Suffolk State last year. When we heard that Mosby University was going to open its doors and consider accepting Negroes, we decided to apply for admission and see what would happen. We were excited when we were accepted here."

Clyde said, "Reggie tells me that practice starts this coming Monday afternoon. Both of us are going out for the team, so why don't the two of you come out and join us?

Ted looked at LeRoyce and said, "I'm willing to give it a shot. How about you LeRoyce?"

He laughed and said, "I might as well. I don't want to have to sit around and listen to you moanin', groanin' and complainin' about all your bumps and bruises, and me not have anything to complain about myself.

The four of them agreed to meet at the cafeteria at six o'clock that evening and have dinner together. Then they headed back to their respective rooms to continue getting settled in.

When dinnertime rolled around, the four new arrivals noticed that, while the vast majority of the other new students at the cafeteria were white guys, there were several other coloreds there as well. Seeing them made them feel a lot more comfortable about their decisions to attend a formerly all-white university.

After dinner, the four of them hung around out in front of the cafeteria on that warm late summer evening. It wasn't long before they had a chance to meet some other new students, including Voshon Rice, who was a big tall guy and Shakur Wade who was lean, but very solidly built. They discovered that both of these fellows had played freshman football at a couple of small, predominantly Negro schools. It didn't take too much prodding to convince them to come out for the Mosby team and join their new friends.

The six of them seemed to enjoy each other's company, and their new found friendships made any feelings they were having of homesickness and anxiety disappear. As they were enjoying the evening, Ted Thigpen turned to his room-mate and said, "Hey LeRoyce, look at the size of that fellow over there. I bet he's played some ball in the past." Voshon overheard them and said, "I saw that big guy when I was checking in. He's kinda dark, but he's no colored man. He looks like some kind of Indian or something."

"LeRoyce laughed and said, "I don't care if he comes from Borneo. He looks pretty big and strong, and I wouldn't mind having him on my side in a rumble or on my football team either. Why don't we wander over to where he's sitting by himself and introduce ourselves and try to persuade him to join us at practice?

"Great idea," said Reggie. "Let's go say hello and meet him."

The rest of the guys tagged along. As they got closer, the big fellow spotted them coming and stood up with a frown on his face. Maybe he thought the six of them were going to gang up on him, but he sure didn't look scared. He was about 6' 3" and looked like he weighed about 300 pounds. He was huge, and frankly a little scary looking. Reggie quickly diffused the tense situation by smiling and extending his hand and said, "Hi there. We noticed you sitting all by yourself. Since we are all new here, too, we thought we'd come over and say hello. As soon as those words were out of Reggie's mouth, the frown on the big man's face was replaced by a warm smile, much to the relief of everyone there.

"My name's Reggie and this is my room-mate Clyde." The big fellow shook hands with both of them and said, "My name is Tane Maaka. Nice to meet you!" Then Ted and LeRoyce introduced themselves as did Voshon and Shakur. There were smiles all around, and Tane seemed very happy to have made some new friends. He hadn't really met anyone since he arrived at Mosby. Everyone seemed to give him a wide berth, but perhaps that was because everyone else was intimidated by his appearance.

"Reggie said, "I've never heard of anyone by that name. How do you spell it?"

Tane replied, "It's spelled T-A-N-E but is pronounced like I said it, TAWN-NEY. It's a New Zealand native Maori name and it means "Fierce Warrior." My parents were originally from there, but we live in Hawaii now. My last name is spelled Maaka, but all the syllables are pronounced like a lot of other Hawaiian words as MA-AH-KA."

Clyde spoke up and said, "Tane, all of us are going out for the Mosby football team on the day after tomorrow. Have you ever played? You sure look like you might have."

Tane, laughed and said, "I only played my senior year in high school, but I mainly concentrated on wrestling. I've just transferred here from a community college that didn't have any sports teams so I haven't done much, other than working out the last two years."

LeRoyce said, "How did you do in wrestling?"

Tane smiled as he modestly replied, "I was the Hawaii state high school heavyweight champion in both my junior and senior years."

Voshon was grinning and said, "Come on out with us Tane. We'd like to have a "Fierce Warrior" on our team." Tane liked these guys and it didn't take too much arm twisting for him to agree to join his new friends for the first day of football practice.

8

Not only were the dorms opening in anticipation of the student's arrivals for the new school year, but the lodges were opening up, as well. Mosby University had a long-standing policy of not permitting Greek fraternities at the school, but had allowed the establishment of "lodges" which were very similar. All the lodges had been built by the university, who owned the structures. They tended to attract young men who shared similar interests with the existing members. Residents of the lodges would pay a monthly fee to reside in them that was slightly higher than students paid to live in the dorms, but since the lodges had larger common areas and were much more comfortable, the additional fees were worth it. Newcomers to the University could choose to live in the dorms throughout their entire time at the school. However, if they received a bid from one of the lodges in the spring of their first year, they could live at the lodge in subsequent years. Some students just preferred to remain independent, and either live in the dorms, or at off campus apartments during their time at the school.

The Serpents Den Lodge, which proudly included Mosby's President Robert Howard IV as one of its member alumni, was made up of a diverse group of young men from all over the country. It included a mix of serious students in a variety of fields of study from the arts and sciences to engineering, but many of the schools jocks, party animals, and student leaders were also among its members. The general consensus around the *Estate*, as the campus at Mosby was called, was that the Den had the best parties at the *Estate*. In past years, they had featured a jovial band of lodge brothers called the Snake Charmers, who played old time sing-a-long music. Since the last of them graduated the past semester, they wouldn't be back. However, their wild and crazy social chairman seemed to always be able to find outstanding musical groups to come to the lodge and play on home football game weekends. That meant the lodge was usually packed during these events, and fun times were had by all.

The nearby Muse Men Lodge mainly attracted men who were drama and music majors. A good number of the highly acclaimed Mosby University orchestra were members there, as well. Most of the men who appeared in dramatic productions at the school's 500 seat theater were Muse Men, too. The lack of women at the all-male University was a production problem though, and often resulted in the casting of slender men in female roles. However, it was not unusual for the school productions to recruit local women from the area or coeds from nearby Mary Washington College to appear in their productions.

The Aristotle Abode had more than its share of students majoring in Psychology, English and History. While their parties were generally not that exciting, their lodge grade point average was usually up near the top of all the students around the *Estate*.

The Galileo Gables Lodge seem to naturally attract science and engineering majors from Mosby's highly regarded, technically oriented schools. Their lodge was next door to the Aristotle Abode and the members of the two lodges got along with each other very well.

Naturally, the Stallion Stable Lodge was where most of the members of the University's outstanding polo team resided. Many of them were Latin American horsemen and more than a few Hawaiian cowboys called paniolos from the Big Island were members too. Some people thought the idea of Hawaiians playing polo was odd, but they were good horsemen and very adept at the game. In addition, the Stallion Stable had quite a collection of young men from the northeastern part of the country, who were mostly of Italian descent. Apparently, many of them loved being designated as being a member of the Stallion Lodge. Their parties were also among the best at the *Estate* and usually featured bands from Philadelphia or the Jersey shore.

The Moses Manse was a beautiful lodge and enjoyed strong alumni support. It always attracted the cream of Mosby's Jewish students and they were proud to claim that they had many lawyers and doctors who had been members during their undergraduate days. They also generally excelled in their studies and had been frequently recognized as having the highest percentage of Dean's List members of all the lodges at Mosby.

In sharp contrast to both the membership composition and architecture of all the other lodges at the school was Saint Bartholomew's Hall. Generally referred to as St. B.'s Hall, its membership was almost exclusively comprised of young men from the state of Virginia. Many of their members traditionally hailed from the Richmond or the Tidewater area, and several of them had attended the same prep schools and known each other for years. Some of their families were even listed as being among the FFV's (First Families of Virginia.) They were regarded as being very preppie, but also were thought to be rather snobbish by most of the other students at the university. Their lodge's brick exterior had been painted white, and it was the narrowest building at the *Estate*. Because of the building's narrow interior, the lodge was often referred to as the Hall. Its narrowness didn't lend itself architecturally very well to hosting parties, which was fine with many of their members. Most of them were more than content to just talk to each other on party weekends at the Hall. Needless to say, some of their dates were not impressed by their self-obsession, but for those girls who came from families just like those of the young men at St. B.'s, they usually managed to be fairly comfortable being there in spite of that rather stuffy atmosphere.

Since Mosby University was an all-male school, the students in Warrenton often had to venture out to many of the women's colleges around the area to find any female companionship. In honor of Colonel Mosby's exploits, these road trips were referred to as *raids,* and attractive girls were usually referred to as being *ghostly* if they were pretty and were judged to be lovely spirits. As for the girls that didn't qualify as being *ghostly,* they were sometimes called by other names. On many occasions, the most unattractive girls were sometimes cruelly described as being *ghastly.* No doubt, many of these young women had their own descriptive appellations for the Mosby men, who considered them to be unworthy of their time and affections.

Mary Washington College was located in Fredericksburg, Virginia. That city was only 38 miles away, and due to its close proximity, it was the main place to find girls for many of the men at Mosby University. Marymount College was located in Arlington, Virginia, just across the river from Washington D.C. It was the preferred destination for many of the Catholic men at Mosby University. Madison College was located about an hour and a half south in the Shenandoah Valley; being so remote, the lonely girls there had a reputation for being very friendly. Mary Baldwin College was located in the hometown of former President Woodrow Wilson, even further south, in scenic Staunton, Virginia. It was about a two hour drive away. Among its distinctive landmarks were the pair of large bronze dogs on either side of the steps to the main residence hall. Legend said that the dogs would always bark any time a virgin passed by.

The farthest women's school that the Mosby men tended to visit, was lovely Sweet Briar College, located all the way down Route 29 past Charlottesville and near Lynchburg. The young ladies, who went to this very exclusive and expensive school, were the daughters of extremely wealthy parents. Many of the guys who went there and fell in love, often found that their lives changed dramatically if they married any of these young ladies. Despite that, very few Mosby men traveled there very often due to the distance and the fact that they faced strong competition from the men at the University of Virginia, who only had to make about an hour's drive.

First year students at Mosby University faced a tough challenge because of the rigorous academics at the school. It was not uncommon to see about half of the entering first year class flunk out at the end of the first semester. Entering freshmen students also had the social handicap of not being able to drive a vehicle of any kind in Fauquier County during their first year at Mosby. However, the school would often host mixers in the beautiful large reception space at J.E.B. Stuart Hall during the fall on away football game weekends. Young ladies would be bussed in for the evening from the various women's colleges in the area for an evening of dancing and socializing.

Aside from the lodges being a place where social events occurred, many of the students at Mosby often liked to hang out at Fannie Sue's Tea and Crumpet Room, located just a short distance out of town to the West on Route 211. While the name implied that it might be a dignified establishment, in reality it was just an old barn-like place that featured keg beer, hot dogs and little else, other than the music on its jukebox. The men's room there spoke volumes about the class of Fannie Sue's. It had a metal urinal trough attached on one wall that was higher on one end then the other. Water ran slowly, out of a faucet above the high end, toward the drain pipe at the other end, where the fluids ran out through a hole in the wall. The owners were reportedly former Mosby students and were said to be doing quite well with their business there. The place frequently advertised in the *The Ghostly Vision*, which was the student newspaper, that there was "No Fannie Sue, no Tea and Crumpets and no Room!" It was grubby, but the beer was cheap and the fact that most of the patrons were under the legal age for alcoholic consumption didn't seem to be a problem. Loud rock 'n roll and blues music blared from its jukebox, and dancing was okay, if you could find enough space to do it. The owners employed some burly young local men to serve as bouncers to deter patrons from getting into fights, after a rather notorious incident between a group of St. B.'s and a couple of Serpents Den men in the fall of 1957.

9

On Monday afternoon August 17th, quite a large group of students began to gather on the athletic practice field near the Mosby Memorial Gymnasium. They had been told to show up in shorts, tee shirts, and wearing sneakers, but some failed to get the word. They were sent back to wherever they were staying to put on the proper gear and then return. Head Coach Willie Hairston introduced himself to the assembled group, and then introduced all of the assistant coaches.

Willie said, "This is Coach Johnson. He is our Defensive Coordinator and Assistant Head Coach. Coach Freeman handles Special Teams. Coach Horne is my Offensive Assistant and is in charge of conditioning. Since we will be doing a lot of running and drills this week, all of you are going to get to know Coach Horne very well. Coach Crocker is in charge of linebackers, and Coach Benson will be responsible for the Offensive line."

"We have a pretty small staff in comparison to most of the colleges we play. That puts us at a disadvantage compared to some of our opponents. Another disadvantage we have is that we don't award athletic scholarships. Most of the teams we play do. In spite of that, we feel that we can compete by working hard, being smart and giving 100% out there on the field of play. While I realize that the majority of the players who have come out here today are from last year's team, I see that there are a number of newcomers, and we welcome you. I want to assure everyone that the competition for positions is wide open, and anyone that shows the coaches they can play, will play."

"Practice begins at one o'clock each day this week." Willie continued, "Anyone who shows up one minute after the hour will be considered late and should have a good excuse. Both today and tomorrow's practices will be devoted to testing, conditioning, and drills with Coach Horne in charge. We will issue pads and helmets at one o'clock on Wednesday afternoon and began contact drills later that day."

"We were fortunate enough to enjoy a very successful season last year. It, culminated in our beating Oakmont University, our biggest rival. The Piedmont Pinnacle Trophy is the prize for winning that game; it is now on display in the trophy case in the lobby of Mosby Memorial Gymnasium. Go by and check it out sometime. All of us are hopeful that this season will be a success as well, but it won't happen without a lot of hard work and dedication."

"Okay men, let's get started with a little paperwork," Willie concluded. "The coaches will be passing around a clipboard where you should put down your name, where you are currently living, and your year in school. Also, you should list what position on Offense and Defense or Special Teams that you think you would like to try out for. While that is being completed, Coach Horne will begin the conditioning and testing of speed and strength.

"When Willie was finished talking, Dan Kojak, the previous year's offensive team captain and the center on offense yelled out the school cheer, "Here we go Mosby Men…Here we go!" The rest of the players joined in. The practice was underway.

Rod Horne told the men to run a warm up lap around the field. Then he broke them into smaller groups and asked the other assistant coaches to help him time all of the players in the 40-yard dash. Following the sprint timing, there were some strength and weight lifting testing and also some agility drills. Coach Bobby Freeman took the kicker and the punter off to the side along with the snapper and practiced some kicking and punting. Fortunately, Manny Morales, a former Argentinean soccer player, who handled the kick-offs and long field goals the previous season, was back, and his leg was looking very strong. The team's outstanding punter from last year, long legged Dick "Cadillac" deVille was back. Seeing him out there put a big smile on Coach Freeman's face.

The coaches noticed several new faces. Some looked like they might be good athletes. All the coaches, including Head Coach Willie Hairston, with the exception of Ray Crocker and Dan Benson, were colored. All the players the previous year had been white, but it looked like this year's team would be more diverse, as there were several young colored men on the field. Crocker and Benson had come to the team from Oakmont after last season, and had added a lot of skills and knowledge to the staff. One of the perspective players was identified to be as Tane Maaka. He was clearly the biggest man out there. He also looked like he was very strong and extremely quick for his size. Maybe he might be able to fill the void left when Hank Warwick had graduated. Hank was such a standout the previous season, that his loss had been a major concern prior to the start of practice.

When the practice ended, most of the new players headed back to the dorms, but the majority of the returnees were prepared to shower at the gym. The coaches went back inside to the conference room near their offices to review what they had observed that day. The players seemed to be in a good mood and excited about getting ready for a new year at school and on the gridiron. Most of them were also anxious to hear how their buddies spent the summer. Al Nelson called out to Johnny Baugh, "Hey Johnny, did you bring the Snakemobile back to school this year?"

Johnny laughed and said, "You betcha! That thing is the ultimate party machine. In fact, Jack Delaney, Eddie Ferrous and Parker Boardman got a ride up to my place just northeast of Pittsburgh, and they all rode down to school with me in it this year." The Snakemobile was a used 1950 Cadillac hearse which Johnny picked up at a used car lot during mid-semester break the previous year. A big red wiggling snake was painted down both sides. It usually was outfitted with wall to wall mattresses in the back and could haul a lot of folks around.

"Hey Garrett, I bet you didn't have as much fun this summer as I did. I must have played golf about 50 times, "said lanky "Cadillac" deVille to the Raiders sure-handed receiver and outside linebacker Garrett Gassman.

"Naw, Cadillac! I probably didn't. I just worked at my job as a lifeguard and spent most of the summer evenings cruising around in my Mercury convertible picking up chicks," Garrett replied.

Jack Delaney laughed and said, "Yeah Garrett. That sure sounds boring. How about letting me join you on your next raid at Mary Washington? I bet that all you have to do is put the top down, turn up your radio, and then try to keep all those good looking *ghosts* from climbing into your car." Garrett nodded and looked at him with a sly grin on his face.

Billy Vorache piped up and spoke to Manny Morales, the team's kicker and said, "What did you do this summer Manny? Manny replied, "I went back home to Argentina and froze my butt off. It's winter down there now, and it was a tough one. It's pretty hot around here now in Virginia, but it sure feels good to me." The other guys laughed.

Running backs Freddie Lammhandler and Ironhead Ferrous were kidding each other about who was going to gain the most yards during the coming season while defenders Ashton Fincie and Mac Gordon were joking about who was going to make the most tackles. The whole gang of returnees was in a good mood and looking forward to another great season.

Once the coaches returned to their conference room, Willie was the first to speak, "Well men, how do you think it went out there today?"

Defensive coordinator Jack Johnson spoke up. "We will learn a lot more once we start practicing in pads, but I liked what I saw out there today. The guys seemed to be excited to be here. Having a positive attitude is something we preach around here."

"I was really excited about Reggie King coming here this year. I kept an eye on him as he was going through his paces. He handles himself very well, and he showed me a lot of speed and agility," said Dan Benson.

Rod Horne laughed, "I guess he did. He clocked the fastest time of anyone out there today in the 40-yard dash."

Willie said, "Let me see that sheet with the times on it, Rod." Rod handed it to him and Willie broke out into a big grin. "Men, I've got good news. Last year, Kenny Lynx was our fastest player with Ironhead Ferrous and Butch DeRose about a tenth of a second behind him. Garrett Gassman and Ronnie Wall were each only about a twentieth of a second behind them. We had some good speed on that team, but this year it seems that Kenny is now the fourth fastest player on the team and Reggie King is on top with Ted Thigpen and Shakur Wade behind him. I'm getting excited about our prospects after seeing these numbers, but we still have to see if they can play."

Coach Ray Crocker said," I was watching the guys trying to bench press 200 pounds. That big Hawaiian guy made it look like a piece of cake. He pumped the barbell up over and over until we made him stop. He is one strong fellow; I see him becoming an anchor on our defensive line. He also seems to have lightning cat-like reflexes, which is pretty amazing for someone who weighs about 300 pounds. I don't know many offensive linemen who would enjoy trying to block him.

Willie interrupted him, "Men, I'm glad everybody's excited about our prospects this year, but we've got a long way to go and a lot of work to do before we get there, so maybe we ought to curb our enthusiasm until we see how they do once they put on the pads and start hitting." Everyone nodded in agreement.

The next day, the practice was minus a couple of guys who changed their mind about trying out, but that was okay with the coaches. Always better for them to quit right away than once the season started. The prospective player's measurements and weights were recorded. The coaches discovered that, since Tane Maaka wore a size 8 ¼ hat, they were going to have to special order a helmet that would be big enough to fit him.

The coaches had the players do some warm up laps before starting the agility drills. Some of the guys complained about soreness, but didn't get any sympathy from Rod Horne. He had warned everyone to come back to school in shape. Once the agility drills began, it was pretty clear who the skill position players on the team would probably be.

However, the coaches knew that drills didn't always translate into ability on the field and drills didn't measure toughness and heart. Even more important was having a positive attitude. They would find who did and who didn't soon enough. The coaches and the team had a lot of work to do to be able to get ready for the season, since their opening game against Piketown College would be coming up soon on Saturday September 12th. Since it was a road game, they would have even less time to get their offense and defense installed and be ready to play.

10

Things were very different at Oakmont University in Pennsylvania. Their football team had been practicing for over a week, and their twelve coaches were working the 85 young men who had turned out really hard. The temperature and the humidity was high, but Head Coach Irv Swindle didn't believe in anyone getting any water until the end of practice. The players were very thirsty, but there was no sympathy or relief to be found. Most of the players were on scholarships, although walk-ons were welcome. The coaches would find out rapidly if the newcomers had any talent. Few walk-ons were willing to take the abuse the coaches were handing out, so most of them quit. Most of the scholarship players seemed to hate Swindle, since he treated them so badly and threatened them constantly. He was obviously still steaming over the loss to Mosby in last season's finale, which marred a previously unbeaten record, and he was determined to get revenge.

The strength and conditioning coach had been working the squad hard on the weights since the previous season and was feeling confident the team had the ability to steamroll most of their opponents. Both the offensive and defensive lines were going to average around 280 pounds. That was perfect for their smash mouth brand of football. Swindle was up in his twenty foot high "tower" at midfield with a megaphone. He shouted at the coaches and the players whenever he saw something he didn't like. It appeared that there must have been a lot of things going on that he didn't like, since he was yelling almost constantly. Swindle always wanted to crush any and all opponents, but this year, he really want to put it to Mosby's team. His main goal for the season was to take that Piedmont Pinnacle Trophy back home to Oakmont where it belonged, and nothing was going to stop him. He also wanted to teach Mosby's uppity coach a lesson that all his "fancy schmansy" stuff wasn't going to work this year. He was still fuming that Mosby didn't "man-up" and play straight ahead smash mouth football like the game is supposed to be played. One thing was for sure. As Swindle put it, "My team will be ready when we play Mosby this season. If they try any of that crap again, Oakmont will be ready for it."

Swindle was pleased about one addition to the team that he felt was going to make a real impact. Sophomore middle linebacker and running back, Horsie Dann, had enjoyed a great freshman season, and was looking even better this year. Dann weighed between 235 and 240 pounds most days, and was a real stud out there on the field. He also had a mean streak. He would just as soon try to knock someone's head off as look at them. He was going to play a lot on both sides of the ball since he was just too good to keep on the bench. Swindle planned to use him extensively, except of course, when Dann needed a breather. Horsie made the coach grin one day during a contact drill when he ran over the player who was opposing him and then hit him again with a forearm when the player tried to get up. That was the kind of player Swindle wanted on his team. One who was tough and mean and didn't take any prisoners. It was a damn shame he didn't have more guys like Horsie Dann out there. In reality, Swindle had plenty of good tough players, but he always had room for more.

Oakmont, due to its size and reputation, had a tradition of fielding strong teams, but after a mediocre 6-4 record back in 1950, the school had fired their coach. They lured Swindle away from a Big Ten team, where he had compiled an impressive record after being there only three seasons. Oakmont offered him the job as Athletic Director in addition to being the Head Football Coach and that, along with the fat contract, was enough to persuade him to come to Oakmont. Despite numerous complaints about his abusive behavior and irascible temper over the years, his record of success had made the university officials look the other way. They were obviously proud of the fact that Oakmont had become a powerhouse once again under Swindle, so he was very secure in his job.

The Oakmont Outlaws hadn't begun preparations for its home opener against the Cedaredge Yellow Jackets on September 12th, but Swindle was sure they would be ready to put a licking on them when the time came. When the practice ended that day, he made the players do another lap before they could finally get a drink of water. Several threw up during their journey around the field. Swindle watched them from his tower and laughed.

"What a bunch of sissies out there. We want real men on our team here," he thought.

11

Mosby President Robert H. Howard IV was in his office early on August 19th. He was very pleased about how smoothly registration for new students had gone but wasn't surprised since he knew he had a very capable and professional staff. The campus had also been spruced up in preparation for the arrival of the students and their parents. The maintenance and gardening crew had done a good job; Bob Hamilton was proud of how gorgeous the *Estate* looked. The lawns were trimmed, the flowers were blooming, and everything was beautiful. That impressive bronze statue of John Mosby on horseback, which had been unveiled during the 50th Anniversary and created by the acclaimed young female sculptor, J.R. Eason, was especially beautiful. The bronze patina on the statue was even prettier now than the previous fall. The statue reminded all who saw it of the legendary old Gray Ghost, John Mosby.

Bob Howard had made a decision, with the board's approval, to expand the scope of the university by adding a School of Law in 1960. He and his staff were busy working with the architects in planning the construction, which was scheduled to begin in November. It was only fitting, since John Mosby had practiced law in that area for many years. In addition, Mr. Howard and his administrative staff would be reviewing candidates for professorial jobs and working diligently to find ways to attract the best faculty possible. It was an immense task that weighed heavily upon him, so the thought of how the football team was going to do that season was probably one of the furthest things on his mind. Nevertheless, President Howard had been pleased by the performance of Willie Hairston. Willie, the school's first Negro graduate, had done a superb job of coaching the team the year before. In appreciation, he had been signed to a five year contract. President Howard wanted to make sure Mosby kept him, and he knew that Willie Hairston was going to do a great job. He also was pleased that his efforts to desegregate Mosby University had apparently born fruit. Frances Bidwell had informed him about the number of applications for enrollment by colored students that had been received that summer. Apparently, his speech before the NAACP had paid off.

President Howard picked up the phone shortly after 9AM and put in a call to Troy Barksdale II, the alumnus who was the president of Tidewater National Bank in Richmond.

Their loan to finance the construction of the new Law School and some other planned new buildings was going to be the largest loan in the history of the bank. It would also be quite a feather in the cap of both Bob Howard and Troy Barksdale. The terms had already been negotiated, and a handshake deal had been made, but the lawyers hadn't drawn up the documents yet. Bob Howard wanted to put that detail behind him. November would be here before they knew it and he wanted them to be able to break ground on time. When Barksdale's secretary put him on the line, Bob Howard said, "Hello Troy! I thought I'd give you a call today to see how our loan agreement is coming along."

Barksdale laughed and replied, "Nothing to worry about Bob. You know how those doggoned lawyers like to dot all the i's and cross all the t's. We've got a handshake deal, and if that's good enough for you, I hope you know that it's good enough me."

President Howard chuckled and said, "I know we have a deal Troy, but my lawyers would like to have a document to review. Any idea when we could expect one?"

The banker replied, "Should be any day now, Bob. I'll let you know as soon as I hear. While I've got you on the phone, let me ask you, how's the football team going to do this year? Oh, and by the way, did you hear that the bank recently bought one hundred season tickets and that we are now your biggest corporate supporter?"

"No Troy, I didn't know that, but we sure appreciate your support. As for how the team is going to do, it's anybody's guess. Every season is a new one. With graduations and personnel changes, I guess one never knows. However, we had enough confidence in our coach, Willie Hairston, that we recently gave him a five year contract," Bob Howard said in reply.

"Well Bob, there's no question that the team had a good year last season, and times in the USA are changing. But some folks wondered why you would go out and hire a colored boy and his three colored assistants to coach at an all-white men's school that has an outstanding reputation for academic excellence. It seemed kind of strange."

President Howard said, "Troy, times *are* changing, and we are doing our best to change as well and stay up with them. We wanted to hire the best man for the job. Frankly, the color of his skin wasn't a consideration, but his character and his coaching ability certainly was important to me. Our coach, Willie Hairston, is every bit a graduate of Mosby University as you are. He is really proud of that fact, and I am, too."

"On that subject, I don't know if you are aware of the fact that I spoke at the NAACP convention in June. I talked about the need for many fine schools, including Mosby, to make an effort to increase their admission of Negro students and give qualified ones the opportunity to attend their institutions. As a result, we received a number of applications from prospective Negro students and have accepted several of them into Mosby this year."

There was a long pause on the other end of the line. When Troy Barksdale finally spoke he said, "Bob, I must admit I'm a little surprised by this decision. Mosby has always been a school for Virginia gentlemen and I, for one, hate to see those traditions change. However, you are the president there, so I'm sure you know what you are doing and what would be best."

"Thanks for your support Troy. I am always going to try to do the right thing and what is best for Mosby University. You can count on that, "Bob Howard replied." Troy Barksdale ended the call as he said, "I'll be in touch."

As President Howard hung up, his longtime secretary Ann Been came in. She looked at him and said, "Is there a problem Mr. Howard?"

He looked up, smiled and replied, "I certainly hope not Ann, but I must admit I am anxious to get this construction loan nailed down."

She looked at him and said, "Mr. Howard, don't you go worrying about that. You know it's going to get done, now that you've made your mind up. You always get things done."

12

Wednesday afternoon August 19th was even hotter and muggier than the previous two days. Some of Mosby's prospective players were concerned about having to wear pads for the first time. It didn't take them long to find out that those concerns were justified. The coaches put them through a series of hitting drills after they ran a lap to warm up. Some of the guys liked the contact, but several first timers seemed to shy away from it.

One of the newcomers appeared to like the physicality. Not many of the others were excited about going head to head with Tane Maaka, who was wearing a brand new helmet, which fit him perfectly. He was the biggest man out on the field. Defensive Coach Johnson watched and said to Head Coach Hairston, "I think we may have found the perfect nose tackle to take Hank Warwick's place. That's sure a load off my mind."

Willie smiled and said, "Make that two of us. I think Maaka's going to be a real force out there."

At the end of practice, Willie called the team together and said, "Good job out there today men. A lot of you are going to be sore tomorrow, but if we keep working hard, the soreness will get better. Our first game is at Piketown on Saturday September 12th. The Pharaoh's

Phans are notorious for all the noise they make at their home games. You can also count on their excellent coach, Billy Reid, having his team ready to play and trying to avenge their 28-10 loss to us last year here in Warrenton. We will start putting in the offense and defense on Monday. Everybody hit the showers and get ready for more hitting tomorrow."

Dan Kojak, the always energetic returning center, had a booming voice. "Come on men," he yelled. "Let's do our Mosby cheer today before we take off." The entire team joined in as he led them in three rounds of, "Here we go Mosby Men…here we go!"

Willie turned to the other coaches and said, "That's the kind of spirit I like to see out there. Let's head back to our conference room and talk about what we saw out there today." They all nodded in agreement and headed there as the players made their way back to the gym for their showers. Some of the coaches grabbed a drink out of the water fountain while others reached for a soft drink from the fridge at the back of the room. Then, all gathered around the conference table.

Willie spoke first, "I know it's too early to tell, but I am encouraged by the turnout and the looks of some of the newcomers. How do you men feel about our prospects?"

Defensive Coordinator Jack Johnson said, "I was really worried about some of our losses to graduation on defense this year, but I'm feeling a lot better now. That Maaka kid is a stud. He's going to be a player, and looks like a great replacement for Hank Warwick. Also, I like the speed I've seen from King, Wade and Thigpen. If they can tackle, my concerns about our defensive backfield might not be anything to fret about."

Willie laughed, "Hey Jack, don't go assuming that you will get all of these guys on your defensive team. Some of them might end up being offensive players this year."

Jack replied, "That's true, but we had a lot of two way players last year and maybe some of them might divide playing time on both sides of the ball."

Willie nodded his head in agreement, "Good point, but we just may just be getting ahead of ourselves. We will get a clearer picture next week when we put in some offense and defense and see how they catch and run with the ball. I just hope it all shakes out. We need to get prepared for Piketown, because I have a strong feeling they are going to be prepared for us." After about an hour of discussion about what they saw out there, the meeting broke up and everyone headed home.

When Willie arrived home, Sally was working in the kitchen. Willie came through the door, approached the kitchen area, and said,"Hey honey, something smells mighty good in there. What's for dinner? I'm starved."

Sally gave him a hug and replied, "It's going to be a surprise, but I bet you are going to like it. Speaking of smells, could you go check Bobby's diapers? I didn't want to do it right now while I'm preparing dinner, but I think a big strong man like you can handle the job."

Willie grinned and said, "That's just what I was hoping to do when I got home today. Okay boss, I'm on my way to his crib to check him out right now." Once he got there, he discovered Sally was right, but since she handled this parental job most of the time, he didn't mind doing his fair share. Little Bobby gave him a big smile and a couple of giggles after he was all cleaned up, powdered, and in a fresh diaper. Willie looked down and smiled back. He sure loved that little boy of his.

That night, after a delicious meal of short ribs, cornbread, mashed potatoes, and collard greens, Willie grabbed Sally and gave her a kiss as they were cleaning up the dishes.

"Hey baby, that was delicious, but I think you taste even better."

She smiled at him and said, "You slick talking devil. I might even have something better for your dessert later tonight if you keep that up."

Willie replied, "I'm kind of tired, but don't you worry, I'm not that tired," as he gave her another kiss.

13

Friday's practice was the last one that week, but also the hardest. The coaches were pushing the players to see how they reacted, providing them with a clearer insight as to who their starters were going to be. A lot of the players got banged up during the hard hitting drills, but fortunately, aside from some bumps and bruises, there were no serious injuries during that first week. Nearly all the retuning offensive linemen were talking about how tough it was to go head to head against that new Maaka guy. Big offensive tackles CC Rider Snyder and Henry Frumzeist called him a "beast." Joe Delaney, Dan Kojak and Charlie Giordano, who were significantly outweighed by Maaka, said that hitting him was like hitting a wall. They also surmised that it was probably going to take three players to block him. However, the coaches watching them out there were smiling at their frustration. Next week's practices would see the players assigned to their positions. The coaches would start putting in the offense and defense in preparation for the season opener.

As the players stripped off their gear that afternoon and headed to the showers, it was obvious that all the new colored players were hanging together at one end of the locker room. The other players on the team were spread around in the rest of the space. Tane Maaka's locker was near most of the colored player's lockers, but not in the middle of them. There had been some hard hitting out there, and while it was not uncommon for tempers to sometimes flare, there hadn't been any fights on the practice field as yet. Coach Willie knew that cliques were commonplace, but the last thing he wanted, was for the team to be divided along racial lines. By the time the season started, he also hoped that all of them would be teammates, even if they weren't close friends.

After Tane showered and got dressed, he went over to his original buddies at Mosby and said, "Anyone up for going over to D.C. tomorrow night with me and hitting some of the rock 'n roll bars there on 14th Street?

One of the guys gave him a confused look and said, "We heard at the orientation that first year students couldn't drive or operate a car in the town or even the county here."   Tane laughed, "That's right, but I'm a junior and that rule doesn't apply to me. My dad gave some money to buy a car after I got to the mainland. I bought a '58 Volkswagen mini-bus in D.C. before I came down here to school. It may be slow and funny looking, but it has plenty of room inside. I even plan to use it for some camping trips up near Skyline Drive. Only Shakur Wade and Le Royce Forsett told Tane that they might like to go. The rest said they were short on cash, and so they would pass on the invitation. Beer drinkin' was legal at age 18 in D.C., so getting in those rock 'n roll bars wouldn't be a problem.

Tane said, "I used to work at places like that. I like the scene at those places and all the chicks that come there."

Upon hearing that, Ted Thigpen piped up and said, "Hey Tane! Would you have room for me too?"

Tane laughed, "You kiddin' me bruddah? That VW's got tons of room. My Hawaiian bruddah, Kevin Kahana, just got into town. I've been wanting to hit the town and have some fun with him. You guys are welcome to join us. I figure we could rest up tomorrow afternoon and then head to D.C. around 7PM. We'll hit the bars, have fun, and drive back to Warrenton later that night. "

A lot of the other players on the team had plans for the weekend, too. With no school until classes began early that year on Monday the 24th of August, it was a great time to blow off some steam. A number of them belonged to the Serpents Den Lodge. Most of them were talking about running down to Richmond to go to a HUGE rock 'n roll show at the Mosque. It was a big theater, not far from Monroe Park, in the middle of Richmond. Performers like Elvis Presley, the Champs and Chuck Berry were just a few of the big names who had supposedly appeared there in the past. The Mosque had formerly been a Shriner Temple, built in a Moorish style. After the City of Richmond bought it, they into a performance theater which hosted a number of big name shows every year. R.T. Mueller, the rather bizarre Serpents Den Lodge social chairman, was a huge fan of rock 'n roll music. After he heard about the big show, he put up a flyer on the lodge's bulletin board and a lot of Serps were planning on going.

Ashton Fincie, whose locker was adjacent to Tane Maaka's, overheard what Tane was saying about going into D.C. He said, "If you guys like rock 'n roll music, you ought to go with our gang at the Serpents Den to Richmond tomorrow night and see a really big show. It should be a fabulous event with all the stars that will be performing there."

Tane listened to the description of the event and turned to his buddies and said, "Hey guys, why don't we pass on D.C. tomorrow night and head down to Richmond instead?" He called Ashton over to tell them about it and they all agreed they wanted to go. After hearing about it, Voshon Rice and roommates Clyde Langston and Reggie King decided they wanted to go, too.

Reggie confided to Clyde that the reason he didn't want to go to the bars in D.C. was that he didn't drink. However, he loved music, so going to the show sounded like a great evening.

Tane asked Ashton if getting tickets was going to be a problem. Ashton told him that R.T. had said that the place seated about 5,000 people, but a lot of people would want to see the show. He suggested that to be on the safe side, everyone ought to be there to buy their tickets about an hour before the show began at 7PM.

As the players left the locker room, some were heading over to the dorms while a number of them headed to the Serpents Den Lodge near the center of the *Estate*. It had the largest percentage of players of any lodge at the university. President Robert H. Howard IV, had been a member there as well. In addition to Ashton Fincie being a Serp, CC Rider Snyder, Johnny Baugh, Garrett Gassman, Kenny Lynx, Cadillac deVille, Jack Delaney, Fred Lammhandler, Baldwin Tucker, Mac Gordon, Billy Vorache, Dan Kojak, Ironhead Ferrous, Parker Boardman, Ron Wall, Henry Frumzeist, and room-mates George Maizely and Al Nelson were Serps too. The Den's comfortable lounge area was packed with students who were sharing tales about their summer experiences. Kenny Cade had Russell Tad and Pete Huckleberry's attention as he talked about the catapult the Serps had built last year. He had used it to send a message to the Saint B's who had been messing with them. Since Peter Suntart , Dunhall Binkeg, Nelson Linkous, Kenny Lynx, and Baldwin Tucker all hailed from Virginia, they didn't have far to travel to come back to school. Some of them had even gotten together over the summer break.

Roger Rambeaux was back for his senior year along with his dog Spooky, who was almost like the lodge's official pet. For that matter, Spooky was almost like the school's mascot as well. Roger, who hailed from New Orleans, had already started trying to persuade the gang to come to Mardis Gras during the mid-semester break next year instead of returning to Lauderdale. He said he could mount the catapult on the floor of his pickup truck so they could shoot beads into the crowd during the parade. Roger figured that would attract a lot of flashers.

Bill Fryer, whose amazing ability to read lips had been a secret weapon for the football team last year, had just got back into town.

Bill reported that he had visited a cousin in Birmingham, Alabama in July. While there, his uncle had taken him to have breakfast at a place called the Club. It was on top of a hill and had a fabulous panoramic view. "I actually ate some grits," he said. That brought a big laugh from Garrett Gassman, Johnny Baugh, and Cadillac deVille who seemed very skeptical of his claim.

Everyone had registered by the end of the day on Friday and were all set for classes beginning on Monday August 25th. Despite all the fun times at Mosby, all of them knew that their classes would be a challenge. Students there had to manage their time and if they had to "sneak study," they better do it if they wanted to graduate. R.T. Mueller had come back to school from his home near Philly with a new stack of rock 'n roll records on 45's. He was telling everyone about some of the acts that he saw down on the Jersey shore. He also posted a list of the combos he had hired for the upcoming home game Saturday night parties at the Den that year. R.T. was rather bizarre, often rude and crude, but he was also very organized and a hell of a social chairman. His abilities enabled most of the guys to overlook his often strange behavior. The Dean of Men at Mosby, Robert P. Funk, had the nickname of R.I.P. Funk, since he had the power to sound the death knell of expulsion for any students who embarrassed the university by behaving badly. R.T. Mueller had never been disciplined so far during his stay at Mosby, but he was certainly on R.I.P.'s "watch list."

Meanwhile, over at Saint Bartholomew's Hall, roommates Troy Barksdale III and Tom Throckmorton were getting settled in their quarters. Tom said, "Did you hear about that big rock 'n roll show they are having tomorrow night at the Mosque?"

Troy replied, "I saw something about it in the Richmond *Times-Dispatch* last week, but who would want to go to that thing?" Since most of the entertainers will be coloreds, he knew they would probably relax the usual rule that required colored spectators to sit up in the segregated section in the second balcony. That area has crappy views, so they let them sit anywhere they wanted down below with the rest of the people during shows featuring a lot of colored performers. "Of course, in Richmond, the presence of whites at a so called colored program is always viewed as an honor by the attending Negros," Troy said. Some whites, will attend anyway so they can feel superior, but it won't be anyone we know, for sure.

Tom laughed and said, "You can bet that no descendants of any of the First Families of Virginia will be there. Can you imagine spending the whole evening sitting next to people like that? Besides, we have been in Richmond all summer and just got back up here. It would be kind of stupid to turn around and go back down to Richmond now."

Troy went on, "Speaking of music, Preston Wickersham told me that he had a superb string quartet all lined up for Saturday night after Mosby's first home football game of the season. Preston has done a great job as our social chairman, and he really knows how to find the talent. It ought to be a smashing good time. Do you have a date lined up yet?"

"No," Tom answered. "I really need to get on the stick and call Buffy. She's the girl I was thinking of asking, and I hope she can make it down from Vassar for the weekend."

14

Late Saturday afternoon, a huge contingent from Mosby University headed down Route 17 towards Fredericksburg, and took Route 1 from there to Richmond. Garrett Gassman had Cadillac deVille, Kenny Cade, Mac Gordon, and Kenny Lynx with him in his yellow Mercury convertible. Ashton Fincie managed to cram CC Rider Snyder, Dan Kojak, and Henry Frumzeist into his little Volkswagen Bug. They looked like one of those circus clown acts when they finally emerged in Richmond. Johnny Baugh filled up the Snakemobile with Parker Boardman, Al Nelson, George Maizley, Fred Lammhandler, Ronnie Wall, and Jack Delaney, but was careful to leave enough room in the back for a case of beer.

As for the newcomers, Tane Maaka was able to take Kevin Kahana, Voshon Rice, Shakur Wade, Ted Thigpen, Clyde Langston, LeRoyce Forsett and Reggie King in his little VW Microbus. They were jammed in, but they were also pretty fired up about the show, so they didn't mind. The trip wasn't too long, and all appreciated the free ride.

The show was going to be a BLAST! When the curtains opened, the beautiful Raelettes led the blind Ray Charles out to his piano. He smiled, clapping his hands to a rhythm, as he started the show by playing ***I've Got a Woman***. The show was underway, and it continued rockin' for the next three hours. The show featured performers like ol Fats Domino who sang **Blueberry Hill** and Mickey and Sylvia who sang **Love is Strange**. Every guy in the place probably wished that the beautiful Sylvia would say to them…."Come here Lover Boy!"

Seeing the guys on the team from the Serpents Den Lodge, Tane and his gang grabbed some seats near them. Thus, most of the team who attended, were sitting together, and everyone there really enjoyed the show.

Following the show, some trouble almost erupted when a redneck attendee, who went to high school with Al Nelson in Richmond, came over to him and said "Hey Al, what were you doing sitting over there by all those spades?"

Al looked at him and calmly said, "These guys are my teammates. Do you have a problem with that?"

The redneck gave him a look of disgust and walked off. It was a good move on that fellow's part, because he was about ready to get his butt kicked. Al's comment made a lot of points with the newcomers. You could bet they were going to be behind him as their quarterback out there on the field.

Richmond had been the capital of the Confederacy. Some of the old traditions and feelings toward race relations obviously still prevailed. There were still even some water fountains around town which were designated as being for whites and coloreds. This was 1959, and long after school desegregation had been mandated by the Supreme Court in 1954 in the *Brown v. Board of Education* case. However, racism wasn't surprising since there had been massive resistance to school desegregation in Virginia by many of the most prominent politicians in the state, including the current governor and a U.S. Senator.

All the young men who attended the show were raving about it on the trip back to Warrenton, and glad they hadn't missed it. They didn't get back until around midnight. Since most of them were still sore from the week's practices, their beds felt really good. They hit the sack with smiles on their faces, but most were thinking about the challenges that lay ahead. School was starting on Monday and practices, too.

    Reggie remembered that Head Coach Willie Hairston had pulled him aside after practice on Friday. Willie said that he had heard from Coach Benson that Reggie was a regular church goer in Pittsburgh. After Reggie affirmed the fact, the coach had invited him to join he and his wife on Sunday at the 9AM service at the Second Baptist Church in Warrenton. Reggie accepted the kind offer and was told to be out in front of his dorm at 8:45 on Sunday morning. Reggie made sure to set his alarm. He asked his roommate Clyde if he wanted to come too, but Clyde said he was tired and maybe he'd come another time.

15

Reggie was waiting out in front of his dorm the next morning, a beautiful sunny day, when Coach Hairston and his wife pulled up in their car. After introducing Reggie to Sally, Willie made the short drive over to the Second Baptist Church. Sally, who was holding little Bobby in her arms, would be leaving him at the church's day care during the service. Everyone enjoyed the pastor's sermon and the spirited music. Following the service, several people came up to Willie and wished him a lot of luck on the upcoming season. He proudly introduced Reggie as being one of his new players on the team. He also told them that there were several other Negroes on the team this year, and that he hoped they would come out to support the team. Many of the folks seemed surprised. There had never been any colored players on the team before, but having Willie and his assistants on the sidelines last year had been an even bigger surprise. Willie said as Reggie was getting out of the car, at the dorm after church, "I hope you can encourage some of the other young men on the team to join us in the future. I think it would be a good thing for everyone."

Reggie had a serious look on his face," I will try to do that Coach. I've even thought about going into the ministry myself someday, so I think I might as well get started right now on trying to bring people to the Lord."

Willie said, "What made you think about the ministry, Reggie?"

The young man replied, "Having lost my daddy when I was just a kid, I saw how my mama's faith enabled her to keep our family together. She made sure we all went to church, too. Also, one of my daddy's cousins went into the ministry. He is now down in Atlanta doing God's work. Nice meeting you Mrs. Hairston, and thanks for taking me today."

As they drove away, Sally said, "Reggie sure is a polite young man. I really like him. I hope he turns out to be a good a ball player, too."

Willie replied, "We are going to find out soon enough. Reggie was not only an excellent football player and basketball player back in high school, he also ran track. He was the fastest player on the team when we timed everyone last week. I have to get going tomorrow and start putting our offense and defense together. Our first game is away on September 12th. It's going to be a challenge. We don't have much time left to be ready.Monday August 24th was the first day of classes at Mosby University. Football practice was scheduled for 3PM to give everyone time to get there. The school had a well-earned reputation for academic excellence. Anyone who hoped to stay in school, had better hit the books hard, or else they would join the ranks of the ranks of many others who had come there in the past and flunked out.

Al Nelson was the team's senior starting quarterback. He was thinking about going to dental school following his graduation, and had been taking all the required pre-dental courses he needed while in school. However, he had one more hurdle to jump over: Organic Chemistry. Al had postponed taking that course until his final year. At Mosby, the course was taught by a diminutive and demanding professor named Dr. Albert Bernstein. He was notoriously tough and didn't grade on a curve. Some thought he was kidding when he informed each entering class that only half of them would pass his course, but it was the truth. Al went to the first class and was shocked by what he heard. He was even more shocked when Dr. Bernstein immediately got down to business. He started writing chemical formulas on the blackboard with his right hand and erasing them with his left hand as he moved from left to right. It got Al's attention and all of the other students, too.

That afternoon, when the team showed up for practice, several guys were a few minutes late. Coach Horne was on them like flies on molasses. He had them run a couple of laps around the field before they could come over and join the rest of the team. He also informed them that they would run two more laps after practice that day. The rest of the team took notice. You could bet they were going to make sure they weren't late.

The coaches separated the players into groups. Offensive linemen would go with Coach Benson; defensive linemen and defensive backs would go with Coach Jackson, who was the Defensive Coordinator. Linebackers would go with Coach Crocker; special teams players with Coach Freeman. Receivers were assigned to Coach Horne while running backs and quarterbacks would report to Head Coach Hairston. Because Mosby's team didn't offer athletic scholarships, they usually had fewer players than most of the schools they played. Because of that, some players had been designated for both offense and defense, so they would be dividing their time between coaches.

As the practice continued, the coaches began to introduce some of the kinds of plays that would be used on both sides of the ball. Practices for the rest of the week followed the same pattern but saw more plays added and some players re-assigned to other positions. By the time the week ended on Friday, the coaches had a pretty good idea as to who was going to play what position on the team. They also knew who would be starters, and who would be backups. Things could change in the two weeks remaining before their first game with the tough Piketown Pharaohs, who usually fielded a big and talented squad. Willie knew the Pharaoh's big stadium would be packed. The home crowd would be looking for revenge, after their loss last year at Mosby Memorial Stadium.

Just as the coaches were getting ready to leave on Friday afternoon to go to their homes and enjoy the weekend, a plump looking student wearing glasses appeared at the door to their conference room. He looked at Willie and said, "Hi Coach, remember me?"

Willie smiled and said, "Of course David. How was your summer?" David Seligman said, "Great coach, but I'm ready to help you with your scouting again this year if you need me."

"Willie replied, "That's great David. You and your lodge brothers at the Moses Manse really helped us a lot last year. Of course we'd love to have your assistance again. Our first game against Piketown is two weeks from tomorrow at their home field, but we will be playing the Lockridge Eagles here the following Saturday.

David grinned. "I've already seen the schedule and even have it up on our bulletin board at the Manse. A couple of our guys don't have classes on Thursdays. I was thinking that maybe they might make the three hour drive up to Piketown and scout out one of their practices. We sure don't look like coaches, so if they saw us hanging around they would probably figure that we are students there. As for the other games, I've already organized a scouting team for each game. I hope we can get the same deal on those great tickets as we did last year." Willie shook David's hand. "You bet. You've got that deal, David."

As Willie headed home he heard the Coasters singing **Charlie Brown** on the car radio and smiled. It reminded him of some of the clowns he knew back in school. Sally was waiting for him with a hug and kiss. All was good in his world as he picked up little Bobby, bounced him gently, and softly sang, "Bobby, Bobby….you're such a Clown," to the cute little guy in his arms. Sally said, "Don't sit down and get too comfortable, Willie, I picked up some steaks and you are grillin' out tonight. Go get the fire started because the baked potatoes are already in the oven."

"Yas-um Miss Sally….ol Willie's doin' that right now," Willie said as he did a little dance move in the kitchen before heading outside to his back patio and lighting the fire.

After a delicious dinner, Sally asked him, "Well, Willie, any predictions about how the team is going to do this year?"

Willie looked at her as he shook his head, raised both hands, and said, "Honey, your guess is as good as mine, but I'm feeling pretty good about the team right now. We've picked up some new players who look like they are going to help us this year, but until we've played a game, anything I might say is pure speculation."

16

As Willie was leaving his office, and preparing to go outside to run the practice on the following Monday, he saw a familiar face heading his way. Bill Fryer called out, "Hi Coach. I wanted to stop by today and see if you think you will need my help this year."

Willie replied, "Good to see you Bill. Hope you had a good summer vacation. You really helped us a lot last year. We would welcome you back on our sideline again for sure."

Bill shook hands with Willie and said, "I had a great summer, but it's good to be back at Mosby. I hear your first game is coming up pretty soon."

Willie nodded his head and said, "We open at Piketown on September 12th and have a lot of work to do to be ready for them and not much time to do it." If you want to ride up there to Piketown with us on the team bus, you're more than welcome. "

He said, "Just let me know when and where to catch it, and I'm onboard, Coach."

Bill, a member of the Serpents Den Lodge, had a special talent that had been very helpful the previous season. Due to a congenital problem as a young child, he had become deaf by the time he reached grade school. He learned to read sign language and read lips as well.

Fortunately, through some advances in medicine and the care of an outstanding E.N.T. doctor, his hearing was later restored. Standing on the Mosby Raider sideline with a pair of binoculars, he had been able to read the lips of the opposing coaches. He passed on that information and gave his coaches a heads up on what to look for on the field. Bill was an International History major, but had always aspired to be an F.B.I. agent. He was fascinated by the challenge of intelligence related things, but knew that he could never become an F.B.I. agent. It was common knowledge that they only hired ex-police officers, C.P.A.s, and lawyers. Willie had given Bill the title of Special Advisor, and tried to keep his role a secret. He figured that someone would catch on sooner or later. In the meantime, the team might as well continue to use his services.

The coaches had the offense running some plays against the defense and assigned various players to various positions. Since some were going to play on both sides of the ball, the coaches would periodically have them swap sides during breaks in the action. It was starting to become a lot clearer as to who would be playing what position. On Thursday, the coaches announced the starting line-up for the upcoming game. They announced that they planned to work the players as a unit on both sides of the ball the following week. Hopefully, the team would be ready to play on Saturday the 12th when they took the field against the powerful Piketown Pharaohs.

On Offense, the starting line-up had Al Nelson at quarterback with Reggie King as his backup and George Maizley as the disaster backup. Fred Lammhandler, Shakur Wade, and Eddie Ironhead Ferrous would split time as running backs. The duo of Johnny Baugh and George Maizley would alternate at fullback. Ronnie Wall, Garrett Gassman, and Kenny Lynx were returning and would share receiver duties. Parker Boardman was back, after an outstanding sophomore year at tight end, and he would be joined at that position by 6'5", 230 lb. newcomer Voshon Rice who would try to offset the loss of Robbie Gunderson to graduation.

The offensive line would be anchored by the return of big Dan Kojak, who had missed his sophomore year due to an injury and had one more year of eligibility. He was taking a light load that semester and planning to graduate at the end of the first semester. He would be backed up by newcomer Clyde Langston, who also could play guard. The starting guards would be Charlie "Radar" Giordano and scrappy Jack Delaney with Baldwin Tucker as a utility lineman, who could play either guard or tackle as a backup. Big tackles CC Rider Snyder and Henry Frumzeist had been solid performers the previous season and Willie was real glad they were back.

The Defense had a new look for the new season. Instead of a four linemen-three linebacker scheme, the loss of team captain and defensive tackle Hank Warwick to graduation had prompted the change to a three linemen-four linebacker scheme. One of the keys to this alignment was having a powerful nose tackle playing over the opposing offensive center. The coaches felt confident they found one in the person of newcomer Tane Maaka. He was incredibly strong and very quick as well. He was going to be a load for opposing linemen to deal with. Offensive tackles Snyder and Frumzeist could fill in if needed to give Tane a break. Returning veterans Ashton Fincie and Billy Vorache would man the defensive end positions with Baldwin Tucker as their backup.

The outside linebacker positions would be Mac Gordon and two-way player Garrett Gassman. The middle linebacker positions would be handled by two-way players George Maizley and Fred Lammhandler and newcomer LeRoyce Forsett.

The defensive backfield looked like it would have more speed that than the previous year. Reggie King would be at one corner and two-way player Kenny Lynx would be at the other. Ironhead Ferrous would serve as their backup. Reggie chose the uniform number 13, much to the surprise of his room-mate, Clyde Langston.

Clyde said, "Why would you pick a number like that Reggie? It's unlucky."

Reggie laughed and replied. "I'm not superstitious and I don't believe in luck. I believe you make your own luck in life and on the field through your performance.

The safety positions would be manned by Johnny Baugh and newcomer Ted Thigpen. As for the kicking game, Manny Morales would handle kickoffs, extra points and field goals. Lanky Cadillac deVille was an outstanding punter, and he gave the team great field position on many occasions last year with his deep kicks. As for the rest of the players, Willie promised them that they would get plenty of playing time on special teams. Also, whenever the team had a two touchdown lead, backups would have the chance to work into the lineup and replace the starters on the field. Willie felt that everyone on the team had an important role to play in the team's success.

Willie liked what he saw, but knew they had a lot of work to do to be ready. In the week leading up to the game, he and his assistants worked on devising and executing their game plan. David Seligman and one of his fellow lodge members went up to Piketown and watched one of the Pharaoh's practices. He passed along their findings to Willie. After reviewing the notes, Willie and his assistants felt that trying to run into the heart of Piketown's big defensive line might be tough. However, they thought they could probably attack the edges and downfield against their smaller defensive backs. Jim Jankowski, their big strong armed quarterback, provided most of their offense, since the notes indicated that their running backs were not very fast or effective.

17

 Roger Rambeaux was sitting in the lounge at the Serpents Den petting Spooky, his big Rhodesian Ridgeback-Rottweiler mix dog. Lance LaRue came in the door looking for him. Roger was the head cheerleader at Mosby University and Lance, along with his three fellow Muse Men Lodge members, Horace Butterworth, Percy Pankey, and the amazing Bruce Springhopper, were the other four members of his team. Lance said, "Did you hear the latest? After Spooky ran over to Piketown's sideline last year and toppled their *Pharaoh* off his throne, Piketown has just announced that Mosby's cheerleaders and Spooky will not be welcome at the game? I'm so mad, I could just spit."

 Roger laughed as he remembered what happened and said, "Well, who wants to go up to Piketown anyway? The place is a depressing coal mining town. Our first home game will be the following week. I will have Spooky all dressed up with his custom silver coat with the Serpents Dens snake on one side and a big M on the other side. He will be excited about running out and grabbing the kicking tees. Since a lot of the players belong to our lodge, I will tell them of Piketown's slight. Maybe that will give them an added incentive to go there and kick Piketown's butt." Upon hearing Roger, Lance almost wanted to do a cartwheel.

Kenny Cade was sitting on a nearby sofa and studying. After Lance took off, he turned to Roger and said, "Maybe we ought to load up our catapult, take it up to Piketown and give their administrative offices the treatment we gave the St. B.'s last year."

Roger said, "Naw, people would notice it in the back of my pickup truck and I doubt we could get away with it up there in hostile territory. I'll just tell the guys to win one for ol' Spooky. Besides, after hearing we wouldn't be going up there, I made a date with a real *ghost* over at Mary Washington. Pete Huckleberry is going with me. Why don't you and Russell Tad, Peter Suntart, and Nelson Linkous try to get dates over there and join us? We can make it a party at that little jukebox joint near Hartwood just off Route 17. I bet someone could even talk Johnny Baugh into loaning them the Snakemobile, if you put some gas into it. "

Kenny replied, "That sounds like a plan. I took a real *ghost* from Mary Washington to that place last year. I'd like to get back together with her after the summer break."

Roger grinned, "I'll try to gin up some interest with the other guys. I might even tell R.T. Mueller about the proposed *raid*, too. On second thought, after the stunt R.T. pulled with his date in the movie theater there with the popcorn box, I don't think I'll mention it. I don't know all the facts of that incident, but I do know that he is banned for life at that theater in Fredericksburg. I hear that they even have his picture on the wall in the ticket booth. Who knows, maybe he's been banned at Mary Washington, too."

Kenny laughed and said, "Yeah, you are probably right. R.T.'s a great social chairman, but he can be pretty bizarre sometimes, as well as lewd and crude. His "bota bag" that he uses to transport his liquor, is more commonly used for feminine hygiene. He sure loves to whip it out and shock people. Most of the other guys will think it's a great idea to make that *raid*, so I bet they get on the phone and round up some dates."

R.T. had put up an announcement on the lodge bulletin board telling everyone that he had hired the sensational **_Tommy and the Tomahawks_** to return to the Serpents Den Lodge for the third straight year. They would be there for the party on the Saturday evening of the Mosby Raiders first home game. The wild and crazy **_Tomahawks_** featured the flamboyant Tommy on lead guitar and three other colored guys dressed up like Indians playing great dancing music with a strong beat. That was another good reason for the Serps to get on the phone and line up some dates. It was going to be a great party and they didn't want to miss out on all the fun.

18

On Friday afternoon September 11th, the air was filled with excitement as the team had a final light run through, before a team meeting in Mosby Memorial Gymnasium to go over the game plan. Instead of going up to Piketown and spending the night before the game, Willie and the coaches had decided to wait until 8AM Saturday morning to load the team onto a couple of busses to take them there. Since it was only about three hours away, they would have plenty of time to get into their uniforms and warm up before the scheduled 2PM kickoff. Big coolers filled with sandwiches and bottles of carbonated water were put on both busses. The team was fired up. Some were understandably nervous, but most seemed ready to get out there and start hitting some other people rather than their own teammates.

After kissing Sally and little Bobby goodbye, early the next morning, Willie left home to head to the parking lot near the coach's offices. He got his playbook and the folder with his game plan before boarding the bus. Having been warned about the importance of punctuality, all the players and the coaches were there by 7:45AM and ready to go. The ride up to Piketown was uneventful. They arrived around 11AM, early enough that they didn't encounter any pre-game traffic around the stadium. The Raiders went directly to the visitor's locker room and began to suit up. The team trainers were busy taping players and getting them ready for the contest. Willie and the coaches were working the room and reminding the players of what they had to do out there. Everyone appeared confident and ready.

As the players went out on the field for their pregame warm-up, the stands were somewhat empty, but Willie knew they would probably be full by game time. The Piketown Pharaoh's Phans were notoriously strong supporters of their team. He had been told that less than a thousand of Mosby's fans had ordered tickets, so it was going to be a hostile environment. Willie was prepared. He had had the team work on some silent counts in the event they couldn't hear the signals.

Willie took the opportunity to talk to Piketown's coach, Billy Reid, whom he had met the previous season. Both coaches wished each other good luck. Willie also introduced himself and chatted with the referees. He told them about his 5 Yard Maker Play, so they wouldn't be surprised if he used it. It was a beautiful, partly cloudy day with temperatures in the high 70's. It looked like it was going to be a good day for the spectators and the players alike.

After the Piketown Pharaoh arrived wearing his Egyptian headdress and sitting on his throne, he was transported by four burley attendants to the podium behind the Piketown bench. The National Anthem was played, and then the team captains met at midfield and the coin was tossed. The Pharaohs won the toss and elected to receive the opening kick-off, much to the delight of the approximately 35,000 fans in the stands. Manny Morales, the little Mosby soccer style kicker from Argentina, boomed it five yards deep into the end zone. The Pharaoh kick returner foolishly tried to bring it out, only to be brought down hard on the 16 yard line by the fast-moving Voshon Rice.

Piketown's big quarterback Jankowski had been briefed that Mosby had lost some of its defensive backs to graduation, so he decided to test the newcomers right away. He noticed that his split end on the left side had a lot of room in front of him. Reggie King, the Mosby

Raiders cornerback, was playing about ten yards back. Reggie noticed the quarterback glance at the receiver he was covering and decided to see if he could bait him into making a throw to his man. Immediately upon taking the snap, Jankowski took a quick three step drop and fired the ball out to the receiver, who had taken off about 5 yards downfield and turned to receive the ball. Just as Jankowski prepared to release the ball, Reggie exploded forward with incredible speed, and snatched the ball in front of the surprised receiver and easily took it for a 21 yard Pick Six touchdown. The raucous crowd was shocked and still silent when Manny Morales added the extra point to give Mosby a 7-0 lead with less than one minute gone in the game.

Willie glanced over at Bill Fryer. "Nobody can blame that one on you Bill."

Bill laughed and said, "Their coach had his play card in front of his face, so I couldn't see anything anyway."

Following another deep Morales kickoff, the Piketown return specialist smartly took a knee and the Pharaohs got the ball on the 20 yard line. Not risking being burned down deep at his own end of the field again, Jankowski tried to establish a running attack without much success. His fullback was smashed in the hole by Tane Maaka for no gain. The next attempted run was stopped by Ashton Fincie and Mac Gordon after only a two yard advance. When Jankowski's pass on 3rd down was overthrown, the Pharaohs had to punt.

Ironhead Ferrous fielded the punt on the Raiders 40 yard line and broke a tackle, as he brought the ball back to midfield. From there, Al Nelson mixed some pinpoint short passes to Gassman and Wall before hitting Kenny Lynx with a 20 yard touchdown pass on a post pattern in the center of the end zone. Morales quickly made it 14-0 after his extra point kick. The Raiders already had a sizeable lead less than halfway through the first quarter.

Willie began substituting some backup players, but after Piketown scored and made it 14-7, the starters returned and dominated the game. Fred Lammhandler rushed for 70 yards, and *Ironhead Ferrous* rushed for 85 yards including breaking a 55 yard run for a touchdown to blow the game open. Al Nelson was sensational as he completed 18 out of 21 attempts for over 250 yards. Willie was confident that Al was going to have a great season. Mosby wide receivers Lynx, Gassman, and Wall caught 13 passes between them. Tight end Parker Boardman had a great game, too, as he caught three passes. Two of them went for touchdowns on play action passes close to the end zone. Mosby went onto win 31 to 14.

After the game, Piketown Head Coach Billy Reid met Willie at midfield and congratulated him on the win. "I thought we would give Mosby more of a game, being at home this year," Reid said. "But the speed of your defensive backs caught us off guard. Both wished each other luck for the rest of the season.

In the jubilant locker room, following the game, Willie was feeling in good spirits as he awarded game balls to Al Nelson, Fred Lammhandler, Eddie Ferrous, and Parker Boardman on offense. He also awarded game balls to newcomers Reggie King, who picked off two passes, and Tane Maaka who dominated the middle of the line on defense. There were a lot of cheers afterwards as the Raiders ebullient senior center Dan Kojak led everyone in a round of "Here we go Mosby Men… here we go!" The team had made reservations for dinner that night in a ballroom of a local hotel. Following that, the buses took the tired but satisfied players back to Warrenton. Everyone agreed it was a great start to the season.

19

The team wasn't the only group of happy Mosby students that night. The big gang of members from the Serpents Den Lodge had made a raid on Mary Washington that was a smashing success as well. Pete Huckleberry and Roger Rambeaux had talked their dates into fixing up the rest of the gang with dates. As it turned out, Russell Tad, Kenny Cade, and Nelson Linkous liked their girls so much, they invited them down to Warrenton for the home opener the following Saturday against the Lockridge Eagles. Everyone enjoyed the hamburgers, beers and dancing at the jukebox joint not far from Fredericksburg where the gang had taken their dates. Some of them must have gotten pretty tired, since they took turns taking breaks and going out to the Snakemobile with their dates to "rest up" before returning to rejoin the group inside.

Because they had to have the girls back at the dorm by midnight to meet the curfew, the Serps were able to get back to Warrenton before 1AM. They were surprised by the news they heard from some of the guys who were still up and playing cards. They told them that the lodge members who were on the team had already returned from their game and had hit the sack. They also learned that the team had pulled off an opening game victory on the road.

Both *The Fauquier Times-Democrat*, and the school newspaper, *The Ghostly Vision*, had complimentary articles about the opening game victory over Piketown College. Single game tickets for the home opener on Saturday September 19th against the Lockridge College Eagles were reportedly selling fast, so there ought to be a good crowd at the game. Not having actually seen the new team, there was not much said about the new group of players. There was also no mention of the fact that there were some colored players on the team for the first time in history. Some of the Mosby's fans were unaware of that change and were going to be shocked when they found out. After the first home game, the attendees and the press would learn about the changes to the composition of the team soon enough.

Over at the St. B Lodge, Troy Barksdale III had some good news for his roommate Tom Throckmorton. Troy said, "My dad's bank has bought a big block of primo season tickets on the 50-yard line so they can take board members and important clients to the games. He and a big gang of people are coming, but he told me that he has six extra tickets available. I can select anyone I want to join me. That means we wouldn't have to sit in the student section with the rest of the cretins. How would you and your date Buffy like to join me and my date at the game? I've invited Rebecca Buckingham from Sweet Briar up for the weekend. I'm sure she's going to love that string quartet that Preston Wickersham hired to entertain us that evening."

Tom said, "Wow, Troy! That would be smashing. Thanks! What are you going to do with the other two tickets?"

Troy replied, "I was thinking of asking Preston if he would like to join us. I'm not sure if he really likes football, since he's kind of stuffy, but it might impress his date. Since we both know he's pretty horny, anything he can do to impress a date might help him when he tries to make out with her later."

Tom laughed and said, "Preston needs all the help he can get. Despite his frantic efforts over the last couple of years, I think old

Preston doesn't know how to score with the women. Frankly, I suspect that he's still a virgin." It was Troy's turn to laugh.

Sunday morning seemed to come way too early, but Reggie woke up and got dressed and was out in front of his dorm when Coach Willie and Sally came by to pick him up. He had been able to persuade his roommate, Clyde Langston, to come along, too and that seemed to make Willie happy. The pastor's message during the service at the Second Baptist Church was really inspiring. The young players thought that the music was even better. Clyde told Reggie afterwards that he was glad he got out of bed and went with them that morning.

Feeling a little stiff and tired following the game the afternoon before, both of them took a nap later Sunday afternoon, after sitting outside under a tree and doing some studying. Reggie wasn't about to lose his academic scholarship. He already knew he liked Mosby University better than Oakmont, so he planned on hitting the books hard in his free time.

A lot of the local residents in the Warrenton, Middleburg, and Manassas areas were probably going to be in the stands on the upcoming Saturday after reading about the Raiders victory over Piketown in the *Fauquier Times-Democrat.* Student interest was probably high as well after they read about the opening victory in *The Ghostly Vision*. With the mild weather forecast for the weekend of September 19th, the papers even speculated that John Singleton Mosby Memorial Stadium might even sell out all their 25,000 seats. The Lockridge Eagle team wasn't predicted to be that strong of an opponent, since they were coming off a 4-6 year. However, Willie and his staff weren't about to take any team for granted. They remembered the close call they had against Radford the previous season when they went down there overly confident and had gotten down 14-0 early in the game.

David Seligman showed up at Willie's office before the start of practice on Monday and said, "My guys were at the Eagles home game against Frostburg on Saturday. I've brought you the scouting notes that we made. Lockridge managed to pull out a 17-14 win, but it could have gone either way."

Willie reviewed the notes and asked some questions. He came away with the impression that the Eagles were pretty conservative offensively. They apparently liked to grind it out if they could and didn't throw the ball very often. On defense, they played back and tried to guard against the deep pass, but Frostburg had enjoyed success running the ball against them. In spite of that, if it hadn't have been for some untimely turnovers, they probably would have won.

He thanked David and told him to call the ticket office and speak to Justin down there. Willie would have six prime seats reserved for David and his helpers near midfield and real close to the action.

David had a grin on his face as he was leaving and said, "Thanks Coach! I already have a couple of guys set to scout out Greenville this weekend for you." Willie smiled and gave David a thumbs up as he went out the door.

Practice on Monday was a light one with an emphasis on running, stretching, lifting weights and talking about the good things that happened on Saturday. Willie told the players where they needed to improve. They would put in the game plan for Lockridge as the week went on and, he hoped, the team would be ready to play in their home opener on Saturday. Coming into the game with a 1-0 record was sure better than the other way around. Willie hoped that could make it two in a row with a win against Lockridge. Practices went well enough that week that Willie felt confident their game plan was solid, and they were ready to take on the Eagles.

20

    The Stallion Stable Lodge members were planning for a big weekend when the Lockridge Eagles came to Warrenton. Their social chairman, Joey Gallata, had booked the fabulous ***Atlantic Surf Kings*** to play on Saturday night. This gang of five guys, in tee shirts with duck tail haircuts, was very popular on the South Jersey shore and in the Philadelphia area. Their classic rock 'n roll songs were also great for dancing. Ricky Russo and Mike Marino were bringing some chicks down from Philly for the weekend while Vinny Del Vecchio and Joey had dates coming all the way from New York City. Since none of them were college girls, who had to stay at approved homes, the guys had reserved motel rooms for them in Culpepper. They were looking forward to a big weekend. Boda Bing…Boda Boom!

    The Stallion Stable Lodge's two Hawaiian former paniolos, Alan Akamu and Kevin Kahana had dates with a pair of roommates from Mary Baldwin they had dated the year before. Kevin would be part of the festivities on Saturday at the game. He would be reprising his role as the GRAY GHOST and would be riding his horse out onto the field prior to the game's start. The girls always thought he was pretty dashing with his sword, hat, and cape. Kevin had invited his good buddy from Hawaii, Tane Maaka, to come to their lodge for the party on Saturday night. Kevin was hopeful that the other guys would like him and extend Tane an invitation to join the lodge when bids went out in the spring.

Hearing that social chairman R.T. Mueller had hired the sensational **Tommy and the Tomahawks** to play at the Serpents Den Lodge on Saturday night, most of the members at the Den had arranged to get dates and made plans to bring them into town. As usual, Cadillac deVille was observed making a lot of last minute phone calls as he scrambled to come up with one. Most of his buddies thought that the odds were not very good. George Maizley had invited Judith, his long-time sweetheart, down from Sarah Lawrence and would be doubling with his roommate Al Nelson. Al seemed to have a thing for cute little Sandi Lee from Richmond and had invited her up for the weekend. Garrett Gassman had fixed up Jack Delaney with a girl from George Washington University, who was the roommate of his date. Garrett had met her that spring and assured Jack that she was a certified *ghost*. Many other girls from Mary Washington would be there for the game and the party later that night. After the successful raid some of the Serps had pulled off the weekend before, the party was going to be a blast. Fortunately, several of the guys had persuaded R.T. to drop his plans to get the party rolling by using the lodge's catapult to shoot off a fuselage of flaming old jockstraps wrapped around some oranges into the pond near the lodge. R.T. was disappointed and wondered why some of the guys thought the idea was just a little too strange. However, he went along with their desires and told them that maybe he would do it another time. Most of the guys in the lodge were probably thinking that R.T. ought to wait until the middle of the summer break to try that trick.

On the game day Saturday morning, Troy Barksdale II showered after breakfast and got dressed for the day's activities. When he finished the task, he couldn't help but admire the image he saw in his closet's full length mirror. His lightweight wool black blazer, with the bright silver buttons, had been tailored to fit him perfectly at the exclusive men's shop where he bought all of his clothes. His crisp grey toned Pima cotton button-down shirt was fashionably accented with silver cuff links, which had black inserts. He wore a silk black and silver grey rep tie, which he had put on with a perfect Windsor knot. His lightweight grey wool slacks were sharply creased, and his black Bass Weejun loafers were shined to perfection. He smiled at the image in the mirror, because he knew that he looked terrific. He said to himself, "Well, just look who is the Rep Dreath around here today."

In stark contrast to the kick-off spectacular that R.T. had envisioned, numerous mimosas and Bloody Mary's were being served, along with some delicious catered hors d'oeuvres to some other stylishly attired people. This affair was going on in the beautiful center courtyard at the corporate headquarters of Richmond's big Tidewater National Bank late that Saturday morning. The mid-September day was warm, but not unduly so, and since the majestic magnolia trees provided plenty of shade, relief from the sunshine was readily available. Light classical music emanated from the courtyard's sound system to provide some additional ambiance.

Barksdale, the bank's president, wanted to celebrate the bank's purchase of one hundred season tickets to Mosby University's home games by having this event. He had invited a number of the bank's most important customers to join him and the executives of the bank, all with their wives, to attend the reception that morning. Following the reception, everyone would be driven up to Warrenton in chartered luxury busses to enjoy an afternoon of action on the gridiron. He hoped the Mosby Raiders wouldn't spoil the fun and would win their home opener against the Lockridge Eagles. This day was sure to engender a lot of goodwill, and because it was a write off, Troy didn't care how much it cost. He was proud of the record the Raiders had compiled the previous season, but still not sure he liked the idea that the school had employed a colored coaching staff to coach the team. He felt there had to be a number of qualified white coaches available. He also thought most anyone could have done a good job in replacing old Buddy Hendricks, who had run out of enthusiasm as the former coach of the team. He should have been fired years ago.

Another sizable group of people were also enthused about going to Mosby's home opener. The large congregation at the Second Baptist Church in Warrenton was already very proud that Coach Willie Hairston and his wife Sally were regular attendees. After seeing Coach Hairston bring a couple of young colored players to church with him, and then learning that there were several others on the team, made a lot of people in Warrenton's Negro community interested in going out to see the Mosby Raiders. In the past, there were not many of them who cared to watch Mosby's all white team play. The team had traditionally struggled to win any games, and that was another reason for the lack of enthusiasm. Seats, in the open seating bleacher section in the north end zone were available for only a dollar a piece. That's where most of the congregation was going.

As for the student section at John Singleton Memorial Stadium, it was located on the west side, behind the home team bench between the goal line and the 35 yard line at both ends of the field. Being the home opener, the stadium was expected to be packed with fans. The visiting team fans were usually located high up on the east side of the field near the goal line. The number that actually would show up varied from team to team. Lockridge had requested all of their allotment of 5,000 tickets, due to their strong fan support, so there would be some cheering out there during the game for the Eagles that day.

In the locker room prior to the game, Willie went over the game plan and reviewed the kind of plays they would feature on both offense and defense. The players seemed pretty clear about what they had to do. After big Dan Kojak led them in the Mosby cheer, the team was all fired up and ready to go. Once they emerged onto the field, they saw that the gridiron was in great condition. As usual, it had a big black M painted in the middle of the field in the center of a gray circle. It was going to be a perfect day for football. Rather than wear their black jerseys with the silver gray numbers, the team was wearing their light gray jerseys with the black numbers due to the warmer weather. The stands were somewhat empty for the most part, but a steady stream of spectators was coming in. As the Raiders went through their stretching exercises and warm up drills and plays, the Lockridge Eagles came out onto their end of the field wearing their red jerseys. Willie noted that they had about double the amount of players that Mosby did. That wasn't surprising since most teams did. However, he did worry that the warm day might tire his players out, and Lockridge might have enough quality substitutes to make a difference in the outcome. Those worries were short lived as he concentrated on making sure his team executed the game plan. Willie made a point to go introduce himself to the referees and greet the opposing coach before the game. That tradition had started the previous season and he wasn't going to stop doing it.

Prior to the start of the contest, the five man Mosby all male cheerleading squad was trying to fire up the home crowd. The squad was led by Roger Rambeaux, a member of the Serpents Den Lodge, and the other four members of the team, were members of the Muse Men Lodge. Lance LaRue, Horace Butterworth, Bruce Springhopper, and Percy Pankey always delighted the crowd with their enthusiasm and creative choreography. They were well known for doing amazing handsprings and backflips on the sideline prior to and during the games. Roger had his dog Spooky out there with him. Spooky had on a silver grey coat with a big M one side and a black snake on the other, since he was also the unofficial mascot of the Serpents Den Lodge. Spooky routinely barked after every cheer and he also loved the crowd's enthusiasm.

About ten minutes prior to the scheduled kick-off, the five members of the Fabulous Flugelhorns came proudly marching out onto the field waving their shiny brass instruments up and down in time with their steps. Their trumpet-like horns featured extra wide cones, or flanks and were generally thought to be of German extraction. One of the history professors at Mosby had once informed his students that flugelhorns were traditionally used on the battlefield to summon the troops to the flanks of the enemy. Having them there was only fitting, since Colonel Mosby always seemed to outflank his opponents. These five young talented musicians, like most of the cheerleaders, were also members of the Muse Men Lodge. As they marched out onto the field, they assumed positions at the five points of the big letter "M" at midfield and then began to loudly play Mosby's school song.

Suddenly, Kevin Kahana, the student who played the part of the Gray Ghost, came thundering out onto the field riding a handsome black horse. He was wearing a silver gray outfit and black boots. His big black cape waved in the breeze as he brandished his sabre in the air. Upon seeing him appear, the Mosby fans exploded into enthusiastic cheers and applause. The school band played the National Anthem, the captains of both teams met at midfield with the referee, and the coin was tossed. Mosby won the toss and elected to defer to the second half, so they would be kicking off to the Eagles.

The game got underway as Manny Morales boomed a kick deep into the end zone. The returner wisely elected to take a knee and not try to make a return. The Eagles would take over on offense on their own 20 yard line on their first offensive possession. Immediately after the kickoff, Roger released Spooky onto the field. He ran out, retrieved the kicking tee, and brought it back to Roger to the cheers of the home crowd.

The Eagles went on offense. They tried a run on first down, but linebacker George Maizley was coming hard on a run blitz and stopped the ball carrier after a gain of only one yard. Then, their quarterback attempted a quick look-in pass to their tight end, only to see big Tane Maaka bat it down. The quarterback's pass on 3rd down with 9 yards to go sailed wide and out of bounds, forcing them to punt.

Bill Fryer came over to Willie. "Sorry, coach. I can't seem to be able to help you out. The Eagle's coach always holds up a folder in front of his face when he sends in the plays.

Willie replied, "That's okay Bill. Just keep watching and maybe you might pick up something for us as the game wears on."

After the Eagle's soaring punt, Ironhead Ferrous called for a fair catch, and the Raiders took over on their own 38 yard line. On first down, Al Nelson dropped back looking to pass, but instead he gave the ball off to Fred Lammhandler on a draw play that went for nine yards. Nelson threw deep on second down and narrowly missed hitting Kenny Lynx on a go pattern. That attempt loosened up the Eagle's defenders. On third down, Baugh punched straight ahead for three yards and a first down as a big cheer went out from the crowd.

Al Nelson began to fire a series of precision short passes in the flats and crossing patterns to his wide receivers Wall, Gassman, and Lynx in addition to quick look in passes to his tight end Boardman. He also mixed in some quick hitting off tackle runs by Ferrous, Lammhandler, and Wade with fullback dives by Maizley and Baugh who were alternating at that position. These plays resulted in a series of Raiders first downs as they marched steadily down the field. Nelson completed the drive when he threw a touchdown pass to Gassman in the flat on a play action fake. The Raiders went out in front, 7-0 after Morales kicked the extra point. The 62 yard drive had taken a lot of time off the clock and about half the time in the first quarter was gone.

The Eagles fought back valiantly. They moved the ball from time to time during the game, but never seemed to be able to sustain a drive. Their runs would often be stuffed, and the speedy Mosby defensive backs thwarted their attempts to complete most of their passes. Mosby's nose tackle Maaka, despite having both offensive guards and the center trying to block him, disrupted many running plays. The outside pressure from Vorache and Fincie often forced the Eagles quarterback to rush his throws. The game mercifully ended with a 24-3 win by the Mosby Raiders. The score was deceptive, and might have been higher if Mosby hadn't been so conservative on offense. The team seemed content to just chip away at the Lockridge defense and eat up the clock with long drives instead of trying to score quickly. Willie met the Eagle's coach at midfield following the game and they wished each other good luck in their remaining games. Since so many players had contributed to the win, Willie decided to award the game ball to Jack Johnson, his Defensive Coordinator, for his efforts in holding Lockridge to a single field goal. The players applauded the selection. Jack had a big smile on his face in appreciation of the honor.

Most of the Mosby fans were delighted in what they had viewed on the field that day. The students were always happy with a win and not a loss, which would have put a damper on their plans for the post game and evening parties. The Negro fans, who had been sitting in the north end zone bleachers, were really excited about seeing some colored players out there on the Mosby gridiron for the first time. They planned on telling all their friends about what they saw and hoped more would come out for the upcoming games that season.

However, not all the Mosby fans were happy with what they observed that day. Mitchell Montague IV, a 1938 graduate, had come with the big contingent on the chartered Tidewater National Bank busses from Richmond. He pulled Troy Barksdale aside after the game and said, "Did you see all those colored people down in the end zone today? The next thing you know, they will be sitting up in the west stands with us. Now that the university has decided to admit colored students, and they have them out there on the football field, are we going to start scheduling some colored schools to play? I'm not happy about this development. I'm going to have to look long and hard at whether or not I want to come back to any more games in the near future."

Troy Barksdale nodded his head in agreement. "I understand how you feel. Frankly, I don't know what foolishness got into Bob Howard's head to make that damn speech at the NAACP convention this year. All I know is that it has resulted in a number of colored students enrolling in our school, and I don't like it one bit. I think this all started because he allowed that Willie Hairston to come to school here and become a graduate. We both know that the coloreds have their own schools, so why should they be coming here? It was already bad enough that we had to play schools like Oakmont, up there in Pennsylvania. They have had colored players on their teams for some time, but fortunately, none of the other teams we play in Virginia or Carolina have any Negroes on theirs. I wonder how they are going to react when they see them on Mosby's team this year?"

Montague replied, "Yeah! It's a damn shame. Those people ought to go to their own schools with their own people. They fit in there. They should not be coming to a fine institution like Mosby University."

"Just hiring Hairston to replace Hendricks after he retired wasn't bad enough in itself," Barksdale responded. "Letting Hairston hire three other Negros as his assistants last year was the last straw. President Howard even twisted my arm into giving Hairston a mortgage on a house that he and his wife bought here in Warrenton. It was the first mortgage the bank has ever given to a colored applicant. If this trend continues, it's going to dramatically change the university we both love. At least, I see that they have added a couple of white assistant coaches this season. President Howard knows that the bank is the largest season ticket holder, so you would think that he ought to appreciate our support. Don't worry Mitchell, I'll be talking with Bob Howard very soon and will share our concerns with him."

21

Following the game, the mood around the *Estate* was joyful. Many students were still cheering as they headed back to their dorms or lodges. At the Stallion Stable Lodge, Joey Gallata, their social chairman, had arranged a post-game cocktail party where they they served Chianti with delicious antipasto. Kevin Kahana was still wearing his Gray Ghost outfit; several of the member's dates were admiring it. Kevin's roommate, Alan Akamu asked Joey if maybe they could have some pineapple and guavas added to the post-game nibbles next time.

Joey laughed. "You kanakas are all alike. You can take a guy out of the islands, but you can't take the islands out of the guy."

Ricky Russo, Vinny Del Vecchio, and Mike Marino, hanging out near the food and wine with their dates, overheard what Joey said and laughed.

Vinny said, "You got that right Joey. I'm surprised that Kevin and Alan didn't bring their surfboards with them and try to do some surfing up at Great Falls on the Potomac near D.C.

Kevin replied, "I invited my Hawaiian bruddah Tane Maaka to come over tonight to hear the **Atlantic Surf Kings** play. Better be careful and don't call him a kanaka, since some natives over there in the islands think it is insulting. We Hawaiians call each other kanaka's all the time, but you haoles better not do it. You saw him kickin' butt out there on the field today; I don't think you want to be next. He's a big tough dude!"

"So Kevin, you think maybe I ought to bring my tire iron to the party tonight, just in case we have a rumble?, Mike Marino asked.

Kevin laughed and replied, "Naw Mike, leave it in your car. Tane's a good guy and you're going to like him, but only a fool would want to mess with him."

Meanwhile, at Saint Bartholomew's Hall, most of the lodge members had taken their dates back to their approved homes and would be picking them up later to escort them to dinner prior to the evening's festivities. The string quartet that Preston Wickersham had hired wasn't scheduled to start until 8PM, so there would be plenty of time to have a civilized dinner at a nice place. Following that, they could return to the Hall for the music and some stimulating conversation during the quartet's breaks.

Troy Barksdale III, and his roommate Tom Throckmorton were planning on taking their dates to the exclusive private Huntsman Club, just up the road near the Plains, Virginia after the game. Troy's dad was a member. Tom's date Buffy had raved about the venison that both she and Troy's date Rebecca had enjoyed there last spring, after attending the Virginia Gold Cup with the two St. B. roommates.

The scene at the Serpents Den Lodge was festive as well. Their houseman, Cary Fredericks, was wearing his white serving jacket and was pouring French 75's for the members and their dates. Assuming that not many would succumb to the temptation to drink too many of these sneaky, but potent concoctions, the members and their dates would be back later to do some serious partying and dancing to the hard driving rhythms of **Tommy and the Tomahawks**. The members who were on the football team were returning from showering at the gym. They were in a celebratory mood as they received pats on their backs and congratulations for a great win. Several of their dates were happy to see them, too. Most of the dates had been brought to the lodge by some of the other members so that they could enjoy the French 75's while waiting for their heroes to return. Instead of pats on the back, the girls were kissing the triumphant players. The guys enjoyed all the adulation. Peter Suntart was in a corner talking to Nelson Linkous and his cute date Joanie, from Mary Washington, when the players arrived. He asked Henry Frumzeist if he minded having those new colored players on the team this year.

Henry laughed. "I might mind if these guys couldn't play, but most of them are talented. They have been working hard out there and have done a good job for us. I don't care if they are purple or green, they are my Mosby Raider teammates and so I like 'em."

Al Nelson and his room-mate George Maizley came in about that time. Al's date Sandi and George's longtime girlfriend Judith, had both been brought over to the lodge by the suave and gentlemanly Bill Fryer and his date Dovie Eckstrah. Pretty Dovie had been sitting with them in the stands. Sandi and Judith almost jumped for joy as they ran over and gave the guys a big hug and a kiss. Bill had been down on the sidelines after he showed his date to her seat in the stands where the girls were all sitting together. Both George and Al were naturally quiet and reserved but both had big grins on their faces. Bill's amazing ability to read lips had given him the ability to screen potential dates from a distance and find out what they thought of him. As a result, he was usually able to find himself some real winners. Dovie Eckstrah, Bill's beautiful date for this weekend, was positive evidence of that ability. He had flown back home to New York from D.C. earlier that year and thought one of the stewardesses was really a ghost. When he observed her talking to one of the other attendants up in the galley, he saw her tell her friend that she thought he was a handsome guy. That prompted him to write his name and phone number down on a piece of paper and give it to her as she disembarked. He was delighted when she called a few days later and told him her name was Dovie. After a nice phone conversation, he made a date with her on a weekend when she was going to have a layover in D.C. They had a ball as evidenced by the fact that she was there for the home opener. Wow, talk about a Smooth Operator! Maybe someone might even write a song about him some day.

That night, when the parties at the lodges began, a lot of unaffiliated students were wandering around, looking for good places to come inside and enjoy the fun. Mosby University encouraged nearly all parties on football game weekends to be open to all students to be able to attend. However, local young men from town were not welcome. There had been problems in the past, and some fights had resulted. The locals eventually learned that if they tried to crash a party, the sheriff would be called. Besides, being outnumbered, they might end up in the hospital before the police arrived.

The Moses Manse had a party going on, but they didn't hire a combo. They used the money they saved to do a wine tasting. The father of one of the members was the CEO of a large wine distributing company in New York City. He had arranged for them to be able to sample some excellent vintages. This event was limited to their members and their dates.

Over at the Galileo Gables Lodge, the members had hired a magician to perform some scientific magic tricks to see if any of the members could figure out how he did them. After the rousing victory on the field that day, many of the members were fired up, ready to exercise their brains and show their buddies just how smart they were.

Neither the Aristotle Abode Lodge nor the Muse Men Lodge hired any outside entertainment, but the Aristotle Abode had a keg of beer and some lively Scrabble games going, so they were having fun. Meanwhile, the Muse Men were playing some slow dance music on their Hi-Fi system with the lights turned down low. It was a very romantic environment.

Elsewhere around the *Estate* that evening, the St. B's and their dates were absolutely enthralled by the classical string quartet that

Preston Wickersham had hired. Their renditions of Beethoven's "Razumovsky" and Schubert's "Death and the Maiden" almost brought everyone to tears. Their moods were enlightened when the quartet played Mozart's "Haydn" and then again as their final selection was "Air on a G-String" before they took a break. As he listened to "Air on a G-String" by Johann Sebastian Bach, Preston wondered if the day would ever come when he might ever see a G-String in person. Although roommates Troy Barksdale III and Tom Throckmorton enjoyed the music, they were much more concerned about trying to impress their dates. Despite having been treated them to a great meal at the club prior to returning to the Hall, both Buffy and Rebecca were starting to look a little bored. Buffy even asked Troy if there was going to be any music that they could dance to that evening. How gauche, Troy thought.

Finding suitable dance music wasn't going to be a problem at the Serpents Den Lodge after the energetic and talented **Tommy and the Tomahawks** began playing. As usual, the shirtless Tommy was wearing a full Sioux headdress, while singing and playing lead guitar. He and his combo began pounding out the music. They always featured a strong beat, perfect for dancing. Fortunately, no one put Spooky up on the fireplace mantle as they had done one time the previous year. Upon hearing the music start, he had wisely retreated to Roger's room and climbed up on his master's bed to take a nap. The dance floor was crowded; everyone was having a ball. Johnny Baugh dazzled his lodge brothers and their dates when he performed his "patented" swirl around move while dancing with cute little Alice Ainsworth from Mary Baldwin. Johnny had told the guys that Alice had been a little leery about getting into his Snakemobile the first time he took her out, but later discovered that its roominess and comfort had some exciting advantages.

Since it was customary for the parties at the lodges at Mosby to be open to all students and their dates, it was not uncommon for all the Mosby students to move around from one place to another.

Some Serps took advantage of a **Tomahawks** break to head over to the Stallion Stable to check out the **Atlantic Surf Kings**. The **Surf Kings,** with their falsetto harmonies, were fun to listen to, but most of the Serps thought the **Tomahawks,** with their strong beat, were better for dancing. Also, the **Tomahawks** were fun to watch. Ronnie Wall and Parker Boardman, who didn't have dates that night, went to the Stallion Stable. They were greeted by the team's kicker, Manny Morales, as they came in the door.

"Great to see you guys," said Manny. "Welcome to the Stable. Tane Maaka just showed up and is out their dancing with Kevin Kahana's date. You ought to go over there and see it. She is only about five feet tall and a hundred pounds. She looks like a midget compared to that huge guy, but he is amazingly agile and quick for someone his size."

Ronnie and Parker hung out for a while and had fun watching Joey Gallata and Ricky Russo try to outdo each other on the dance floor. Meanwhile, Vinny Del Vecchio and Mike Marino were hanging out in a corner, trying to put some smooth moves on their dates. Ronnie and Parker enjoyed the party, but only stayed for about a half an hour before heading back to the Den. Before departing, they invited their buddies at the Stable to come on by and hear the amazing **Tomahawks**. They invited Tane to come as well.

Ronnie said, "You would like seeing these guys, Tane. They pretend to be American Indians, and since you are of Maori descent, you would get a kick out them. They are pretty wild."

Tane laughed and said, "They sound crazy too, but they better watch out because us Maori's can also be pretty crazy." He made an angry looking face, squatted down, slapped his thighs and then his arms, and rolled his eyes. Then he stuck out his tongue and began making a loud grunting noise.

Parker and Ronnie looked at him in shock and Parker said, "Wow, Tane that was crazy. If you did that out on the field to the other teams before we played them, you would probably scare the Hell out of them."

Tane looked at him and said, "That's not a bad idea. We call that kind of thing the Haka. Since it was originally a war chant, it's perfect for getting ready for combat on any field."

Ronnie replied, "You ought to show the coach and maybe we might start doing it someday if he thought it would fire us up and scare our opponents." Tane grinned and nodded in agreement before returning to the dance floor. With that, Ronnie and Parker waved goodbye to Manny and headed back to the Den.

The action at the Serpents Den Lodge was starting to heat up. Long legged Cadillac deVille, although dateless, was trying to do the Limbo. Naturally, every time he tried to go under the bar, he ended up flat on the floor. He had consumed enough beer on top of the earlier French 75's, so he didn't mind a bit. R.T. Mueller was down in the bar in the basement of the lodge feeling very satisfied that hiring of **Tommy and the Tomahawks** had been a smashing success. Their rendition of the Isley Brothers' smash hit song, "Shout," seemed to go on for about a half an hour. When it was over, everyone, including the band was soaked in perspiration and needed a break. Meanwhile, downstairs at the bar, R.T. periodically squirted Scotch into his cup from his unusual rubber *bota*. The Serps houseman Cary Fredericks was ready to set him up with more ice and water whenever he needed to refill his cup. R.T. was still a little miffed, after his idea for using the lodge catapult had been turned down. Blaaaah! Some people around at the lodge just didn't understand him.

Not all the students at Mosby were hanging out at the lodges and partying that evening. The new colored enrollees at the university were just staying in their rooms at the dorms. They were probably uncertain about how their attendance at any of the lodge parties might be received. Despite the Supreme Court's *Brown vs. Board of Education* ruling in 1954, most of the schools in Virginia were still segregated, because many politicians were resisted obeying the edict.

None of the young men had dates, and the idea of their asking any of the lodge member's dates to dance was out of the question. Mosby was a good school and forward looking, but it was also in the South, and there were still many deep seated prejudices. Tane Maaka was a newcomer who had gone to the parties. Although he wasn't white, he wasn't a Negro. In addition, being as big and strong as he was, not many people were going to question his being there.

Reggie had told the coach that he and his roommate Clyde would like to ride with the coach and his wife to church again on Sunday morning. Could someone pick up Ted Thigpen and LeRoyce Forsett too, he had asked.. Coach Hairston had been pleased to hear that. He had arranged for another member at the Second Baptist Church to meet him at the dorms on Sunday morning and give Ted and LeRoyce a ride. All of them seemed to enjoy the service. They also met some of the folks in the congregation and had nice conversations with them following the service. Willie was hopeful that more of the newer team members would want to come in the future.

22

Coach Willie Hairston was in the process of going over the Lockridge game with his assistant coaches when David Seligman showed up at the door of the conference room. Willie saw him and said, "Come on in David. You and your guys did a great job of scouting the Eagles for us. I hope your buddies enjoyed those prime seats I arranged for them."

David grinned, "My pleasure, Coach, and the seats were great. Thanks. I brought some notes on the Greenville Titans for you today. My friends watched them go on the road last Saturday and put a 28-7 licking on Red Rock College." He handed the notes to Willie, and went over a few of them before he left.

After reviewing the notes with his assistants, Willie concluded that Greenville had improved quite a bit over last year's team. In 1958, they had not been able to overcome some injuries to key players during the season. However, he also recalled that Mosby had beaten the Red Rock Rockets 31-7 last year so maybe Greenville's win was not unexpected. Nevertheless he remembered the close call the team had at Radford last season, when they got down 14-0. They had expected an easy win. Willie was determined not to let that happen again. He also knew that going into Greenville and playing them there would be a lot tougher task than they had in the game against them the previous year in Warrenton. David's notes indicated that they had a balanced offense and an aggressive blitzing defense, which enabled them to get some sacks on the Rockets' quarterback. Willie figured that the Raiders might have to counter that with quick hitting runs and quick passes.

Bill Fryer showed up at the practice field that day. He went over to Willie and said, "Coach, I'm afraid I haven't been much help to you these first two games. Both opposing coaches were careful to keep a play sheet in front of their mouth when sending in plays. I'm beginning to wonder if the word is out about what I was able to do last year? Do you still want me to try to read their lips on the sidelines?"

Willie replied, "I appreciate all the help you have given us Bill, and if you are willing to keep trying, I'd like to have you do it. You never know. Someone might slip up. You might pick up on something that would give us an edge. However, it wouldn't surprise me if the word about you leaked out. Maybe I had better be careful out there calling plays on the sidelines as well, since other teams might be trying to do the same thing to us."

Bill smiled and said, "You got it Coach. I'm happy to do it, and besides, I kind of like that view from the sidelines."

It was the team's usual brief Monday practice without helmets and pads and with an emphasis on stretching and loosening up. That was combined with a post-game review. The coaches announced they would be putting in the game plan starting on Tuesday.

Following the practice, Willie got a surprise call from the secretary to Mosby's president, Bob Howard. She said that the president was in a meeting, but wanted to talk to him. She asked Willie to wait at his office for the call. A half hour later, Willie's phone rang. President Howard was on the line. He said, "Willie, we have a problem. I am very disturbed and almost embarrassed to tell you about it."

"Well sir, you've made me curious," Willie said. "Go ahead and fill me in on what the problem is, and if I can be of any help, let me know."

Bob Howard said, "I appreciate your attitude Willie. This is something I have to handle, but I would like your input before I make a decision. I got a call today from Charles Collins, the president of Greenville University. He informed me that, due to the fact we have four colored coaches and several colored players this year, the hotels in their town have told him that they cannot accommodate the team. If we are willing to have the white coaches and players stay in one place and the Negro coaches and players in another motel, perhaps that might be a way to solve the problem. I told him that I was not happy to hear this, but would get back to him tomorrow morning. He also informed me that he hoped we would understand and not choose to forfeit the game instead."

Willie replied, "That's one option that's off the table because, after I inform the team about this, I can guarantee they will want to play the game."

Upon leaving his office and heading home, Willie chuckled as he heard Guy Mitchell singing his hit song, **Heartaches by the Numbers.** He thought to himself, "You got that right. Why can't some people realize that the Civil War ended a long time ago? Aren't all decent human beings worthy of respect?"

Sally looked at Willie's frown when he walked in the door and said, "What's the matter, honey? Did you have a bad day at practice?"

Willie finally managed a smile, "Practice went fine. Some other stuff has me upset." He went on to tell her about his conversation with President Howard and the lodging problem for the team in Greenville.

Sally listened and then said, "I can understand your being upset, but I'm sure there is a solution. Come here and give me a hug. We can talk more about it after I serve you a nice dinner." Willie did as he was told and began to feel better immediately. After going and getting little Bobby out of his crib and holding him, he had nothing but smiles on his face for the rest of the evening.

The next morning, Willie went into his office to start working on the game plan. The phone rang. "Good morning Willie," said President Howard. "I've come up with a solution. I had my secretary make some calls and we have found a very nice hotel in Asheville that would be more than happy to have all the team stay there. It's only about an hour away from Greenville so the team can go and spend Friday night there. The team can take the busses to the game the next day. Following the game, you can return to Asheville, spend the night, and come back to Warrenton on Sunday. It will mean two nights on the road, but the team would be able to enjoy a victory dinner all together at the hotel on Saturday night."

Willie responded, "That sounds like an excellent solution Mr. Howard, but how do you know it would be a victory dinner?"

Bob Howard laughed, "I just figured that after you told the team why we would not be staying in Greenville, they would be pretty fired up about beating the university down there."

Willie said, "I think you're right, but I can guarantee you that they won't be as fired up as I will be to post a win. I do plan to tell them why we are staying in Asheville."

"Good luck to you and the team. I won't be there, but I will be listening to it on the local radio and hoping for a victory," President Howard said.

Practices went well that week in preparation for the game against Greenville on Saturday, September 26th. The hitting was very intense. A fight almost broke out between Ronnie Wall and Ted Thigpen after Ted put a hard hit on Ronnie during Thursday's practice. Ronnie got up and gave Ted a vigorous shove. Ronnie got one back in response from Ted, and both of them pulled their helmets off. Some of Ronnie's white teammates came over to support him. Seeing that, some of the new colored players rushed over to back up Ted. Fortunately, Tane

Maaka stepped in and separated the players. In a loud voice, he said, "Hey! Knock that stuff off. Save your aggression on the field for Greenville. We are all teammates here." Immediately, the situation was defused, and the two players shook hands. It seemed that all those watching agreed with Tane's statement. They knew that they were all Mosby Raiders and teammates. Also, all of them were anxious to get after the Greenville Titans.

The Raiders, upon arriving in Greenville, were fired up and ready to play. Despite a hostile home crowd loudly cheering for the Titans to win, it was no contest. The Mosby Raiders romped to an easy victory and beat the stunned Greenville Titans 49-3. After Al Nelson tossed touchdown passes to Parker Boardman, Garrett Gassman and Kenny Lynx to go up 21-0 in the first quarter, he was replaced by Reggie King at quarterback. From then on, the team seemed content to pound away on the ground with strong running by Fred Lammhandler, George Maizley, Johnny Baugh, Shakur Wade and Ironhead Ferrous behind some great blocking. The team's big tackles, Snyder and Frumzeist, gashed huge holes for the runners in the middle of the line. Starting center Dan Kojak, along with starting guards Giordano and Delaney got the job done, too. As the Raiders made substitutions, guard Clyde Langston made some great downfield blocks on wide runs, pulling out and leading the way. Reggie King caught the Titans off guard twice by deftly faking runs into the center of the line and, then, throwing short "Alley Oop" touchdown passes to his tall tight end, Voshon Rice. The Titan's six foot tall safety and their linebacker, who were trying to cover him on both occasions, had no chance of defending those passes against Rice's jumping ability. Seeing Rice effortlessly soar skyward to snag the TD passes from Reggie brought a smile to Willie's face.

On defense, Greenville tried to control Tane Maaka with their center and their two offensive guards blocking him without much success. He pushed the pile backwards all day. Mosby's defensive ends Fincie and Vorache, along with their linebackers Gassman, Maizley, Lammhandler and Gordon pressured their quarterback. They made a lot of tackles and kept Greenville from having any consistency on offense.

Following the game, Willie met Greenville's coach at mid-field and apologized for appearing to run up the score. He told him that after his team got out in front 21-0, he had substituted extensively. The players he put in were excited about playing and had simply executed very well. The Titan's coach understood. After hearing that the Raiders couldn't stay together in Greenville, he also apologized. "I heard about that snub by the local hotels around here. That sure didn't help us any. It must have fired your team up. I hope things will be different when your team comes back in a couple of years. We'll see you next year in Warrenton. Good luck on the rest of your season." Willie wished him and his team good luck as well. The Titan's coach was a class act even if some of the folks in the hotel business around there weren't.

Rather than change out of their uniforms in Greenville, following the game, the team got in their busses and headed back to Asheville. Upon arriving, they showered in their own rooms prior to coming downstairs to a banquet room where a big buffet dinner was served. The players were a little tired, but everyone enjoyed the great food after Willie asked Reggie King to offer up a blessing. Following the meal, Willie singled many players who had made great contributions to the winning effort. Game balls were awarded to both quarterbacks Nelson and King, the defensive line of Maaka, Vorache and Fincie, and also to Voshon Rice for his fabulous leaping touchdown catches.

The next morning, the team enjoyed a big breakfast buffet before getting on their busses and heading back to Warrenton. Upon arriving there, most of the players took naps that afternoon, did a little catch up studying, and prepared for their classes the next week. With a home game coming up the next Saturday, the week wouldn't be so hectic.

Sally greeted Willie with a kiss when he came home and told him that she had listened to the game on the local radio station. She said,

"I guess you showed Greenville that it doesn't pay to be inhospitable to you and your team."

Willie laughed and said, "It wasn't Greenville University's fault that the people running the hotels around there are racists, but their team paid the price for it. Our guys were pretty fired up and ready to play. The only negative was being away from you and Bobby for two nights. I really missed you guys."

Sally kissed him again and said, "I hope you will show me how much you missed me tonight." The Fleetwoods were playing **Come Softly to Me** on the stereo as Willie grabbed Sally, danced a little and whispered in her ear, "Count on it, babe."

23

David Seligman's report on Red Rocks College was on Willie's desk when the coach got back from lunch on the Monday after the Greenville game. Mosby had beaten the Red Rocks Rockets pretty decisively in an away game last year. In reality, he wasn't too worried about playing them at home this season. However, he didn't want to take them for granted either, so he carefully went over David's report. Apparently, Red Rocks had bounced back from a defeat the previous week with a good win over Radford. They had also shown a strong passing attack. They had a big strong defensive line, but David had noted that their defensive backs were a little undersized and didn't seem to be particularly fast. He also mentioned that Red Rocks had an outstanding kicker. He had a strong leg and could kick away from the player who was going to receive a kickoff. Willie began to mull the information over in his mind. He had a pretty good idea about what he was going to tell the team on how to approach this opponent.

Practice went well that week, and some new plays were introduced. Some old plays that hadn't been used so far during the new season were reviewed and practiced as well. By the time Friday October 2nd rolled around, Willie and his staff felt that the team was prepared and ready to take on the Rockets that Saturday.

The *Estate* looked beautiful with its lush green lawns and majestic oak trees. Some of the trees were beginning to turn vibrant colors. The game time temperatures were projected to be in the high 60's. It felt even warmer in the sunny east stands at Mosby Memorial Stadium when the crowd began filing in. The north end zone bleachers had an even bigger crowd than had attended the opening game. It was apparent that the majority of the spectators were Negroes who seemed excited about seeing some of the new players on the team perform for Mosby University. The fact that Mosby's Head Coach was a regular attendee at the Second Baptist Church in Warrenton and had brought a few of his new players with him was probably a major reason why many of the church attendees showed up.

Unfortunately, not all of the attendees rooting for the Mosby Raiders were happy about the changes. Troy Barksdale II was there again with of all his executives and their wives, as well as several very important clients of the bank. Their block of one hundred V.I.P. tickets was right on the fifty yard line. They had ten rows of ten seas each from row 5 up to row 15, and the viewing was perfect. As usual, Marshall Holcombe and his wife were sitting directly behind Troy Barksdale at the game. He was a senior member of the bank's board of directors. Prior to the kickoff, Troy turned and spoke to his old friend Marshall. "Look at all those coloreds sitting over there in the end zone. If the team keeps adding those kind of people to their roster, the next thing we know, they will be over here sitting with us."

Holcome had a surprised look on his face as he replied, "I know just how you feel. Trust me, I'm aware that some people are not happy about what is happening to our team and our school as well. However, I think Bob Howard has done a great job as president of the university so he must have some good reasons for the changes that have been made." Troy Barksdale seemed to scoff at the idea and said, "I bet John Mosby must be turning over in his grave." His wife nodded her head in agreement.

Barksdale went on to say, "President Howard has applied to Tidewater National for a loan to finance some expansion projects, and I plan on discussing this matter with him next week. Maybe I can talk some sense into him. I think I speak for all of us who went to school here when I say that I hate to see the fine traditions we've held sacred be abandoned in the quest for shallow victories on the gridiron. Rather than discuss this anymore now, why don't we defer it until dinner tonight at the Huntsman Club."

Marshall said, "Good idea Troy. The game is about ready to start."

Meanwhile, in the two student sections, the mood was ebullient. They were enthusiastically responding to the cheers that Roger Rambeaux and his merry band of cheerleaders were leading. Roger's dog Spooky barked loudly every time a cheer went out, and the dynamic foursome of Horace Butterworth, Percy Pankey, Lance LaRue, and Bruce Springhopper did a series of cartwheels that brought forth a roar of approval from the crowd. It was looking like a party out there, but everyone hoped for a good football game as well.

It wasn't long before Kevin Kahuna came riding out onto the field playing the part of the Gray Ghost. He appeared right after the Fabulous Flugelhorns had marched out to midfield and played the school song. The team captains met at midfield. After Red Rocks won the toss and elected to receive the ball, the game was underway.

Manny Morales kicked off but didn't hit the ball as good as he usually did and the Rockets' kick returner brought the ball back to the 35 yard line. On first down, the Red Rocks quarterback faked a handoff before rolling out and hitting his tight end on a go pattern right down the middle. The tight end rumbled all the way to just past midfield before Johnny Baugh finally tripped him up. The 3,000 Red Rocks fans in the north end of the east stands let out a cheer. After an attempted run up the middle that was stuffed for no gain by Tane Maaka, the Rockets' quarterback dropped back to pass on second down. He had to get rid of the ball, which fell incomplete, just before he was hit by a blitzing Garrett Gassman from his blind side. On third down, with almost ten yards to go for a first down, the quarterback rolled out to his right and pump faked a pass to his top wide receiver, who had split out on that side. The receiver had gone downfield about 12 yards and cut sharply to the sideline. Mosby's cornerback, Reggie King , who had been dropping back in coverage, closed fast to break up a pass to the sideline, only to see the receiver make a double move and take off quickly down the field. The quarterback launched a beautiful spiral deep downfield which landed softly in his receiver's hands around the 20 yard line. Reggie King was in hot pursuit and caught him around the 3 yard line, but the Rockets player's momentum carried both of them into the end zone for the first score of the game. After the successful extra point was converted, the score was Red Rocks 7-0 over the Mosby Raiders. Suddenly, the joyous mood in the west stands of the Raiders fans was muted, but the Rockets fans in the east stands were jubilant.

Troy Barksdale was furious. He turned to Marshall Holcombe and said, "Did you see that stupid boy fall for that fake out there? They need to put him on the bench and put a real player out there. Kenny Lynx would never have messed up like that."

Few people noticed another unfortunate event that occurred on the touchdown play. Mac Gordon, Mosby's outstanding left outside linebacker, was blocked down low by the Rockets tight end. Afterwards, Mac had to be taken off the field with a possible knee injury. LeRoyce Forsett was his backup; Coach Johnson told him to be ready to go in the next time the Raiders were on defense. Prior to the kick off, Willie told the team, "Hang in there. There's a lot of football left to play."

Because the Red Rocks Rockets kicker was reported to have a strong and accurate leg, Willie planned on having two kick returners back on kickoffs. Each would be standing on the goal line at the hash marks. He had assigned speedy Shakur Wade to be back there with dependable Ironhead Ferrous to handle the job. The Rockets kicked off. The ball went to Shakur's side of the field. He caught the ball and turned on the jets. He flew up the field, and then cut sharply to the sideline where he saw an alley forming. That alley began to close near midfield so Shakur cut back toward the sideline once again, only to be met by a crushing tackle. The ball flew loose. It was a fumble. After the officials pulled the players off the pile, they discovered that the Rockets had recovered the ball on their own 45 yard line. Red Rocks was back on offense again. It got very quiet in the west stands , but the Red Rocks College fans in the corner of the east stands were still jumping up and down and cheering loudly.

Troy Barksdale was furious. He yelled loudly, "Get those damn colored boys out of there and put some real men in the game." He then turned to his wife and said, "I'm beginning to think that buying all these tickets this season was a mistake. If this keeps up, we might not be coming back to many more games this year. Look! They have sent in another colored player to take Gordon's place. The way things are going, I wonder how long it will be before that coach makes the whole team colored."

As the Raiders got ready to play defense once again, Freddie Lammhandler said, "Come on guys, we are only down one touchdown. Let's get the ball back and win this game." That must have inspired the players. They held the Rockets to a three and out that series and forced them to punt. Mosby's dependable Ironhead Ferrous was back to field it, but let the ball go into the end zone for a touchback, so the Raiders took over on offense on their own 20 yard line. The Rockets big defensive line had a reputation for being nasty. Following a quick dive play for 3 yards by fullback Johnny Baugh, one of their defensive tackles tried to spear Johnny on the ground after the whistle had blown. He had to be helped off the field. However, the 15 yard penalty after the play moved the ball to the 38 yard line.

Raiders quarterback Al Nelson called a trap play on first down. When Henry Frumzeist let the big defensive tackle slip by him into the backfield, Raiders guard Jack Delaney pulled out and cut him down at the knees as Ironhead Ferrous rambled through the hole for an eight yard gain. The Rockets defender was limping badly and had to be taken off the field. In the huddle Delaney laughed and said, "That ought to teach them to take any cheap shots against our guys."

On second and two yards to go, the Raiders lined up in a tight formation. Speedy Kenny Lynx split out wide to the left on the tight end side of the formation and was double covered by the cornerback and the Rockets safety. Never the less, the Rockets were probably still expecting a run by the Raiders to try and get a first down. The ball was snapped. After Nelson faked a handoff to Lammhandler going left behind guard Charlie Giordano, who pulled to lead the way. Al bootlegged the ball and ran to the right on a waggle play. Ronnie Wall had lined up only about three yards from right tackle Frumzeist. He fired off downfield looking like he was going to block the cornerback, who was covering him. The cornerback thought he was trying to knock him toward the sideline away from the direction the run was going. The defensive cornerback deftly avoided Wall's attempted bock and headed toward the middle of the field. Wall ran right by him and took off deep up the right sideline just as Al Nelson launched a beautiful pass that Ronnie caught on the dead run. He easily outran the cornerback, who had been fooled and was desperately trying to catch up. The play went for a 50 yard Mosby touchdown. After Morales made the conversion, the score was tied 7-7. The west stands finally had something to cheer about. Amazingly, even the Tidewater National Bank contingent seemed happy for the first time that afternoon. Barksdale cheered in the stands and turned around and said to his friend Marshall, "See, that's what you get when you when you let our white players get the ball and play the game."

The turnaround seemed to inspire the Raiders on defense as they stiffened. For most of the rest of the game, they were able to stop the Rockets and limit any gains they made to short ones. Meanwhile, the Raiders offense mixed quick hitting runs by Ferrous, Lammhandler and Wade with quick passes to their receivers, Wall, Lynx and Gassman and their tight ends Boardman and Rice. Although the Rockets managed to score three points on a 48 yard field goal, that was the end of their scoring that day.

When the game ended, the Mosby Raiders had pulled out a 28-10 victory. Both Reggie King and Shakur Wade atoned for the mistakes they had made earlier in the game. Shakur broke off a 40 yard touchdown run on a draw play and Reggie picked off a pass and broke up several others in the second half. LeRoyce Forsett even did a good job of filling in for the injured Mac Gordon at linebacker and came away with a sack.

Despite those efforts, the win didn't elicit much praise or cheers from some folks sitting near midfield in the west stands. However, up in the president's box, Bob Howard seemed happier as the game wore on. He had invited Kevin McDonald, president of Red Rocks College, to be his guest. President McDonald was happy about the way the game started, but not so much about the way it ended. At the game's end, he congratulated Bob Howard, who had been a superb host, on the Mosby victory.

Al Nelson finished with three touchdown passes and was the recipient of the game ball by Head Coach Willie after the game. He only played three quarters before being replaced by Reggie King, who didn't even attempt a pass. Once Reggie got in the game, the Raiders seemed content to try and run out the clock on the ground. Bill Fryer told Willie after the game that someone must have let the word out about him. Once again, the coaches on the other sideline had been careful to keep their mouths covered whenever they sent in a play. Willie said that was okay, and if Bill was willing to keep trying, he'd like him to be there.

The Mosby Raiders were off to a great start as they moved to a 4-0 record. They would later learn that their record had been matched by the mighty Oakmont Outlaws. Oakmont, who had crushed their first four opponents, was rolling along with an undefeated record and had won big once again.

24

After the game, Troy Barksdale II, Marshall Holcombe and their wives left the crowded parking lot. They headed north up Route 17, instead of going south on 17 to pick up Route 1 and go to Richmond. They arrived at the exclusive Huntsman Club near the Plains, Virginia before sundown. Upon their arrival they relaxed in the comfortable leather sofas and chairs in the bar and ordered drinks. Troy preferred good single malt scotch with a splash of soda. Marshall liked fine bourbon on the rocks. Since they had a good variety of only the best at the club, he was very pleased with his drink. As for the ladies, both Emily Barksdale and Gladys Holcombe preferred a glass of properly chilled chardonnay. They didn't have to wait long before they were joined by their friend, Thomas Bracewell III and his lovely wife Eunice who came over and joined them. The Bracewells were delayed by the traffic going out of the stadium.

The three couples socialized for about half an hour before being shown to their table. They all enjoyed some taste tempting delights that evening, perfectly paired with excellent wine. It was a good thing they had made reservations, since the place had a big crowd now that the fall fox hunting season had begun. Naturally, the conversation centered on the changes that had transpired at their beloved alma mater and what they could do about them. Rather than drive back to Richmond that night, they had all reserved rooms at a lovely Bed and Breakfast Inn just off Route 50 near the quaint town of Middleburg. Around that part of the country, Route 50 was more commonly known as the John Mosby Highway. Upon arriving at the B and B, all of them were tired and a little tipsy, so everyone said goodnight and turned in for the evening.

Meanwhile, earlier in the evening back in Warrenton, the Serpents Den Lodge didn't hire a combo to play that Saturday night. Their social chairman, R.T. Mueller, was saving the money in his budget for the upcoming Homecoming Weekend on October 17th. He was planning a big party at the Den after the game that day against the Radford Rascals. As for the current evening, he felt that just playing some music on the lodge's Hi-Fi system would be adequate entertainment for the members and their dates who wanted to relax and hang out there. However, many of the Den's members were planning to go over to the Stallion Stable Lodge and join their buddies there. They had heard good things about the fabulous group from Asbury Park, New Jersey that would be at the Stable. Their social chairman, Joey Gallata, had brought a group back after their smashing performance the previous fall. **Bobbi and the Ball Busters** were widely considered to be the best band on the Jersey shore. Their lead singer, Bobbi, was a real *ghost*, and the rest of the members of the all-girl band were pretty hot, too. All of them could really rock out, dance, and sing. The dance floor at the Stallion Stable was jammed, and everyone was getting pretty sweaty and having a ball.

The St. B.'s didn't have any entertainment planned that night either. They felt that an evening of exciting discussion about their genealogy would be more fun. Then their dates would learn just how lucky they were to be able to come and hear all about it.

The Moses Manse was having a combo from Culpepper come and play, but no one knew much about them. As for the Galileo Gables Lodge, the Aristotle Abode Lodge, and the Muse Men Lodge, none of them had hired any entertainment, so the Stallion Stable was pretty crowded. Some people gave up on trying getting in, and went on down the road to Fannie Sue's Tea and Crumpet Room, where they were featuring ten cent draught beers that night.

As for the new students and those unaffiliated with any of the lodges, many of them usually wandered over to where the lodges were in search of a party. Others just hung out in the dorms. Tane Maaka had told some of his friends on the team about the fun he had at the Stallion Stable on the night after the first home game. He talked LeRoyce Forsett, Vashon Rice and Shakur Wade into going over there with him that night. Kevin Kahana saw them come in and welcomed the gang, but some of the other students looked at them with a wary eye. They only stayed about thirty minutes and enjoyed the music before they headed back to the dorm. Tane wanted to dance a little bit, so he decided to stay longer. Some of the other students realized they were on the team and were friendly enough to come over and congratulate them on the win that day. That brought a smile to their previously serious looking faces. There weren't any problems, so that was a good thing.

Sunday morning found most of the students sleeping in, but Clyde Langston and Reggie King were out in front of their dorm bright and early along with Ted Thigpen. The three of them caught a ride to and from church with Coach Willie and his wife that day. Many people came up to them after the service to say hello. The pastor even commented on the success of the team, its new found diversity, and the leadership of Coach Willie Hairston. That brought a smile to the faces of the players and Willie and Sally, too. On the ride back to the dorms, Reggie commented on the pastor's words that day. He told Willie and Sally how much he appreciated their taking him and the other guys to church each Sunday.

Willie said, "Reggie, aren't we all supposed to spread the Word? I'm just passing the buck to our pastor. He can do a much better job than me. I'm just a football coach and he's a professional."

Reggie went on and said, "Coach, I was wondering if we shouldn't have a team prayer on a regular basis, both before and after our games?"

Willie thought about it for a couple of seconds and then replied, "That's a great idea Reggie, but I don't think I should lead the team in the prayer. The team hears enough from me already. It should be handled by a player and I nominate YOU!" Clyde and Ted both jumped on the idea and agreed with their coach that Reggie would be the perfect choice. After a little more verbal arm twisting, Reggie agreed to handle the task. His Head Coach looked at Reggie in the rear view mirror with a pleased smile on his face.

25

It was not uncommon for the president of Mosby University to get into his office early, but he was there earlier than usual on Monday October 5th. After reviewing some notes and papers, he phoned the school's law firm right after they opened up that morning. The normally calm and mild mannered Bob Howard was obviously agitated as he spoke to the head of the firm.

"The time seems to be getting away from us. We need to nail down that loan agreement for the construction of the new law school and the other buildings here at Mosby," President Howard said. "The law school is supposed to open next fall; we have already lined the construction company and some professors. What is taking so long?"

Senior partner Alfred Redding replied, "The lawyers for the bank keep dragging their feet, telling me that the bank's board hasn't signed off on the loan yet."

"I don't understand why that should be the case. Troy Barksdale is the president of the bank and he has assured me that there's no problem," Bob Howard said in response.

Alfred Redding said, "Maybe you need to get in touch with Barksdale to get the delay resolved."

"I think you're right Al," President Howard replied. "I will take care of that today and will be back in touch." Shortly thereafter, he put in a call to Troy Barksdale at Tidewater National Bank. When Barksdale came on the line, Bob Howard said, "Good morning Troy. How did you enjoy the game on Saturday against Red Rocks? Although we got off to a slow start, I was pleased that we finished strong and came away with a win."

Troy Barksdale replied, "It was a good win, but I must confess that I'm a little concerned about the direction the team seems to be taking. With the infusion of all these new colored players on the team, and the reality that the team's coach and some of his assistants are also colored, I am worried about the image this is going to project of our beloved school. Mosby University has always prided itself as being a quality institution of higher learning for young gentlemen. I'd hate to see it turned into another Tidewater State."

Bob Howard listened carefully and then said, "Mosby University only has slightly over one hundred Negro students here now out of the student population of roughly three thousand. I hardly think we could be compared by anyone to Tidewater State down there in Richmond which is a one hundred percent Negro school. I must admit that the idea of increasing the diversity at Mosby was my idea, but it was a move that was long overdue. The times we live in have changed. I feel that we all need to adapt to the times, quit resisting, and accept the changes that have taken place."

Barksdale replied, "There are many people right here in the state of Virginia these days who might disagree with your assertion that we need to accept the changes that have been forced upon us by the Supreme Court and the Federal government. I'm sure you're aware that our governor here in the Old Dominion is one of those people.

President Howard responded, "It is not uncommon for any change to be met with resistance by people who prefer that things stay the way they always were. While I don't necessarily agree with that kind of thinking, I can understand why they think that way. However, sometimes change brings opportunity, and I don't see why qualified people should be denied opportunities because of the color of their skin. Coach Hairston broke the barrier at Mosby. He is not only the first Negro coach in the history of the football team, he is also the first Negro graduate of the school. I'm sure that you will agree that he has done an outstanding job as Mosby's coach. As for the new colored players on the team, all of them are excellent students, or else they would not have been accepted for enrollment. They also have been good citizens since arriving at school. None of them have gotten into any trouble. They have been a positive factor on the team, so I find it hard to imagine why anyone would have a problem with them being here."

Barksdale replied, "I, along with many of my friends in the west stands at the game on Saturday, couldn't help but notice the number of colored fans in the north end zone bleachers. We saw that there were many more there than we had observed at the opening game this season. Frankly, we were a little worried that the way things are going it might not be too long before they are sitting in the west stands right next to us."

"Troy, I know that your bank currently owns one hundred season tickets," Bob Howard said. If you are truly concerned about what you just told me, one solution would be to buy an additional block of tickets next year. You could leave those seats adjacent to yours empty at the games. That way, no one, be they white or colored, would be seated beside your people. Your area in the stands would be very exclusive. Actually, you might need to buy twenty more seats in order to have the row behind all ten of your people empty as well as the row in front of them too."

"That's a ridiculous idea, Bob! Rather than go to the trouble and expense of doing something like that, an easier solution would be for us to not renew our tickets next year," replied Barksdale.

President Howard responded "I certainly understand, but hope that would not happen and you will continue to support the team.

However, that is your decision to make. Due to the success the team has been enjoying, I suspect that there would be many people interested in acquiring your choice seats next year. But, enough talk about football this morning, because I know you time is valuable. The reason I called today was to inquire why it's taking so long for your attorneys to draw up the loan agreement for the university's proposed expansion. We want to break ground in November. Since we are already in October, we're rapidly running out of time."

"Frankly Bob, some of the members of the board here at Tidewater National, including myself, have strong concerns about the direction the university seems to be taking," Barksdale said. We are also wondering how admitting these colored students will impact future enrollment and the university's success. Because of those concerns, I'm not sure that we can resolve this issue in time to meet your target date."

A stunned President Howard replied, "Troy, I must tell you that I find what you're telling me, to be very disappointing. I thought we had a gentleman's agreement on the matter, and it was a done deal. Now, after hearing what you're telling me today, it may force me to look elsewhere for the money, so the project can go forward."

"I think we both know that Tidewater National and Mosby University have had a long standing relationship with each other. I certainly hope that it continues, but I understand that you have to do what you feel you have to do," Barksdale said. "Bob, it's been good talking to you this morning, but I have to run now since I am already five minutes late for a scheduled meeting." With that, the conversation ended.

Upon getting off the phone, Bob Howard paged his secretary and said," Get me Ralph Mitchell at Benjamin Franklin National Bank in D.C." It only took a couple of minutes before she buzzed her boss and said, "Mr. Mitchell is on the line, sir."

President Howard picked up the line and said, "Good morning Ralph, it's been a while since we have spoken. I hope things are going well."

"Everything's great Bob, how have you been? I would think you must be pretty happy about the success of your football team these days. Being a Mosby graduate myself, I have to tell you that I sure have been excited about the fabulous turnaround the football program has experienced in the last couple of years."

Bob Howard replied, "Ralph, as a businessman you understand that the key to any success are the people running the operation. Our new coach has done an outstanding job. We gave him a five year contract to make sure we didn't lose him to another school. We're also proud of the academic excellence that Mosby students continue to demonstrate. Because of our desire to continue to grow, we have made a decision to add a law school to the University. The plans have been firmed up and we want to break ground on the construction at the earliest possible date. As you probably know, we have had a long-standing relationship with Tidewater National Bank down in Richmond and had hoped that they would be willing to finance its expansion. However, they seem to have some reservations about committing the funds for the project. That's why I called you today. I wanted to see if perhaps Franklin National would be interested in working with us?"

Ralph replied, "Are you kidding me, Bob? We would be delighted to consider financing this project, and because our assets are about five times the size of Tidewater National's, it would be easier for our board to consider this loan request. The only negative would be the fact that we don't have any other business accounts with you at this time. Doesn't Mosby University currently have its business checking account and pension trust account with Tidewater National Bank?"

President Howard said, "You're right about that, but if you were willing to persuade your board to grant us that loan, I would verbally agree to move all our business accounts to your bank. Would that be enough of an incentive for you to get this deal done?"

Ralph replied, "No question about it. Have your lawyer send us the paperwork for the loan request. We'll get right on it. When do you need the money?"

Bob Howard laughed and said, "Yesterday, but next month will do."

Ralph said, "That won't be easy, but I promise you that we will do our best to meet your deadline, if you promise to move the University's accounts as soon as I notify you of the loan's acceptance."

Bob Howard said, "You've got a deal, Ralph. Great talking with you today and our lawyers will be in touch." He hung up with a smile on his face that replaced the look of frustration earlier that morning.

26

Monday's practice was different than the others that season. It was going to be a short week since the away game against the mighty Frostburg Panthers was scheduled for Friday night. Willie knew it was going to be a tough assignment to go in there and come away with a win, but losing to them the year before was an added incentive. He reviewed the notes that David Seligman had dropped off about Frostburg's last game. The notes only confirmed what he already knew. The Panthers were a tough, well coached team with a stout defense and a conservative disciplined offense. Prior to dismissing the team on Monday and letting them head to the showers, Willie told the players about the plan to have a team prayer before and after each game for the rest of the season.

"Although we hope that all players will participate, I will understand if any of you chose not to do so," he told them. Willie went on to say, "And, I won't hold it against you if that's your choice." He didn't detect any resistance to the idea, which made him feel good about his decision.

After he had met with his assistants following the practice, Willie headed home. He heard the Everly Brothers singing their new hit single, "***Till I Kissed You***" playing on his car radio. The song made him want to give both Sally and little Bobby a big kiss once he arrived home. Sally must have been listening to the same song because, she had both a smile on her face and a big kiss waiting for him when he walked in the door.

Willie said, "That was just the tonic I needed after a tough practice today. Thanks Babe, you're the best!"

Sally was still smiling as she said, "That kind of talk will get you a hug too, so come back here, darlin' and get some more sugar." Willie did as he was told.

"Our game this week at Frostburg is on Friday night. We'll be taking off right after lunch on Friday," Willie said. We won't be returning until late that night, so I don't want you waiting up for me. If you have any chores for me to get done between now and then, try to remember to write them down, because I'm gonna be pretty busy and will probably forget them if you don't."

Sally said, "Don't you go worrying about any chores. I want you to be focusing on coming home with a win. I remember that they beat you last year, and I know my man needs to make sure that doesn't happen again this time." Willie nodded in agreement. During the practices that week, Willie recalled that Frostburg hadn't seen their power sweep play with all kinds of players leading the way. The play had both guards and the other running backs going wide. They called it the Saint B. right or left because the players had told him that the members of the St. B. Lodge liked to run around in a pack. Maybe that might kind of strong running might open up their passing attack, which had not been very effective against them last year. However, that was before Al Nelson got his contact lenses, which dramatically improve his accuracy. If the Panthers thought they would be facing the same quarterback this year, they were going to be in for a rude surprise. Willie also made a mental note to talk to the referees prior to the game about their Five Yard Maker play. In last year's game, it had confused the referees. That led to a key penalty which was instrumental in causing the Raiders to lose the game. Since Mac Gordon's injury had put him out for the season, Willie hoped that LeRoyce Forsett could continue to get the job done at the left outside linebacker position. At the conclusion of practice on Thursday, Willie and his assistants felt that the team was ready, but they wouldn't really know until the game began.

The team boarded the busses around 2 PM Friday for the journey up to Frostburg. Everyone seemed to be in high spirits, since they had started the season with four wins and no losses. However, the returning players remembered last year's loss to the Panthers and knew that they would be in for a tough game. Bill Fryer accompanied the team on one of the busses. He was beginning to wonder if his efforts were a waste of time. The opposing coaches had been very careful to cover their mouth when sending in their plays, and he hadn't been much help to the Mosby coaches. Willie had persuaded him to hang in there, so he was going to try, but he was starting to feel worthless.

Prior to going out onto the field of play, Willie announced that Reggie King would like to lead the squad in a prayer. Reggie dropped to one knee in the center of the locker room. Willie was pleased to see that all members of the team followed his example and did likewise.

Reggie prayed for courage and that members of both teams would emerge from the game without injuries. He also asked that all his teammates would be committed to leaving nothing undone on the field that evening. The team needed everyone dedicated to an on hundred percent effort. Following the prayer, Dan Kojak enthusiastically led the team in a cheer before they ran out onto the field to warm-up for the game. Willie went over and greeted the opposing coach, whom he had met last season. He also went met the referees, as had become his custom before games.

The Panthers won the toss and deferred until the second half, so the Mosby Raiders were going to receive the opening kickoff. Eddie Ferrous was deep to receive the kick, but the Panthers, in a shocking surprise, did an onside kick to start the game and recovered the ball on Mosby's 48 yard line. The Raiders went on defense and looking stunned by what had happened. Knowing that Frostburg had a reputation for having a controlled conservative offense, they were surprised when the Panthers' quarterback faked a run and dropped back to pass on first down. He launched a bomb to his receiver, who had taken off downfield looking like he was going to block his defender, but instead, the Panthers receiver kept going down the sideline. It was a perfect pass and it resulted in a Frostburg touchdown in the first minute of the ball game. The fans in the stands went wild, and were jumping up and down in excitement.

Willie called the team over to the sideline. He said, "Men, the game's not over. We still have 59 minutes to play, so let's get out there and do it."

The team lined up as it had a few minutes before. This time, the Mosby up men were very alert, but the Panther's kicker kicked off deep to Ironhead Ferrous. He made a good return up to the 31 yard line. Al Nelson huddled the team up and called for a St. B. Right on first down. Hard running Freddie Lammhandler went for a nine yard gain behind the great blocking of guards Jack Delaney and Charlie Giordano. On second down, the Raiders were content to get a first down on the 43 yard line following a quick three yard dive play by fullback George Maizley.

Nelson called a St. B. Left and Ironhead Ferrous broke it for a 13 yard gain down to the Panther's 44 yard line for another first down. Delaney's block on the cornerback was so hard, the cornerback was shaken up and had to come out of the game. Willie saw the player being helped off the field and a substitute came in to replace him. He immediately got a smile on his face, and it wasn't because he liked to see his opponents get hurt. With the ball on the left hash mark, he sent in a play where with three receivers were lined up to the wide side of the field. That grouping included tight end Boardman and wide receivers Gassman and Wall. Another wide receiver, Kenny Lynx, was split out only a couple of yards from Mosby's big left tackle CC Rider Snyder on the short side of the field. The Panthers immediately shifted their defensive players to the wide side of the field to cover the Mosby receivers before the ball was snapped. Next, the trio of receivers on the right side of the field all ran patterns of various lengths toward the right sideline and drew their defenders with them. Kenny Lynx was almost salivating as he took off downfield, being covered by the substitute cornerback. He made a quick move to the sideline and then ran right by the defensive player as Raiders quarterback Al Nelson lofted a perfect pass. Kenny caught it easily for a 44 yard touchdown, which evened the game at seven all after Manny Morales kicked the extra point.

From the rest of the first half, both teams were able to move the ball, but neither could sustain a drive. Cadillac deVille, the Raiders punter, kept Frostburg pinned down in poor field position with his booming punts. The half ended with both teams tied.

The second half saw more of the same kind of defensive battle out there on the field. Although the Raiders were beginning to move the ball more effectively, they still couldn't finish any of their drives and come away with any points against the strong Frostburg defense. At the same time, Tane Maaka was wrecking the Panthers offensive efforts. He put their starting center out of the game and terrified his replacement so thoroughly that he caused a couple of fumbles between the center and the quarterback.

Finally, at the beginning of the fourth quarter, the Mosby Raiders mounted a successful drive which culminated in a three yard touchdown run by Freddie Lammhandler. Mosby went ahead for the first time that night by the score of 14 to 7. Frostburg immediately responded with a long drive that led to a tying touchdown. With less than three minutes to play, the score was 14-14. Following the Panthers kickoff, the Raiders were able to move the ball by mixing some effective runs by Wade, Lammhandler, and Ferrous with some short play action passes to Boardman, Wall, and Gassman, but after a couple of incomplete passes, Mosby faced a third down and four yards to go at mid-field. Willie called a timeout and sent in guard Clyde Langston with a play. Al Nelson looked at his team in the huddle and said, "Five Yard Maker on five." The players almost broke out laughing.

The Five Yard Maker was as play designed to draw Raiders opponents off-side. If that happened, it would result in a five yard penalty. The quarterback would line up behind the center, but not put his hands underneath to get the snap of the ball. As he began barking signals, he would suddenly take off running to the right behind his lineman in the hopes that the defensive players would react and jump off-side. The center, upon seeing them jump, would snap the ball in order to get the penalty. The backup plan for the play was a direct snap by the center to the fullback. The back would run straight ahead and hope to pick up the yards anyway.

Fortunately, the backup plan wasn't needed. Two defensive linemen jumped when Al took off, and Kojak caught them off-sides as he snapped the ball to Maizley. It was a five yard penalty and a key first down which kept the drive alive.

The Raiders finally fizzled out on the 31 yard line. It was fourth down with 2 seconds to play. Willie called his final time-out. He beckoned to little Manny Morales and said, "Go win it for us kid," as he sent him into the game. Manny was going to attempt a field goal from the 38 yard line which meant it would be a 48 yarder. Kojak's snap was perfect, Nelson's hold was as well, as Morales approached the ball. The excited crowd was on their feet, but that excitement soon turned to disappointment as Manny's kick flew long and straight. It split the uprights and gave Mosby a three point 17-14 victory in a very tough game.

Willie met the Panthers coach at mid-field. The coach said, "This was almost a repeat of last year's game, but this time your kicker made the winning field goal. Good luck on the rest of your season. We'll be pulling for you when you play Oakmont. They really poured it on us a couple of weeks ago and took some cheap shots out there, too. They have a new running back named Horsie Dann. He went for about

150 yards against us. He's a brute. We really had a hard time stopping him."

Willie thanked the Panthers' coach and congratulated him and his team on a good game. He wished them good luck as well. As Willie headed back to the sideline, he saw that all of his team was kneeling in prayer on the sideline with Reggie in the middle of the circle. Willie smiled. He didn't think that God usually took sides in mundane matters like ball games, but he sure was happy the way things had turned out. Once in the locker room, he gave game balls to special team's standouts Manny Morales and Cadillac deVille. He also gave one to Tane Maaka, whose heroics on defense had been outstanding. Center Dan Kojak then spoke up and protested and said that the coach ought to give himself one too for having the guts to call that Five Yard Maker at a critical time in the game. The players all started chanting COACH, COACH, COACH….so Willie relented and accepted one, too. It was an animated and enjoyable ride back to Warrenton that night. Although the players were very tired, they were still pumped up with adrenaline. Willie dozed a little in his seat, happy that his team was now 5-0 at the midway point of the season.

Upon their late arrival in Warrenton, everyone on board the busses took off and went back to their respective dorms or lodges and hit the sack. The adrenaline had worn off; everybody was worn out. Most of them slept them a little bit later than usual on Saturday morning. They had earned it.

27

On Saturday night, while many of the students at Mosby were planning on hitting the road and rounding up some *ghosts* at the nearby girls' schools, most of the team were planning on relaxing in Warrenton. Kenny Cade, upon learning that Johnny Baugh was not going anywhere, persuaded him to loan him the Snakemobile. Kenny and Nelson Linkous, Peter Suntart, and Russell Tad wanted to make a raid on Mary Washington. None of them had dates lined up for the big Homecoming game against the Radford Rascals the following weekend. They were hopeful they might discover some girls worthy of inviting down to school for Homecoming weekend. Since R.T. Mueller had lined up the sensational **Carolina Shagmasters** to play at the Serpents Den, the Serps knew the party was going to be a blast.

When the Snakemobile arrived at Mary Washington, it attracted a lot of attention. Kenny parked it out in front of the Student Union building, and a number of coeds came out to get a closer look. The "slick talking" Serps didn't have to exhibit much salesmanship to convince four of the cutest girls to go out with them. They told the girls they wanted to take them to the little burger and beer joint with a jukebox not far from town. The girls piled into the Snakemobile, and the gang took off. Everyone had a great time dancing with their newly found friends, but the dancing must have worn them out. All of them seemed to need to take turns to go out to the Snakemobile and take some rest breaks that evening. The evening was a smashing success. The guys liked their dates. They invited all of the girls down to Warrenton to attend the game against Radford and go to the big party that night on the following Saturday night.

On the bus ride back to Warrenton after the Frostburg game, some of the players had talked about heading over to Fannie Sue's Tea and Crumpet Room on Saturday night. Jack Delaney persuaded LeRoyce Forsett, Voshon Rice, Tane Maaka, and Shakur Wade to join him and CC Rider Snyder there. Le Royce and Voshon would ride with Tane, and Shakur would catch a ride with Jack and CC. They would pick Shakur up at the dorm and Tane would follow them to Fannie Sue's. Anxious to blow off a little steam after a tough victory, all the guys were looking forward to a little fun that Saturday night. Since there wasn't a home football game that weekend, Fannie Sue's Tea and Crumpet Room was packed with a mixture of locals along with the students.

The "fun loving" trio of Troy Barksdale III, Preston Wickersham and Tom Throckmorton from Saint Bartholomew's Hall were also there. They were always entertained when they watched the crude antics of all the cretins at Fannie Sue's. They couldn't help but notice the arrival of the players. Since most of them were coloreds, the players stood out even more.

Tom said, "Hey Troy, there's your buddy Jack Delaney. Are you going to go over give him a little payback for the rude treatment he gave you the last time you ran into him here?"

Barksdale curtly replied, "Why don't you go handle that for me, smart ass? You think you're a pretty macho guy. Go for it, Tom."

Tom replied, "I have a better idea. Why don't we go around to some of the local redneck guys who are here tonight and try and stir them up? It might be a HOOT!"

Wickersham agreed. They split up and moved around the room making some incendiary racial comments to the rednecks. "Look at those spooks over there." "Who let those jigaboos in Fannie Sue's?" "Did you see that black guy eyeballin' that pretty white girl dancing over there?"

It didn't take long for a gang of about ten of the locals to head over to the players and start making wise cracks. When the bouncers spotted the trouble brewing, they told the guys to knock it off. They told them to take it outside, or else they would call the sheriff. Once everyone went outside, some words were exchanged. The biggest local came over and tried to throw a punch at Shakur. Tane Maaka moved with lightning speed and grabbed him. In the wink of an eye, Tane easily picked the big guy up and body slammed him to the ground. When another local tried to come up behind Tane and try to hit him with a sucker punch, he was met with a right cross by Jack Delaney that dropped him to his knees. At that point, the redneck locals made a wise decision; they backed off and quickly headed to their cars.

CC Rider looked disappointed. He laughed and said, "What a bunch of wusses. They are leaving just as the party is starting to heat up." The St. B's were surprised when the players came back inside. They wondered what had transpired, but weren't about to go over and inquire. After waiting about three or four minutes, the St. B's decided to leave Fannie Sue's rather than stay there in the company of barbarians.

28

That week, there were glowing articles about the team's big win in Frostburg and their 5-0 record in both the local *Fauquier Times-Democrat* newspaper as well as *The Ghostly Vision*. Both papers were predicting a sell out for the homecoming game on Saturday October 17th against the Radford Rascals. Scalpers were even running ads advertising tickets for sale in both the *Washington Post* and the *Fauquier Times-Democrat*. Motels were sold out for miles around. Some spectators were even coming from Washington D.C. to attend the contest.

Coach Hairston congratulated the team at practice that Monday, but warned them about being complacent and taking Radford for granted. He reminded them that they had done that last year against the Rascals and quickly found themselves down 14-0 early in the game. He failed to mention that the Raiders had come back and reeled off 31 unanswered points to win the game. That would have been kind of counterproductive to the message he was trying to convey. The team had had a scare up in Frostburg and didn't need another one at home.

Willie had reviewed the scouting report that David Seligman had brought him and knew what he needed to do to prepare for the Rascals, so the rest of the week was spent doing just that. Bill Fryer dropped by on Thursday and said, "I still think someone has blown my cover Coach. I struck out again up at Frostburg the other night. Are you sure you want me down there on the sideline with you this weekend?" Willie just grinned and nodded his head "yes" in response.

The fall colors were spectacular and at their peak that Saturday on a beautiful sunny day. The temperature was in the mid 60's. A lot of folks showed up early before the game and were busy tail-gating and cooking up all kinds of good things to eat. Mouthwatering aromas wafted in the air. Radford's fans must not have had much confidence in their team, as the majority of their allotted visitor seats were not purchased. The pro Mosby crowd would be like a 12th man for the team that day.

Roger Rambeaux had his team of cheerleaders on the sidelines firing up the spectators well in advance of the scheduled 2PM kick-off. Percy Pankey, Lance LaRue, Horace Butterworth and Bruce Springhopper were unsuccessful in trying to build a human pyramid in front of the west stands. Each time they tried, it would come crumbling down to the delight of all those watching them perform. Later, they drew loud cheers from the crowd as they did a series of cartwheels up and down the sideline in front of the west stands. Spooky barked in response to the crowd's cheers and looked resplendent in his custom coat with a big M on one side and a snake on the other. Roger's big dog really loved game days. Running out and retrieving the kicking tees after any Raiders kickoff had become one of his favorite things to do.

The spectacle continued when the five members of the Fabulous Flugelhorns marched out to the five points of the big M in the center of the field and played the school song. Then Kevin Kahana, playing the part of the legendary Gray Ghost, came roaring out onto the field. His cape was blowing, and he brandished his sword to the cheers of the crowd. Spirits were high. It was going to be a great day.

Meanwhile in the locker room, Reggie King had huddled the players for a pre-game prayer once again. Following it, the Raiders ran back out onto the field to the loud cheers of the spectators. Everyone there in the stadium seemed as fired up as the team.

The stadium was packed. The north end zone bleacher seats were full as well. The crowd there appeared to be made up almost entirely of colored folks from the local area. That day, there were even a number of Negroes in both the east and west stand reserved seats as well. It was obvious that they were excited about the new season's additions to the team. Meanwhile, not all the spectators were happy about the team's success and player additions. The big block of one hundred prime seats at midfield in the west stands appeared to have some no-shows that day. That was a shame, because they were the best seats at John Singleton Mosby Memorial Stadium. Troy Barksdale II was there and was talking to his friend and fellow board member, Marshall Holcombe, who sat immediately behind him.

Barksdale said, "I spoke to Bob Howard a few days ago and told him that a lot of his loyal alumni were not happy with the direction the school is going these days. I let him know that the schools request for funding a major expansion might be in jeopardy as a result."

Marshall smiled and said, "Good job Troy! Do you think you got his attention?"

"I couldn't tell. He heard me, but frankly I think his new obsession with desegregation may have cost him that expansion project he was so enamored with."

Marshall laughed and said, "That would serve him right. Did you place a bet on the game? After Mosby's paper thin victory last week, I thought the local bookies' listing them as 10 point favorites was a joke, so I bet on the Rascals. "

Troy chuckled as he said, "You must have tapped my phone line, I put down a hundred smackers on Radford myself."

After Radford won the coin toss and elected to defer to the second half, Mosby would be going on offense first. Radford had an excellent kicker, who could kick the ball both long and accurately. Both Eddie

Ferrous and Shakur Wade were back to receive the kickoff, as Willie had instructed. Radford's kicker boomed the ball 5 yards deep into the end zone where Shakur Wade surprised the crowd when, instead of taking a knee, he attempted to bring the ball up the field. Troy Barksdale laughed when he saw Wade try to return the ball. He immediately commented to Marshall Holcome, "That stupid boy's going to put the Raiders in a hole right out of the gate. We might as well get our wallets ready to receive some fresh cash."

Their confidence in acquiring newfound riches was quickly erased as Wade followed his blockers. He then found a hole in the wall of defenders and proceeded to run right through it with blazing speed. He outran all his pursuers for a 105 yard kickoff return and a touchdown to start the game. The folks in the predominately Negro crowd in the north end zone were jumping up and down and enthusiastically cheering the play. Shakur ran over toward them and flipped the ball into the crowd. The referee threw a flag, but Shakur didn't care. It felt good, and those fans deserved the ball as far as he was concerned. The referee spotted the ball back further for the extra point because of the penalty, but Manny Morales nailed the kick through the center of the uprights easily anyway. The kick put the Raiders up 7-0 to start the game. Manny followed that kick with another, booming the ball out of the back of the end zone when he kicked off a minute later to the Rascals.

Radford tried a run on first down only to have it crushed by Fincie and Maaka. With a second down and 11 to go, their quarterback tried a quick pass over the middle, only to have it tipped by Vorache and intercepted by Mosby safety Ted Thigpen, who returned it to the 15 yard line. On first down, Mosby's quarterback Nelson called a St. B Right and Ironhead Ferrous took the ball down to the six yard line. On second down and with only a yard to go for a first down, Willie sent in reserve tight end Voshon Rice to pair up with starting tight end Parker Boardman for extra blocking power.

After Rice gave quarterback Al Nelson the play, Al looked at his teammates in the huddle and tried to keep a straight face as he called out, 'Bridal Bouquet' on two!" The players ran up to the line of scrimmage with smiles on their faces and lined up tight. Power runner Freddie Lammhandler was in the I-back position behind fullback George Maizley. The Rascals put eight men in the box and pulled their safeties up close to stop the obvious run.

The fans were on their feet as the ball was snapped. Maizley crashed into the line as a lead blocker. Quarterback Nelson turned to give the ball to Lammhandler, who was following his fullback. But, Nelson didn't give him the ball. Instead, he flipped the ball backwards over his head without looking toward the center of the end zone. There, a leaping Voshon Rice easily snagged it for a touchdown. The Rascals looked shocked as the stands exploded in cheers and laughter. Just as the referees signaled the touchdown, and Voshon was about to leave the end zone, he flipped the ball back over his head into the north stands to the delight of the spectators there. His action immediately drew another flag from the referees, but Manny Morales didn't mind having to kick the extra point a little further out. He had already proved he could do it. He did it once again, putting the Raiders up 14-0 very early in the game.

That was only the start of the rout. Despite Willie playing the back-ups the entire second half and not throwing any more passes, the final score ended up being a 42-7 victory. That win was apparently, much to the chagrin of Troy Barksdale and Marshall Holcombe, who were about the only ones in the west stands who were not smiling and overjoyed with what had happened on the field that day.

Troy had a sour look on his face as he was left the stadium, "Those new boys on the team sure gave the colored folks in the north stands something to cheer about today. A couple of them are probably out in the parking lot right now trying to sell those footballs they got from those hot dog players. If this keeps up, they'll probably be in west stands with us before long. When that day comes, I sure won't be there."

After the game ended, Willie assured Radford's coach that he wasn't trying to run up the score, and told him that his reserve players were just excited about having the chance to play. The Radford coach nodded and said, "I know. I don't think your team even threw a single pass in the second half. You can bet that Swindle up at Oakmont would have been trying to bomb us into the Stone Age." The coaches shook hands and went to their locker rooms. The Mosby team had gone to their lockers just before Willie got there. Prior to their going inside, the Raiders had all kneeled down on the sidelines for a post-game prayer led by Reggie King.

Once in the locker room, Willie congratulated the team on the victory that guaranteed them a winning season. He awarded game balls to Shakur Wade, Voshon Rice, and the entire offensive line, which did a great job of blocking all day. That announcement brought a lot of cheers. The offensive linemen were used to being singled out only when they got penalized for holding.

Before he gave a ball to Wade and Rice, Willie fooled with them a little bit. "Oh wait a minute. I forgot," he said. "You guys already got your game balls, but you foolishly threw them away." He then gave one to each of them, much to their delight.

Bill Fryer poked his head in the locker room on his way to the Serpents Den Lodge. He said, "I struck out again today, Coach." I don't think I am earning my front row view." Willie laughed and said, "Come back, Bill…we want you out there with us…we love you anyway, despite your being totally worthless." Bill laughed, and gave Willie a thumbs up.

29

It was going to be a big party weekend around the *Estate*. Most of the lodges were planning to have some kind of entertainment to celebrate Homecomings. R.T. Mueller had hired **The Carolina Shagmasters** to play at the Den. They were known as one of the top "Beach Music" bands for a long time. They played numerous gigs each summer at places like Myrtle Beach and other towns along the Carolina and Georgia shores.

Joey Gallata, the Stallion Stable's social chairman, had managed to book the popular **Flaming Fignuts.** That group was famous all over the Southeast, and it was going to be hard for any outsiders to get in. The Moses Manse was bringing in a jazz trio from New York City while the Muse Men Lodge had hired the sensational **Velvet Butterfly** group to come back again. They had wowed the Muse Men with their show the previous season.

As for the Aristole Abode Lodge and the Galileo Gables Lodge, they had decided to go together and hire a local blues band from Front Royal and have them play at the larger Aristotle Abode.

Saint Bartholomew's Hall had hired an Italian opera singer from D.C. to sing some romantic arias. They put a notice in the student newspaper *The Ghostly Vision* that indicated it would be a private party, exclusively for members of their lodge and their invited guests. Prospective pre-screened future members, had been invited, too.

All the parties were scheduled to begin around 8PM. That would give time for everyone to change clothes after the game, have dinner and return for the festivities. Manny Morales had told several of his teammates about the **Flaming Fignuts.** He encouraged anyone who wanted to hear them, to come by early in the evening. He knew the place would get packed. A bunch of the Serpents Den members on the team, who didn't have dates, were planning on doing just that before coming back to the Den. As usual, Kevin Kahana had invited his Hawaiian buddy Tane Maaka. He told Tane to come and told him to bring any of his buddies from the team, too. Tane told Ted Thigpen, LeRoyce Forsett, Shakur Wade and Voshon Rice about the party. They said that it sounded like fun, so they would join him. He also asked Reggie King and Clyde Langston. They were unsure, because they had already been invited by Al Nelson and Dan Kojak to come by the Serpents Den Lodge. They said that maybe they might drop by later.

Stallion Stable Lodge members Mike Marino, Ricky Russo, and Vinny Del Vecchio had brought down some hot babes from New York City. They could hardly wait for the **Fignuts** to begin playing. Kevin Kahana and Manny Morales were double dating with a pair of good looking twin *ghosts* from Mary Washington. They returned from having dinner just before the band's opening number. The band always played only one song. It must have had a thousand verses, so it wouldn't matter when they got there. As it turned out, by 8:30 that night the Stallion Stable was packed and the joint was jumpin'.

When the **Carolina Shagmasters** kicked off at the Serpents Den, the dance floor was immediately jammed. Parker Boardman had his hometown sweetheart, Marie Jeanette, out there and they were making some smooth moves. Dovie Eckstrah and Bill Fryer were burning up the dance floor. They had everyone watching them do the shag. Dovie had swapped her planned routes that month with one of her stewardess girlfriends, so she could be there for Homecoming. Johnny Baugh was like a whirling dervish on the dance floor. Everyone was watching as he performed his amazing whirl-around-spin move with the voluptuous Alice Ainsworth from Mary Baldwin. Al Nelson had a sly grin in his face while he was shagging with cute little Sandi Lee from Richmond. His roommate George Maizley wasn't a good shag dancer, but he was still on the dance floor with Judith, his longtime sweetheart.

Cadillac deVille had made about 15 phone calls trying to get a date without any success. Out of compassion, Peter Huckleberry fixed him up with a blind date named Hortense from Mary Washington. Pete was bringing Hortense's roommate Eve up for the weekend. Hortense stood about six feet tall and had very long legs, so it looked like a match made in heaven. Unfortunately, her face resembled that of F.B.I. Director, J. Edgar Hoover. Cadillac was overheard saying to Peter, "HEY Pete, thanks a lot!" Pete figured that Cadillac must have liked her.

Garrett Gassman had a date with a real g*host* named Letta from Averett College down in Danville. Some of the members speculated that she might be of Polish descent because her last name was Kowalski. Kenny Cade, Peter Suntart, Nelson Linkous and Russell Tad were there with the girls they had met the previous weekend at Mary Washington. It had been too late to get them a place to stay in Warrenton, so the guys would have to take them back to Fredericksburg that evening. Fortunately, Johnny Baugh had loaned them the Snakemobile that night.

Dan Kojak spotted Reggie King and Clyde Langston when they came into the lodge. He immediately went over and welcomed them. They looked a little uncomfortable, but several of their Raiders teammates from the Den came over and said hello, so those feelings quickly dissipated. Cadillac deVille was even kind enough to offer them a chance to dance with his date. They just smiled and declined the opportunity. Reggie and Clyde liked the music, but Clyde revealed to Reggie that he liked Rhythm and Blues better. They stayed for about an hour or so before taking off and heading back to the dorm.

Over at Muse Men Lodge, the **Velvet Butterfly** had all those in attendance enthralled with their slow dance music. Everyone loved their velvet precious outfits with the little transparent wings on their backs. It was a very romantic scene, and the lights were turned down low. They didn't have many outsiders come by that evening. That was perfectly acceptable as far as they were concerned.

The St. B's opera singer sang in a loud voice that reverberated off the walls in their narrow lodge building. Several of their dates complained that it was hurting their ears. Some even had the gall to ask if they could go to some of the other lodges to dance. Not wanting to go anywhere near the Serpents Den Lodge, Troy Barksdale III and Tom Throckmorton took their dates, Rebecca and Buffy, to the Stallion Stable. When they arrived, they had to wait about ten minutes before they could get in. Once in, they saw that the **Flaming Fignuts** had the place jumping. Upon hearing them perform, the girls were all smiles. They obviously felt it was worth the wait.

Neither Troy or Tom wanted to get out on the floor with all the sweaty people. They were content to just watch the scene. It wasn't long before they were shocked. A couple of Serps, CC Rider Snyder and Jack Delaney, boldly came over and asked their dates to dance. That shock turned to horror and revulsion when Buffy and Rebecca actually accepted the offers and went out onto the dance floor with them. The song never ended. Finally, about 20 minutes later, the girls returned with big smiles on their faces. For some reason, both Troy and Tom didn't have any smiles on their faces when the girls came back. Instead, they were pretty angry. They yanked their dates out of there and left. While observing the girls having fun on the dance floor, Troy and Tom decided to take them back early to their approved homes. After they told their dates "goodnight," they returned to the Hall and enjoyed the camaraderie of their lodge members for the rest of the evening.

The parties at most of the lodges lasted until around 1AM, but some of the dates had to be taken back earlier to meet curfews. It was a terrific Homecoming weekend, which had been highlighted by another great win by the Mosby Raiders on the gridiron.

30

When Sunday morning rolled around, a lot of the students were sleeping in, but Reggie King and his roommate Clyde Langston were out front of their dorm with Ted Thigpen. Their coach and his wife came by shortly, picked them up and took them to church. Following the service, a number of the attendees came by to congratulate the players and their coach on their great win. This fall had been one of the most exciting ones that many of the members of Warrenton's Negro community had enjoyed for a long time.

Later that day, many students who had invited dates for the weekend, bid them adieu. Most of the others were either relaxing or hitting the books in preparation for the upcoming school week.

Willie and Sally were relaxing, too. They planned to grill some steaks that evening to celebrate the team being assured of a winning season, now that they were 6-0. The Hairstons had truly enjoyed a great year. It had been highlighted by the birth of little Bobby and Willie's graduation from Mosby University. Now that the football team was doing well, everything seemed perfect. Following dinner that evening, Willie began to turn his thoughts to the upcoming road game against the Cedaredge Yellow Jackets. Cedaredge was sporting a 5-1 record and had been a tough opponent the previous season. He was curious about what David Seligman would tell him about them and wondered what kind of game plan he would need for the team to come away with a victory.

Monday's weather forecast called for a front to move into the region later that week with possible rain over the weekend. Everyone had enjoyed the beautiful fall, but it was inevitable that it couldn't last. Willie was in his office when David Seligman came by and brought him his report.

"Well David, how did Cedaredge look this weekend"? Willie said. I see that they have lost only one game this year."

David replied, "They might be the strongest team we have seen this year. Their coach, Dick Myers, has done such a great job; it's rumored that some bigger schools have their eyes on him. Cedaredge might lose him if they can't match the money he could potentially be offered by one of them. Willie said, "It's a shame he didn't get hired away after last year. He's a good guy and a great coach, and I wish him the best of luck, but not this week."

Mosby President Bob Howard had just returned from lunch when his secretary told him that Ralph Mitchell of the Benjamin National Bank in Washington was on the line. Bob picked up the phone immediately. He said, "Good afternoon Ralph. How was your weekend?"

Ralph replied, "Very nice, but probably not as good as yours. I read about your football team's big win in the *Post* yesterday. I bet you enjoyed watching that game."

"You got that right, Ralph. We are now assured of a winning season because of the win over the Radford Rascals. I am very proud of how well they are doing. Personally, I think it is all because of our coach, Willie Hairston."

Ralph Mitchell then said, "I suspect the players have been instrumental in those victories, too. However, that victory is not why I called you today. I wanted to tell you about another win. Your lawyers were kind enough to bring your projections, expansion plans and loan request to my people right after our recent conversation. In consideration of your promise to move your university's business checking account and pension trust if the loan is granted, our board has agreed to finance your expansion. Congratulations! We here at Franklin National look forward to having a long and profitable relationship with you and the good people there at Mosby University."

Bob Howard then asked, "That's wonderful! How soon can we expect to get the money, Ralph?"

Ralph replied, "Would Monday November 2nd be soon enough?

"Thanks Ralph. This news is a load off my mind. I'll sign the loan documents and get them back to you this week if you will give me the name of a contact there. I will instruct our treasurer to call your offices and make arrangements for the moving of our accounts to Franklin National as soon as possible. I want you to know that I really appreciate this. I would like you to be my guest in the Presidential Box at out next home game on October 31st against Klutztown College."

President Howard had a smile on his face after the call. He thought that Troy Barksdale probably wouldn't have one on his face when he heard the news that Mosby University was moving its accounts to Franklin National. He also doubted whether Tidewater National Bank was going to renew their season tickets the following year. However, he thought that Franklin National might be a good candidate to buy them.

At the athletic complex, Willie reviewed the notes with his staff. They all agreed with his assessment that Cedaredge would be a formidable opponent. Even more so since the Raiders would be playing an away game on Cedaredge's turf. Cedaredge appeared to be the fastest defensive team they had encountered so far that season. Their players could really fly to the ball. Willie wondered if misdirection runs and short screen passes might be an effective strategy to counter their strength. Cedaredge seemed to have a conservative offense that featured a very balanced attack. They liked to mix runs with safe short passes, in an obvious effort to control the game clock. They rarely attempted any deep passes and seemed content to try to methodically make first downs and move the chains. They also were obviously very well coached. Mosby's players would have to be disciplined and execute their assignments if the team was going to have any chance of coming away with a win.

Willie had heard the weather forecast, which called for possible wet weather moving into the region. That was a concern for him, too. Mistakes and fumbles are more likely to result under adverse weather and bad field conditions. He would need to stress ball security in practice that week. Conversely, focusing and working on ways to try and strip the ball while his team was on defense was something he wanted as part of his game preparations, too. Practice went well, and by the time Friday rolled around, Willie and his assistants felt the team was prepared. The team would leave Warrenton at 9AM on Saturday. That would give them plenty of time to get to Cedaredge and be ready for the 2PM kickoff.

Willie headed home after practice ended on the Friday before game day. He was glad that they wouldn't have to go to Cedaredge a day early, since it took only about an hour and a half to get there. Johnny Horton was singing his number one hit song on the car radio, **The Battle of New Orleans**. As he listened, Willie's thoughts were on the upcoming battle in Cedaredge; he was feeling a little nervous. Fortunately, after arriving home and getting a hug and kiss from Sally, and holding little Bobby before dinner, he felt better. Seeing them did wonders toward helping him feel more relaxed and confident. After enjoying the great meal Sally had prepared for him, the two of them watched a little TV. Then he turned in early, and got a good night's rest.

31

As the coaches and the team boarded the two busses Saturday morning, the skies were dark, and a light rain was falling. The rain continued to steadily beat down as the team busses drove along the winding road to Cedaredge. With a temperature that was hovering in the low 50's, it didn't offer the prospect of being a pleasant day for either the players or the spectators. When the busses pulled up to the stadium, it was raining harder, so everyone hustled to the door leading to their locker room. After taping and suiting up was completed, Reggie King had the players take a knee. He offered up a prayer, along with the hope that players on both teams would avoid any injuries that day.

Few people were in the stands when the players emerged onto the field for their stretching and warm up drills. The rain was steadily beating down. Most of the fans were probably either tailgating in the parking lot or sitting in their cars until it was time for the scheduled kickoff. By the time the warm up was over, and the team was going to return to the locker room, the stands were about half full. Any of Willie's hopes that the rain would diminish the Yellow Jackets home field advantage were quickly disappearing. He had heard that

Cedaredge had a strong fan base and that they were known for being pretty loud.

After reviewing the game plan one more time, Willie led the team out of the locker room. He saw that, despite the nasty conditions and the steady rain, the stadium now looked pretty full. There were random boos as the Raiders emerged, but mostly silence. Soon, the 5-1 Cedaredge Yellow Jackets came out of a tunnel near the south end zone, followed by Head Coach Dick Myers. Loud cheers erupted from the stands. Willie had previously said hello to Coach Myers and also introduced himself to the officials during the earlier warm-up. Now both teams were on their own sidelines, preparing for the coin toss which would start the game. Ashton Fincie and Dan Kojak were the designed Mosby captains for the game and had the honor of calling heads or tails. Dan called heads. It came up tails. Cedaredge elected to defer to the second half. They obviously wanted to kick off to the Raiders to start the game. With the sloppy field conditions, that was probably the smart thing to do.

The kick off was just short of the goal line. Eddie Ferrous was able to return it back to the Raider's 27 yard line. Mosby quarterback Al Nelson gave the ball off to Johnny Baugh on a quick dive play on first down that went for a couple of yards. He followed that up with a St. B. right following a toss to Freddie Lammhandler that went for a solid five yard gain. Unfortunately, the off tackle run by Ironhead on third down, came up a yard short of the first down mark so Willie sent in Cadillac deVille to punt on 4th down. Mosby's normally reliable punter had a strong leg. But he slipped on the wet turf as he stepped forward to kick the ball and shanked the ball badly out of bounds. The result was a punt that only went for 25 yards. The Yellow Jackets took over in good field position on their 39 yard line. Coach Myers' decision to defer had paid off very quickly.

Once the Yellow Jackets lined up and started on offense, they began to chip away with quick hitting off tackle plays and short passes. They converted several first downs along the way. They also took time off the clock and moved steadily down the field. Both offensive guards and their center were blocking big Mosby's nose tackle, Tane Maaka, which was effective in keeping him from being a factor. They had obviously scouted the Raiders pretty well. Bill Fryer, on the sideline, noticed that Cedaredge's coaches always covered their mouths when they sent in a play. He decided to try a different idea. He watched the players closest to the coach to see if they made any comments to anyone over there. He discovered that he was successful in being able to pick up some of the things they were saying. The problem in doing that was that it gave him very little time to inform the Mosby coaching staff before the Yellow Jackets ran their next play. The Cedaredge drive came to a successful conclusion when their quarterback hit Mike Jenkins, their speedy tall receiver, with a perfectly thrown pass in the corner of the end zone for a touchdown on a play action pass. The conversion attempt was good. To the delight of the diehard fans trying to stay dry up in the stands, the Yellow Jackets went up 7-0. The drive had used up a lot of time. Only seven minutes remained in the first quarter.

Following the Cedaredge kick off, Mosby moved the ball and made a few first downs before running out of steam and was forced to punt again. This time, Cadillac kicked the ball out of bounds down on the four yard line. It nailed the Yellow Jackets down deep. Cedaredge, was careful not to turn the ball over as they ran some very conservative plays. However, they failed to get a first down and had to punt from their 11 yard line. Rather than play for a return, Willie decided to try and pressure the punter in an effort to block the punt. The rush forced the Cedaredge punter to have to kick the ball quickly. It wasn't a very good one. Ironhead Ferrous called a fair catch and caught the ball on the Yellow Jackets 40 yard line. Suddenly, the Raiders were in their best starting field position all day. Mixing short passes and quick hitting runs, the Raiders were able to move the ball down the field, until they ran out of downs and were forced to try a field goal from the 25 yard line. Morales kick was good. Mosby now trailed Cedaredge 7-3.

Not much positive happened for either team in the second quarter, so the score stayed at that number as the time expired, and the first half came to an end.

In the locker room, the muddy players were happy to be out of the elements. They were also disappointed in what was happening on the field. Tane Maaka was sitting by himself and looking furious. The Yellow Jackets had been triple teaming him all day, and he hadn't made a single tackle as a result.

Willie told the team, "Everyone knew we would be in for a battle. Don't let the first half get you down. You still had a half to play. A positive attitude and the faith in your ability to get the job done will be the key to victory."

When the time came for them to go back on the field, something strange happened. It was a surprise to the fans in the stadium and both of the teams, too. A furious looking Tane Maaka ran out onto the field to the Yellow Jacket logo at mid-field. He faced the Cedaredge bench and then squatted down lower with his feet apart. Suddenly, he bellowed loudly. He proceeded to smack himself on his thighs and arms, roll his eyes, as he stuck out his tongue and shouted some more. Everyone who saw the strange display probably thought he had gone nuts. The officials saw it, too. One of them started to approach him. He wanted to tell Tane to return to his bench so the game could get back underway. However, when he got closer to Tane and saw his angry face, the official stopped, figuring this strange display would end soon enough. It did finally end when a bellicose looking Tane shouted, shook a fist at the Cedaredge bench, and stuck out his tongue once again. For all those on the field, the display was a little scary, to say nothing of being very weird. Even the fans in the stands were silent during the unusual performance. One of them turned to the guy next to him and said, "I wonder when the guys in the white coats are going to show up and haul that nutcase off to the loony bin." As it turned out, soon after the second half began, the Yellow Jackets were going to wish that had happened.

Since Cedaredge had deferred to the start the game, Manny Morales kicked off to them to begin the second half. Their return specialist caught the ball two yards into the end zone. Rather than taking a knee, and having the ball placed at the 20 yard line, he decided to run it out. He was met at the 15 yard line by a streaking Shakur Wade, who brought him down with a crushing tackle. The ball flew loose, but fortunately for Cedaredge, one of the Yellow Jacket players managed to fall on it at their 12 yard line. The rain continued to pelt players and spectators alike, as a determined Mosby team went out onto the field on defense. The Yellow Jackets began the second half on offense. Tane Maaka was still looking fierce and crazy and was making strange growling noises when he lined up opposite the Cedaredge center.

After the Cedaredge center snapped the ball on first down, Maaka exploded into him with such tremendous force the center didn't have time to react. The player was knocked backwards into the quarterback, who was attempting to handoff the ball to his running back. The ball came loose during the attempted exchange. There was a mad scramble by both teams. When the officials got to the bottom of the pile, Ashton Fincie was lying on the ball, and Mosby had a first down on the Yellow Jackets 9 yard line. Tane came off the field and received a lot of pats on his back from the Mosby players and coaches on the sideline. Everyone wondered? Was this the kind of break that could turn a game around?

Mosby's quarterback, Al Nelson brought his team out of the huddle and lined up in a power formation with both Parker Boardman and Voshon Rice at the tight end positions. He also had hard-running Freddie Lammhandler at tailback in the I formation behind his fullback George Maizley. At the snap of the ball, Freddie took the handoff and plowed straight ahead for a three yard gain down to the 6 yard line. On second and goal to go, the Raiders lined up in the same formation again. This time, the Yellow Jackets were prepared to meet this smash mouth kind of football. They put eight men in the box and everyone uptight to the line of scrimmage. Dan Kojak snapped the ball and Freddie came hard once again toward the line of scrimmage to receive the handoff from his quarterback. Instead, Al Nelson faked the handoff, stood up and lobbed an Alley Oop pass to Voshon Rice in the middle of the end zone. The Cedaredge defender made a valiant effort to break up the pass but was no match for the 6' 5" Rice and his tremendous vertical leaping ability. It was a Mosby touchdown, putting the Raiders ahead in the game 10 to 7 early in the second half after Morales's extra point.

For the rest of the half, the slugfest continued out on the field and neither team was able to sustain a drive on offense. As time was running out, with less than two minutes to go in the game, Cedaredge finally drove the ball deep into the Raiders territory. The ball was on Mosby's 18 yard line on third down with six yards to go. The Yellow Jackets called a time out with 2 seconds remaining on the clock. They decided to try and tie the game by attempting a field goal. Upon seeing this, Willie sent in Voshon Rice, who usually only played offense. Willie had given Rice some instructions on the sideline and sent him into the game to replace George Maizley at linebacker. The center's snap was good; the hold was perfect. The kicker came forward and stuck the ball cleanly, only to see a soaring Vashon Rice deflect the ball as it headed toward the goal posts. The ball fell to the ground as time ran out. The Raiders came away with a hard fought nail biting win.

Both teams were exhausted. The Mosby Raiders took a knee and huddled around Reggie King on the sideline, who led them in a prayer before going to the locker room. Willie went out to midfield where he shook hands with Cedaredge Head Coach Dick Myers. They congratulated each other on their teams' efforts in a game that could have gone either way. "Maaka's exhibition before the start of the second half was pretty strange," Myers said. "However, if it inspired him to cause that fumble on the first offensive play in the second half, it may have been the key to Mosby's win."

Willie smiled and said, "I agree with you about that. I would like to take the credit for what he did, but, unfortunately, I can't because he did that all on his own. Rice, our backup tight end, also did a great job by catching our only touchdown pass and blocking your field goal attempt at the end of the game."

Myers nodded his head in agreement, "You are right about that too."

They talked a little more before wishing each other the best of luck in their remaining games.

When he returned the locker room, Willie congratulated his players on a hard fought victory. He awarded game balls to both Tane Maaka and Voshon Rice to the cheers of the other players.

After everyone was showered up and dressed, the team boarded their buses for the ride home, where a sumptuous buffet would be waiting for them in the gym. Most of the players were exhausted. Many took naps on the way back to Warrenton, but once they got there, everybody seemed rejuvenated. The mood was becoming very festive as they all enjoyed their dinner. Willie and the other coaches ate with the players. Willie sensed that the team camaraderie had never been greater.

Bobby Darin was singing **Mack the Knife** on his car radio as he drove home that evening. The song reminded him that Cedaredge had almost put a knife in Mosby's unbeaten season. He felt very blessed, but even more so when he got home and found that Sally had waited up for him. She said, "How did my man and his team do today?"

Willie gave her a hug and said, "The team squeaked out a win against a tough team, but I'm not sure that I had much to do with it. I think you've got to give all the credit for the win to the players for this one."

Sally replied, "You're too modest Willie. I'm sure you and your coaches had a lot to do with the victory too." Willie was looking pretty tired, so Sally said, "Come on honey, you look worn out. Let me talk to you in bed."

Willie smiled at her and said, "That sounds good to me, but only if you join me."

She gave him a grin and replied, "Okay Willie, but only because you're such a slick talking rascal."

Willie laughed as he headed to the bedroom. It had been a really great day and it wasn't over yet.

32

President Bob Howard made a call to Ralph Mitchell at Franklin National Bank on Monday. After giving him directions to his preferred parking area near the stadium, he told Mitchell that the attendants would be notified of his arrival.

George said, "I'm pretty excited about coming to the game and seeing my undefeated alma mater roll to victory against the Klutztown College Bears."

Bob Howard laughed, "Don't chalk up a victory for us too soon Ralph. We barely squeaked by last Saturday up at Cedaredge. That's why they have to go out and play the game each week. While I can't guarantee a win this Saturday against the Bears, I will guarantee that our fans will be fired up. Maybe that will help us out on the field."

Ralph said, "I'm happy to report that all the paperwork for the financing and the loan has been completed. You should have it on your desk this week for your approval and signature." Bob thanked him and then ended the call with a look of satisfaction on his face.

Mosby's president wasn't the only person making plans for the upcoming weekend. Most of the students there were excited about going to the upcoming home game to see their undefeated Mosby Raiders take on the Klutztown Bears. Another reason was that they were planning on going to the parties at the lodges that night. The Serpents Den Lodge social chairman R.T. Mueller had pulled another coup. He had hired a fabulous Doo-Wop group called **The Spellbinders** to play at the Den. Most of the members were bringing in dates. However, as usual, Cadillac deVille, was scrambling to find one. Another member offered to fix him up, but he declined. Maybe he feared ending up with another "winner" like the one his buddy Peter Huckleberry had set him up with the last time

At the Stallion Stable, Joey Gallata was bringing the **Fabulous Falcons** down from Philly. Joey told everyone that their lead singer sounded just like Frankie Avalon. Kevin Kahana and Manny Morales were doubling dating the good looking twins from Mary Washington. They even had visions of some serious romance occurring if they got lucky. Hey, as some of the members at the Stable might say, "Boda Bing, Boda Boom!"

None of the other lodges were planning on having any entertainment that Saturday night since most of them had used up their entertainment budget. A few lodges were saving it for the evening after the big final game of the season against Oakmont University.

The excitement and enthusiasm in Warrenton certainly wasn't being felt at the office of the president of Tidewater National Bank down in Richmond. Troy Barksdale II had been informed by his treasurer that Mosby University had just transferred all of their funds out of the bank. When he found out they had moved the money to Benjamin Franklin National Bank in D.C., Barksdale was outraged! He had his secretary put in a call to Bob Howard's office at Mosby University. She reported back that President Howard was in conference and was unavailable at that time. In reality, President Howard didn't feel like talking to him. He figured that he would just let Barksdale stew in his own juice.

Willie got to his office early that Monday and went over the notes from the game against Cedaredge. The more he looked at the notes, the happier he was that the team had come away with a win. That had been a close call for sure. He also knew that Klutztown College would be out for revenge after Mosby's surprising 28 – 0 upset against them the previous season.

David Seligman showed up at his usual time with the scouting notes his guys had made about the Klutztown Bears. Willie reviewed the notes carefully. He noted that the Bears featured a big physical line on both sides of the ball and they liked to run the ball and establish a running attack. He also noted that they rarely threw passes. Most of their runs appeared to be very effective trap plays. When they did pass, their quarterback did not have a very strong arm and tended to float the ball. Willie went over his findings with his coaches, and they came up with a game plan. They hoped it would work and keep their winning streak alive. Maybe it was their imagination, but it seemed that each of their games was getting tougher as the season went along.

Practices went well that week. Coach Johnson, who was in charge of the defense, changed the tactics which would be employed by his starting defensive ends, Vorache and Fincie. Rather than have them try to penetrate into the backfield, he wanted them standing up in a crouched and ready position with their hands in front of them. They would position themselves between the offensive tackles and the ends. They would try to observe and read the tackles' and the ends' efforts to block them. Then they would use their hands to push the offensive lineman away and move laterally in the direction the lineman was trying to block them away from going. By doing that and not penetrating, they would not get trapped. This technique would help them move to the hole were the runner was heading. The outside linebackers, Gassman and Forsett, who was still starting in place of the injured Mac Gordon, would blitz on some plays and flow laterally on others. The defensive backs would play a little tighter to the line of scrimmage than normal. The purpose was not only to stop the runs, but also to entice the Bear's quarterback to throw the ball.

Bob Howard finally took a call from Troy Barksdale on Wednesday morning that week.

In a loud voice, Barksdale said, "Bob, what in the world is going on? I was informed that Mosby has just moved all of its money out of Tidewater National. I'm shocked by this news, since that's where it's been for many years.

President Howard was not surprised by Barksdale's reaction. He replied, "Yes Troy, the money has been there for a long time, and your bank has profited handsomely from it. Since you recently told me that you didn't like some of the changes that were being made at the University, I can understand why you might not like this one either. Frankly, the main reason for the transfer was that I was unhappy with the lack of progress your bank had made on our loan request. Construction was being held up on our expansion project because of that delay. When you expressed some concerns about making the loan, it prompted me to find out if there might be another institution that might be more responsive to our needs. I found that institution in Washington D.C. The president of Benjamin Franklin National Bank is a graduate of Mosby University, like you and me, and he wants our school to grow and be successful. We have enjoyed working with you Troy, but felt it was time for a change. I hope you will continue to support the University, and I look forward to seeing you in the future."

Barksdale couldn't believe what he was hearing. He quickly replied, "In view of this unexpected development, I'm not sure that Tidewater National will be renewing our block of season tickets next year."

Bob Howard said, "I can understand that, Troy. However, as successful as the team has been the last couple years under coach Hairston, I'm sure there will be a lot of takers for those prime seats. Who knows, maybe Franklin National might be interested in them."

Barksdale sputtered and replied, "Now Bob, don't you go jumping to conclusions that we're going to give them up. I just said that I was not sure we were going to renew them. I don't want you promising them to anyone else in the meantime. Okay?"

"That's fine, Troy! We will give you first right of refusal on the seats next season, but if you do want to renew them, be sure to send in the money on time when the renewal funds are due in February," replied President Howard. He was smiling as the call ended.

By the time Friday afternoon rolled around, Willie felt his team was ready for the challenge. He also felt good about the game plan. He had previously told Sally that, if her nurse friend at the hospital was willing to come over and look after little Bobby, he wanted to take her out to dinner Friday night. He came home and showered. Then, after her friend showed up to look after Bobby, he and Sally were off to the Hound's Haven in Middleburg for a great dinner. They each enjoyed a glass of wine to go with the tasty Chateaubriand for two that they had ordered. Willie didn't want to order a bottle and run the risk of having a hangover the next day. His team was 7-0, and he wanted to keep that unbeaten streak alive.

33

Many of the beautiful fall leaves on the trees in Warrenton and the surrounding area had started to fade and fall, but that did not diminish the sheer loveliness of the Virginia horse country. The weather forecast for Saturday October 31st called for temperatures in the low 50s with possible windy conditions. As far as Willie was concerned, most anything would beat the weather he and the team had endured the previous weekend at Cedaredge. The local *Fauquier Times-Democrat* newspaper predicted a sellout crowd for the game, and odds makers had made Mosby a seven point favorite.

On Saturday afternoon, it appeared that much of the crowd had come early. The parking lot was getting full, and many people were tailgating and celebrating Mosby's unbeaten record to date. The north end zone unreserved bleachers filled up early with enthusiastic fans from the local area. Practically all of them were colored. When both teams went out onto the field for their pregame warm up, Willie went over to shake hands with the Bears coach. He also chatted with the referees prior to watching his players go through their stretching exercises and drills. After both teams finished their warm-ups, they retired to their locker rooms for last minute instructions.

Meanwhile, as the Mosby cheerleaders were firing up the home crowd, Spooky was barking excitedly. Roger Rambeaux was leading the cheers, and the other four Raider cheerleaders were delighting the spectators with their antics and cartwheels up and down the sidelines. The *Fabulous Flugelhorns* marched out and dotted the points of the big M in the middle of the field. Then they played the school song to herald the appearance of the Gray Ghost who thundered in the Stadium on horseback. The crowd went wild as he rode, waving his sword and sparking their enthusiasm.

Following the National Anthem, the captains met with the head referee at midfield. The coin was tossed, and the Raiders won it, to the delight of the home crowd. As usual, Mosby deferred to the second half, so they would be kicking off to Klutztown. Remembering the Raiders' successful opening onside kick against them the previous season, the Bears had some of their "good hands" players up on the front line as Manny Morales approached the ball. Having them up front proved to be unnecessary as Mosby's kicker sent the ball deep, out of the end zone for a touchback. A loud cheer went up from the stands when Spooky raced out onto the field, snatched the kicking tee in his teeth, and happily brought it back Roger on the sideline. The game was underway.

It was first and ten to go for Klutztown at the Bears 20 yard line. They pulled their left guard and sent him to block on an attempted off tackle trap play to the right. However, when he got there, there was no one to trap. Ashton Fincie had fought off his natural urge to penetrate into the backfield and also avoided the offensive tackle's attempt to move him out of the hole. With linebacker Freddie Lammhandler's assist, Fincie stopped the Bears big running back after a gain of only one yard. On second down, the Bears tried a similar play to the left side. They hoped to trap Vorache, but he did not penetrate and avoided the offensive tackle's block. He and Garrett Gassman stopped the runner after he gained just two yards. With third down and seven to go, the quarterback attempted a pass, but it fell short of his receiver. It was three and out and the Bears were forced to punt. Ironhead Ferrous fielded the punt at the Raider's 40 yard line and brought it back to the 45 yard line before being tackled.

Since the Bears linemen on both sides of the ball were big and fairly slow, Willie's planned strategy was to attack their flanks and throw play action passes from a moving pocket, forcing the Bears to run. Maybe they would get tired out.

On first down, the Raiders ran a St. B. Left with both guards, Delaney and Giordano, pulling and leading the way. Fullback Johnny Baugh led the blocking for Shakur Wade, who got the ball. The play went for 15 yards to the Bears 40 yard line. Unfortunately, Giordano suffered a knee injury on the play and had to be helped off the field. Clyde Langston, who had been used as a substitute fairly frequently during the season, came into the game. It looked like he might have to play the rest of the game. Following the injury time out, the Raiders ran a St. B. Right with Freddie Lammhandler getting the ball and both guards pulling. The play went for a nine yard gain down to the 31. On second down and one, Raiders quarterback Al Nelson appeared to hand the ball off to Ironhead Ferrous on another St. B Left. The entire Bears team seemed to be moving in that direction to stop it. However, Nelson skillfully ran a naked bootleg as he rolled out to the right. He then hit a streaking Ronnie Wall on a go pattern down the sideline for a 31 yard touchdown. The crowd erupted in cheers and cheered a even louder when little Manny Morales added the extra point to make it 7-0. Mosby had gone out in front on their first offensive series.

Following another deep kickoff by Morales, which resulted in a touchback, the Bears started at their own 20 yard line once again. It was almost a repeat of their first series. They were forced to punt once again after going three and out.

When they got the ball back, the Raiders continued their strategy of running wide and throwing quick passes off of play action fakes. Their fast pace of play seemed to wear out the Bears.

At halftime the score was 21-0 and beer was flowing freely in the stands. Bob Howard turned to his guest, Ralph Mitchell, just as hors d'oeuvres were being served. He said, "Well Ralph, how like the game so far?" Ralph laughed as he washed down a tasty crab cake with a sip of Chardonnay and said, "It's been great. Do you think they can hold that lead?" Bob Hamilton smiled and nodded a yes.

Once the second half began, Reggie King replaced Al Nelson at quarterback. Al had thrown three touchdown passes in the first half to all three of his wide receivers (Lynx, Gassman and Wall). During the second half, when the Raiders were on offense, Reggie didn't even attempt a pass. He was content to hand the ball off to his running backs, who continued to run wide against the very tired and slow Klutztown linemen. This strategy resulted in another touchdown on a dive play by George Maizley to up the score to 28-0 before the Bears finally managed to get a touchdown late in the game. The final score of 28-7 moved the Raiders record to 8-0. Afterwards, Willie gave the game ball to Al Nelson, although he only played half the game. His precision passes for touchdowns had broken the game open and was the key to the win.

There were a lot of happy spectators cheering that day. Most of them stayed to the very end, even after the outcome was pretty much decided. However, some of the spectators seated in the center of the west stands got up and left the game at halftime. That certainly surprised some of the people sitting nearby. Troy Barksdale and Marshall Holcombe and their wives had driven up from Richmond to the game together. They had all had enough of the crowd's noise and all the high spirits in the north stands by halftime. Since the game seemed to be well in hand, they were more than ready to take off and avoid being caught up in the post-game traffic..

Not all the people in the stands were ordinary spectators that afternoon, and some of them were pulling for Mosby to lose. They weren't fans from Klutztown. Instead, they were scouts from Oakmont University, and they took a lot of notes about what they saw that day.

The Raiders still had another game to play against Bloomsburg before they took on Oakmont on November 21st, but Oakmont wanted to be fully prepared when they came down to Warrenton. That big game was going to decide the winner of the Piedmont Pinnacle Trophy. The fabulous trophy, had nearly always graced the trophy case at Oakmont, and Head Coach Irv Swindle was determined to bring it back this year.

34

As the students and the other spectators filed out of Mosby Memorial Stadium following the game, most everyone's spirits were high. The Raiders fans were thrilled that the team was still undefeated after managing to beat a very tough Cedaredge team on the road and then win again against Klutztown College. The season still had two games to go, but everyone knew that the looming showdown against the mighty Oakmont team, would really determine whether or not Mosby's season had been successful.

Mosby's student newspaper, *The Ghostly Vision,* had reported that only two of the lodges would be having any entertainment that Saturday night. Most students anticipated that the Serpents Den and the Stallion Stable were going to be jammed. The Den was featuring **The Spellbinders***,* a fabulous Doo-Wop group, and the Stable had a group from Philadelphia coming into town called **The Fabulous Falcons**, whose lead singer was supposed to sound like Frankie Avalon.

Fannie Sue's Tea and Crumpet Room was also expecting a big crowd, after running an ad in *The Ghostly Vision* stating that they would feature ten cent draught beers for five minutes on the hour and half-hour throughout the evening. There was obviously going to be a lot of celebrating in and around Warrenton that night.

In order to make sure that their buddies got in the door, and didn't have to wait too long in the line outside, the Stallion Stable's social chairman, Joey Gallata, had a plan. He arranged for members to take turns standing at the door with a velvet rope across it. They would monitor who would get in to hear the music, just like they did at the top clubs in Philly and New York City. He had previously discussed this idea with R.T. Mueller at the Serpents Den Lodge. Both of them agreed to give first priority to members from the other lodge in getting in. Once **The Spellbinders** began to perform, the Den's dance floor was immediately packed with members and their dates who liked the group's romantic slow dance music. The Stallion Stable's dance floor was packed, too. The music of **The Fabulous Falcons** was more upbeat; the action on the floor was as well. Being able to go back and forth between the two lodges was a great way to mix up the music. Everyone from both lodges had a ball that evening.

Meanwhile, over at Fannie Sue's, the place was also packed to capacity. There was a line waiting to get in there too. Voshon Rice, LeRoyce Forsett, and Ted Thigpen thought about going there, but they didn't have a ride so they abandoned the idea. The three were feeling a little sore and tired from the game, so they decided to hang out and play some cards. Another reason for not going by themselves was the trouble that flared up the last time they went there. Using some discretion probably made a lot of sense. Being in the minority, anything they did would attract attention, and they wanted to make sure that that the only attention they got was on the playing field.

Quarterback Al Nelson had another date that night with cute little Sandi Lee from Richmond. Since he had the chance to relax in the second half of the game that day, he was feeling in great shape. Sometimes Al didn't feel so great after he had taken a few hard shots on the field. After hearing that he had been awarded the game ball, a lot of the members and their dates came by to congratulate him on his performance that afternoon. Since this was his senior year, finding a good replacement for him next season was going to be a major concern. Hopefully this new player, Reggie King, who was a junior, would develop into a solid player by next year. Everyone knew that Reggie was the backup quarterback and a starting Raiders cornerback. However, since he had not thrown many passes this year, there were some people who had doubts about his ability to replace Al Nelson, who was a star.

Johnny Baugh was feeling good too despite being a two way player. He hadn't had much work at safety that day, since the Klutztown quarterback wasn't a very good passer. Also, George Maizley had carried the bulk of the load at fullback that day on offense. Johnny had a date that night with the voluptuous Lilly Dahlen from Mary Washington. He was looking forward to the opportunity to holding her tightly and doing some slow dancing at the Den. He also was excited about going over to the Stable and performing his trademark "whirling dervish swirl around move" on their dance floor.

R.T. Mueller had even come up with a date that weekend himself. Roger Rambeaux had fixed him up with Jennifer LeNoir from New Orleans, whom he had gone to high school with. She was now enrolled at George Washington University in D.C. R.T. thought she was quite exotic looking and the big black widow spider tattoo on the side of her neck was kind of cute. Roger had warned R.T. to be good to her, because she was rumored to be into Voodoo back in high school. Whether or not R.T. would behave himself was anyone's guess. If he did something bizarre and turned up the next day as a frog, it wouldn't surprise too many members at the Den.

Jack Delaney and CC Rider Snyder had dates with the girls they had apparently snaked away from a couple of St. B.'s earlier that fall. Buffy and Rebecca seemed to be having a great time at the party. Big Dan Kojak was having a ball with his regular girlfriend, Barbara Jo, who hailed from Hamburg New Jersey. Kenny Cade and Nelson Linkous had brought over a couple of *ghosts* named Suzie and Jo from Mary Washington. Judging by their performances on the dance floor, it looked like both couples were hitting it off.

Over at the Stallion Stable the action was heating up. Everyone seemed to love the music of **The Fabulous Falcons**. Joey Gallata was hearing a lot of congratulations from his fellow members. Mike Marino said, "Yo' Joey, you were right. That lead singer does sound just like Frankie Avalon. He and the band are great. Way to go gumbah."

Ricky Russo and Vinny Del Vecchio were really tearing it up out there on the dance floor. Both of them had dates from Marymount they had brought down for the weekend. The only problem was that both of them had to stay at approved houses, meaning they had to be back there by midnight. Not much chance for any romance that night for them. Meanwhile, Kevin Kahana and Manny Morales were double dating again with the cute twins from Mary Washington. Both of the guys and the girls looked like they were having a great time.

No one wanted the parties to end. Unfortunately, like all things, they eventually did. When Sunday morning finally rolled around, a lot of tired young folks were sleeping in late. Reggie King and his roommate Clyde Langton weren't two of them as they, along with Ted Thigpen, were waiting out in front of their dorm early that morning. Soon, their coach and his wife came by to take them to the Second Baptist Church. Following the service, the players and Willie attracted a lot of attention. Many people offered their congratulations on their win the day before and for their overall record that season. All the players appreciated the lavish praise. They had big smiles on their faces when they got back into Willie's car that morning.

35

    Oakmont University's Head Coach, Irv Swindle, had summoned his two assistant coach scouts to meet with him at 9AM sharp on Monday. Upon hearing about Mosby's win on Saturday, he was frowning. Once the scouts arrived at his office, they summarized what had transpired during the game between Mosby and Klutztown. They presented a clear verbal picture of what Mosby had done on defense as well as on offense. Assistant Coach Kirk Robertson described Mosby's offense; a series of runs with the guards pulling to lead the way, combined with periodic accurate play action passes by the Raiders quarterback, Al Nelson, to his wide receivers. Robertson felt that, if Oakmont could pressure Nelson and contain Mosby's passing attack, it would result in a victory.

    Ben Mitchum, the other Oakmont scout, talked about Mosby's defense. He said, "They use a three lineman-four linebacker scheme like we do, but their defensive ends stand up and don't penetrate. Because of that, I don't think our trap plays will be effective against them. I think we ought to play smash mouth football and run right at them with zone blocking instead. Nobody has been able to contain Horsie Dann so far this year, so let's use him to ram the ball down their throats. As for their pass defense, it was hard to determine how good they are since Klutztown's quarterback was so lousy. They have some new colored players on the team. I recognized one of their names and am pretty sure that he used to play basketball for us here at Oakmont."

Swindle, who was smoking a big cigar while listening to their report, immediately asked, "What was that player's name?"

Mitchum then replied, "Reggie King."

Swindle laughed and said, "What position does he play for Mosby?"

Mitchum said, "Mosby's roster is pretty thin. Some of their players have to play on both offense and defense. King is one of their starting cornerbacks on defense, but he also came in and played the quarterback position during the entire second half of the game."

"How did he do at quarterback?"

Mitchum laughed, "All he did was hand off the ball to their running backs.

Swindle said, "Are you are telling me that he never threw a pass?"

Mitchum went on. "That's correct! Even on third down situations, where a pass might have been called for, he still just handed the ball off to a running back. They must not have much confidence in his passing ability. I think the only reason he came in for their starter was that Nelson had taken a couple of late hits during the first half. Their coach might have been worried about him getting injured out there and not be available for the game against us."

Swindle thought about what his assistant had said and replied, "What you're saying makes a lot of sense to me. King was a crappy basketball player for us who liked to run around like a madman and throw hot dog passes. That led to him being benched, and later, losing his scholarship. He stinks! If we can pressure Nelson, and maybe even hurt him with some hard hits, Mosby won't have a prayer of beating us. He's obviously the key to their team's success. I want you guys to go to Bloomsburg this Saturday and scout them again. Then, meet with me a week from today at the same time to go over Mosby's game there."

Both assistants let their boss know they understood what he wanted before they left his office. Swindle was still fuming about last year's game against Mosby. He could hardly wait to exact some revenge against the Raiders and their uppity coach.

In the meantime, Swindle was feeling very good about the way Oakmont's season had been going. They were not only undefeated, but their smallest margin of victory so far that season had been 21 points. More impressively, their largest margin was 48 points. Swindle had a big physical team on both sides of the ball, and they had been beating up their opponents in the process of winning all their ball games. One of the team's brightest stars was his sophomore sensation, Horsie Dann. He varied in weight between 235 and 240 pounds and had excellent speed. He was also the only two way player on Oakmont's roster. Dann had been a star at his high school in Pittsburgh, and several Big Ten schools were interested in him. However, Swindles' former assistant Dan Benson had somehow managed to talk him into coming to Oakmont. That was about the only good thing the turncoat Benson had ever done for him. His departure for Mosby, was good riddance as far as Swindle was concerned. Benson and another turncoat assistant named Ray Crocker had left Oakmont at the same time. It was just one more incentive for Swindle to want to go to Warrenton and kick Mosby's butt.

Horsie Dann was an appropriate name for Oakmont's star player. He was like a runaway horse, and a bruising runner on offense who enjoyed punishing would be tacklers by running over them. On defense, he was the leading tackler on the team at the strong side middle linebacker position. However, the thing that Swindle liked most about him was his toughness. Dann would bite, claw, scratch, spit on or kick any player who got in his way. Sometimes it caused him to get flagged with unnecessary roughness penalties, but he made more than enough big plays on both sides of the line of scrimmage to make his head coach smile. Swindle's teams always played a real bruising style of football and he frowned on doing any of the fancy schmancy kind of stuff that Mosby's coach liked to do. More than anything else in the world, Swindle wanted to teach the Mosby players and their coach a lesson on how to play the game. He was so focused on beating Mosby that sometimes he had to remind himself that he still had a couple more games to play before he took his team down to Warrenton on November 21st.

36

At the same time that Swindle and his assistant coaches were plotting strategy at Oakmont University, Mosby's President Howard was at his desk in Warrenton. He was anxiously waiting for confirmation from his chief staff that the loan funds were available. They had been promised by Ralph Mitchell for that day. About 10 o'clock that morning he got the good news that the money was there. That meant the construction project could begin. He had already retained architects and hired a major construction company that had the capacity to jump right on the project and get it done on the earliest possible date. Since John Mosby had been a practicing lawyer in Warrenton, it only made sense that the University bearing his name should have a law school. In addition to the law school building, some other ancillary construction projects would be done that President Howard felt would be an asset for the University. He called his secretary into his office and dictated a press release to be sent to the major newspapers and media outlets in the area. When he had finished, he let out a sigh of relief. He felt a wonderful sense of satisfaction.

Work would begin immediately, but President Howard planned on having an official groundbreaking ceremony on Saturday, November 14th. That was almost one year to the day of the school's 50th anniversary in 1958. It was at that 50th anniversary celebration that the beautiful bronze statue of John Singleton Mosby, the old Gray Ghost, was officially unveiled, a fabulous addition to the *Estate*. This marvelous work of art had been made by a talented young female artist named J.R. Eason. The patina on the bronze had changed during the last year, but if anything, it had become more beautiful. President Howard never failed to admire the statue as he passed by on the way to and from his office in Mosby Manor. Since the actual groundbreaking would be at the western edge of the *Estate,* Bob Howard decided to have an official ceremony announcing the expansion near the statue. Because the football team had a bye that weekend, a lot of people would be around, so it was a perfect time for the event. Prior to that ceremony, he thought it would be nice to have the Mosby University Orchestra play some selections for the attendees. Their playing would make it a more festive event, like the 50th anniversary celebration the previous year. The plan called for him to go out to the garden at the base of the statue. Once there, he would extract a ceremonial spade full of dirt as a symbol of the start of this exciting new chapter in the history of the university.

At around 1PM that afternoon, David Seligman appeared at Willie's office with his notes on the Bloomsburg Quakers. When he saw Willie, he expressed his appreciation for great seats that been provided for his lodge members efforts. Willie said, "David, it would be hard for me to thank you and your buddies enough for the work you've done for us. However, I can tell you that it has been invaluable, since we don't have the budget or the resources to be able to do it ourselves." After David left, Willie reviewed the notes with his staff. They began to formulate a game plan to work on prior to going up to Bloomsburg that Saturday and playing the Quakers. Mosby University had already been advised by the officials at Bloomsburg that they should not bring their cheerleaders or their annoying dog to the game. Spooky had harassed the horses pulling the Quakers wagon last year and almost caused a serious accident. When Willie told his assistant coaches about that particular edict, all of them who had been there the year before got a good laugh. It really had been quite a spectacle.

David's scouting report revealed that Bloomsburg basically had the same team and used the same scheme on both offense and defense that they did the previous year. He did make a mental note that Randy Nixon, Bloomsburg's outstanding kick returner, ran one of the kick offs all the way back for a touchdown against their opponent that past Saturday. Special Team Coach Bobby Freeman would have to make sure that Mosby's kickoff team would have discipline and stay in their assigned lanes. Willie wanted to make sure Nixon didn't run one back against them. The Quakers had been a tough opponent the previous season. Willie recalled that the key to Mosby's victory in '58 had actually been the punting of Dick deVille. His booming kicks had given the Raiders superior field position throughout the entire game. He hoped that this Saturday the team would not have to punt so often. Another note that David made was about a player named Radcliff, who was Bloomsburg's big and talented defensive right end. David said that he had recorded a couple of sacks and had harassed the Radford Rascals quarterback the entire game. After Willie went over the scouting information about the Quakers with his team, Mosby's quarterback Al Nelson told Willie that Bill Radcliff was his cousin. He also said they weren't that close, since his father and his sister, who was Radcliff's mother, had been embroiled in some kind of family dispute many years ago.

Willie recalled that Radcliff had hit his cousin pretty hard last year and even knocked him out of the game for a while. One would have thought he would have been kinder to his kin folk. The last thing Willie wanted to see was a repeat of that happening again. It sounded like Snyder was going to have his hands full trying to block Radcliff. Maybe the Raiders might have to line up tight end Boardman on the left side of the line to give Snyder some help. As usual, practice went well that week. The team worked diligently on perfecting the game plan they would use against the Bloomsburg Quakers. Coming off his great performance against Klutztown, Al Nelson was looking very sharp, feeling confident, and looking forward to taking on the Quakers. There had been a lot of stars on the team this season, but Al's outstanding play and leadership had probably been the biggest reason for Mosby's unbeaten record.

Since Bloomsburg was a three hour drive from Warrenton, the Mosby team planned to leave Friday evening after an early dinner. They would go up there that night to be rested and ready to play prior to the kickoff, which was scheduled at noon. On Friday, Willie said goodbye to Sally and gave both her and little Bobby a kiss before heading back to the athletic complex. He got there in time to see that everyone boarded the busses and they got away on time. Upon their arrival at Bloomsburg, most of the players hit the sack. However, the coaches got together for about a half an hour to review things one more time before they turned in.

The weather forecast had called for a cold front to move through the area on the weekend. The chill on Saturday morning was proof that the weatherman had actually been right for once. The temperature was in the low 40's, with cloudy skies, but that was at least better than playing in the rain and the mud as they had at Cedaredge. Fortunately, conditions improved, and it had warmed up a bit by the time the players took the field. Willie thought it wasn't going to be too bad of a day for football. He also felt that his team was ready to play.

When game time rolled around, Bloomsburg won the toss and elected to receive. Due to the colder air, the ball didn't fly as far as usual when Morales kicked off. Randy Nixon, the Quakers star kick returner, fielded it on the 5 yard line and took off fast up the field behind a wall of blockers. The spectators thought he might break it for a touchdown, but he was knocked out of bounds on Mosby's 45 yard line. The home crowd in the stands was cheering madly. Bloomsburg mounted a drive that featured a blend of short passes and quick hitting off tackle runs that ended in a touchdown on their first possession of the day. The score put them up 7-0 over Mosby much to Willie's dismay. With only six minutes taken off the clock, he also knew that there was a lot more football left to play.

Following Bloomsburg's kickoff, Ironhead Ferrous did his best to emulate what Nixon had done to start the game. He broke a couple of arm tackles before finally being brought down on Mosby's 42 yard line. Al Nelson lined his team up tight on first down and faked a run to Baugh up the middle before hitting his tight end Boardman in the flat. Kenny Lynx had split out wide to the left side and taken off fast down field. That had opened up the left flat. People in the stands saw Raiders tight end Parker Boardman make a quick block on the defensive end before going into the flat and catching the perfectly thrown ball. It was a gain of eight yards. Following a St. B. right which picked up five yards on a run by Lammhandler, the Raiders had their initial first down of the game. From there, the Raiders moved steadily down the field on a series of short passes by Nelson and some nice runs by Wade, Lammhandler and Ferrous, before they stalled out and had to settle for a 27 yard field goal. Morales' kick split the uprights. The score was 7-3 in favor of Bloomsburg near the end of the first quarter. At least, the Raiders were finally on the scoreboard.

Both team's defenses stiffened and neither could sustain a drive in the second quarter as they exchanged punts several times. The half ended with Bloomsburg hanging onto their 7-3 lead. In the locker room at halftime, Willie encouraged the team to execute better on offense. Missed blocks or assignments, combined with a few penalties had been the cause of their failure to get any touchdowns. Fortunately, they still had a half to play to try and to turn things around.

The game began to turn around very quickly when Ironhead Ferrous took the second half kickoff back 95 yards for a touchdown to put the Raiders up 10-7, after Morales' extra point attempt was successful. It was quiet in the stadium since no Mosby fans had apparently made the trip up to Bloomsburg for the game.

The Raider's defense led by the play of Maaka, Fincie, and Vorache up front proved to be stout, as Bloomsburg had trouble sustaining any drives in the third quarter. Mosby added another touchdown and went up 17-7 on a great 20 yard pass by Nelson to a diving Gassman in the corner of the end zone just before the quarter ended. Having that cushion made Willie feel a little better. Unfortunately, that comfortable margin didn't last long. The Quakers fought back and enjoyed their best offensive drive of the day as they marched steadily down the field. They took seven minutes off the clock at the start of the fourth quarter in the process of scoring a touchdown to narrow the Mosby lead. The stadium's crowd came alive as the scoreboard now registered Mosby 17 – Bloomsburg 14.

When the Raiders got the ball back following Bloomsburg's kickoff, they began executing beautifully on offense. Al Nelson mixed runs with play action passes for a series of first downs. On a second down and six yards to go situation around midfield, Nelson dropped back to attempt a pass to Ronnie Wall. Wall had lined on the right side and gone downfield about ten yards, before he stopped and came back on a buttonhook pattern. Just as Nelson threw the pass, which was tipped by a Quaker lineman and fell incomplete, he was hit hard on a crushing tackle by Bloomsburg's Radcliff. The vicious blow caused Nelson to land on his right shoulder. He lay there motionless on the field. An injury timeout was called. After he got up and was helped to the sideline, it appeared that he had broken his collarbone and was out of the game. The injury to their star quarterback seemed to deflate the entire Mosby team. At the same time it appeared to energize the Quakers. Reggie King took over at quarterback and tried a pass on third down. It was wobbly and fell incomplete, so the Raiders had to punt. Cadillac's punt was really good, going out of bounds at the six yard line with about three minutes to play in the game.

The Quaker fans were on their feet as their team went on offense and attempted to go 94 yards and win the game. On first down, their quarterback faked an off tackle run before dropping back and hitting Randy Nixon on a post pattern for a 30 yard gain up to the Quaker's 36 yard line. Mosby safety Johnny Baugh was shaken up after making the tackle. Voshon Rice, who was a backup at both tight end and safety, came in to replace him. The Bloomsburg drive continued to move steadily down the field. They executed a mixture of some wide runs to get out of bounds and a series of short passes to the sidelines. They were using their time-outs too. Of course, the clock stopped if their passes fell incomplete.

With three seconds left in the game, Bloomsburg called their final time out. Their excited fans were wondering what was coming next. The Quakers were on the Raiders 29 yard line. A 46 yard field goal attempt to tie the game could be tried from the 36 yard line, but since their kicker was not very good, their coach decided to go for the win. Randy Nixon made a great move on the sideline and beat a tired Kenny Lynx who was trying to cover him. The quarterback immediately launched a beautiful spiral to the end zone that looked like it was going to be the game winner. Safety Voshon Rice streaked over, leaped high into the air, and smacked the ball away from Nixon's waiting hands. The game ended as Mosby squeaked out a 17-14 win, but the victory came with a very high price. The Raiders had lost their starting quarterback, and the dreaded Oakmont Outlaws were coming to Warrenton in two weeks. Everyone knew that the Outlaws and their coach would be out for revenge.

Reggie huddled with the Mosby players over on the sideline in the hush that fell over the stadium when the game ended. He led them in a quick prayer of thanks and prayed for the health and welfare of Al Nelson. Afterwards, it was a somber scene in the locker room as Willie awarded game balls to Al Nelson, Voshon Rice and Eddie Ironhead Ferrous. Willie and his coaches had already been worried about the Oakmont game, but they were even more so now. On the long bus ride back to Warrenton after the game, Willie asked all his coaches to think about ways they could get Reggie King up to speed to handle the job of playing quarterback against undefeated Oakmont University. He also knew that Oakmont coach Irv Swindle would probably be preparing a spot in his school's trophy case for a return of the Piedmont Pinnacle Trophy after he heard the news of Nelson's injury.

When they arrived back at Mosby, Willie took Al Nelson to the hospital in Warrenton and checked him in before heading home. Jackie Wilson had just finished singing his hit song, **Lonely Teardrops**, on Willie's car radio as Willie pulled into his driveway. When he came in the door, a smiling Sally was delighted to see him back and gave him a hug and kiss. She asked, "How did the game go up in Bloomsburg? Bobby and I have sure missed you."

Willie had a frown on his face as he replied, "Well honey, we won and lost today."

Confused, she said, "I don't understand. What happened?"

"Well, we were lucky to squeak out a 17-14 victory in a tough game, but we lost Al Nelson to an injury. With Oakmont coming to town in two weeks, I think we are in real trouble," Willie replied.

"Don't you have a back-up player to take his place?"

"We have Reggie King, but he hasn't played much quarterback for us this year and doesn't pass the ball like Al Nelson, who has been our most valuable player,' Willie replied.

Sally said, "I don't know much about football, but I do know that Reggie is smart, and being with him most every Sunday, I also know he's a fine young man. I wouldn't rule him out on getting the job done if I were you Willie. He might just surprise you. Besides, what is this negative talk coming out of you tonight? Aren't you the man who always says that a positive attitude is the key to success?"

Willie smiled for the first time since arriving home. He kissed Sally and said, "You are right, as usual. I'll keep my chin up. My team, my coaches and I are going to find a way to deal with this setback."

Sally laughed and said, "There! That's my man talking now."

37

The following Monday morning the entire coaching staff at Oakmont University met with their Head Coach. Irv Swindle found it hard to suppress the smile he had on his face as he got ready to pass along some news to the men. That was a welcome change to his normal scowl and irascible manner. Most of them figured his change in demeanor was due to the team's lopsided 48-3 win over the Radford Rascals on the past Saturday. He told everyone to sit down and shut up as he prepared to speak.

"As you know, we have sent a team to scout the Mosby Raiders the last couple of weeks. Our scouts watched them luck out and come away with victories. This past Saturday, they barely got by Bloomsburg, who we beat 35 to 7 earlier this year. They squeaked out a lucky 17-14 win. Frankly, from what I heard, Bloomsburg almost beat them before the time expired. But, that's not the good news that I wanted to tell you about this morning. Mosby's starting quarterback, Al Nelson, was injured in the game. I'm sure you defensive coaches remember him, since he carved us up last year. It looks like Nelson will be out for the game against us. Their backup is that pathetic Reggie King. He played basketball here last year and lost his scholarship due to his hot dogging play out there on the court. He couldn't play basketball worth a damn, and our scouts report that he is worse at football. They tell me that his passing attempts have been terrible. Apparently, he is a fairly decent cornerback, but if he tries to play both ways, he will probably get tired. If he's tired he may be lousy at both jobs. We might just plan on burning him with some passes when we play them."

The assistant coaches let out a collective cheer. Swindle's defensive coordinator said, "We ought to stack our players up by the line of scrimmage and dare him to try and throw the ball. We're going to kick Mosby's butt." Everyone was grinning in delight.

Later that afternoon down in Warrenton, Willie had learned about Oakmont's big win when David Seligman brought him his weekly scouting report. What he noticed in the report was what he already knew. Oakmont had a powerful and very physical team and Horsie Dann, their sensational sophomore running back, had been almost unstoppable. As the Outlaws only two way player, he had also powered their defense from the strong side linebacker position and had been their leading tackler. Willie was worried and hoped his team wouldn't get embarrassed like Radford's had that past Saturday. Willie reviewed what he had learned with his assistants and then said, "Well, men, does anyone have any good ideas on how we are going to beat Oakmont?" Everyone looked pretty grim and serious.

Dan Benson, the team's offensive line coach, spoke up. He said, "I might have an idea. Before I went to Oakmont as an assistant coach prior to coming here, I was a head football coach at a high school over in northern Kentucky. There was a team down there, coached by a fellow named Homer Rice, who compiled an unbelievable winning record at Fort Thomas Highlands High School. Fort Thomas is a little town located just south of Cincinnati, Ohio. Coach Rice used an offense that no one had ever seen before and none of the teams they played could seem to stop it. Having lost to him and his team badly for three straight years, I had met him and chatted briefly on the field after the games, so he knew who I was. After I knew I would be leaving my high school for the Oakmont job, I got in touch with him. I wanted to pick his brains, and since he knew I wouldn't be an opposing coach against him anymore, he was kind enough to let me come to Fort Thomas. I listened as he tried to explain how his system worked. I made a lot of notes.

Once I got to Oakmont, I tried to speak to Swindle about the offense. He just laughed it off. He told me that Oakmont played hard-nosed smash mouth football, and he didn't want to hear about some fancy schmancy high school stuff. The reason I'm telling you about this now is that I think it would be something we should look at. I also firmly believe that Reggie King would be the perfect player to run it. Since we have a bye next weekend, it would give us two weeks to look at it and see if it might help us."

Willie listened to Dan and replied, "Men, today we'll have a light workout for the team, with mostly running and stretching to recover from the game against Bloomsburg. After I address the team, I would like everyone except Dan to work with the players. I want to have him come back in here with me and explain how this so-called miracle offense might help us." They nodded in agreement and went out to meet the players.

Once the players were assembled, Dan Kojak asked, "Coach, what's the scoop on Al?"

Willie replied," I took him to the hospital Saturday night. One of the doctors confirmed that Al's collarbone is broken. I'm afraid that his season has ended. He's been a great player for us and will be sorely missed, but I'm confident that our team is going to find a way to offset his loss. I also know that all of you will be ready to play with Oakmont comes to town on Saturday November 21st. Congratulations on a great effort last Saturday. It was a tough game, but we kept our unbeaten record intact. Let's start by doing some stretching exercises. Coach Horne will be in charge today. Coach Benson and I have some work to do. I will see you all tomorrow." Then, Willie and Dan headed back to the coaches' offices.

Once in the conference room, Willie took a seat and said, "Okay Dan, tell me all about this amazing "fancy schmancy" high school offense and how it will help us beat Oakmont." Dan chuckled and went up to the blackboard.

"To begin with, the real name of this offense is The Triple Option. I hope that sounds better to you than calling it the Fancy Schmancy?"

Willie laughed and nodded his head in agreement. "What's the key to the offense?"

Dan said, "The entire team has to understand how it works and their role in making it successful, but there is one position where the player manning that position has to do his job perfectly every time if the offense is to succeed. That position is the quarterback."

Willie said, "That sounds like we are in trouble since we just lost our starting quarterback."

Dan replied, "Al Nelson was an outstanding quarterback for our usual offensive system, but I think we may have an even better one for the triple option on the team right now."

"Who are you talking about, Dan?"

Dan smiled and said, "Our present backup quarterback Reggie King! The person playing quarterback in this system has to be fast, and Reggie is the fastest player on the team. He has to have leadership ability, and Reggie leads the team in pregame and postgame prayers and has the teams' respect. But the main ability the quarterback in this system has to possess would be his ability to read the opponent's defense and make split-second decisions."

Willie then asked, "Why do you think Reggie can do that?"

Dan replied, "Because I have seen him play basketball. He was a fabulous point guard, who could bring the ball down court swiftly. He had the uncanny ability to make a pass at the last possible moment to a player who was open for an easy basket. That is exactly the skill needed at quarterback to make this offense work."

"Okay Dan, I will assume that you're right about that for the time being. Now, how about explaining to me how this offense works?" Dan nodded his head and went to the blackboard and drew some X's and O's.

"To begin with, this offense gives the same exact look to the defense on every down. That's a real positive. It also has the ability to go either to the left or to the right out of the same set up. That's another positive. It's primarily a running offense, rather than a passing one, but passes can be thrown to keep the defense honest."

Willie said, "I think I like what I'm hearing so far, but why is it called the Triple Option?

"Because either the fullback, who is the first option, can carry the ball, or the quarterback can either keep it and run with the ball himself, or pitch the ball to a halfback to go wide on a run," Dan said. So, the runner can be the fullback, the quarterback on a keeper, or a running back on a toss. That's why it is called the Triple Option**."**

Willie came up to the blackboard and said, "Show me these options on the board."

Before he did that, Dan explained that the main idea behind this offense was to leave the defensive tackle and the defensive end on the side the play was going, unblocked. Doing this would enable double teaming of the defensive linebackers and bring a strong element of power to what was really a finesse style of a running attack. Dan then proceeded to show Willie what he meant up on the blackboard. The quarterback would be under the center with the fullback not far away and directly behind him. The two halfbacks would be about midway between their offensive guards and tackles and about five yards behind them and deeper in the backfield than the fullback.

When the ball was snapped, the quarterback would turn quickly to the side where the play is going, Dan explained. He would then put the ball in his fullback's gut. The fullback would have taken off quickly toward the play side guard's position. The play side guard would have chip blocked the nose tackle to assist the center before taking off and blocking the play side middle linebacker. The quarterback would read the defensive tackle on that side and put the ball into the fullback's gut. If the defensive tackle tried to crash down to the inside to go after the fullback, the quarterback would pull the ball out and continue down the line toward the defensive end. Conversely, if the defensive tackle decided to go outside to contain the play to the outside, the quarterback let the fullback keep the ball on an inside run.

Willie smiled as he listened and said, "That is starting to make sense. But what does the quarterback do about a defensive end or linebacker in the 3-4 defense if he doesn't hand off to the fullback? Not only do we use that defensive set up, but Oakmont does as well."

Dan said, "The fullback is the first option, but what you just asked leads me to describe the second and third options. This offense doesn't normally use any wide receivers, but instead uses two tight ends that are split out slightly from the offensive tackles. The play side offensive tackle does not block the defensive tackle in front of him. Likewise, the play side tight end doesn't attempt to block the defensive end or linebacker near him. Both the tight end and the offensive of tackle just go down field and block linebackers or safeties down there. If the defensive end or outside linebacker attempts to maintain contain around the end and goes wide toward the running backs, the quarterback will plant his back foot, cut sharply and go downfield."

"If the defensive end or outside linebacker attempts to tackle the quarterback as he runs along behind the line, the quarterback will toss the ball to the trailing running back behind him. That running back will go wide around the end with the play side running back leading interference for him. He will also have his play side guard, tackle and tight end blocking for him as well. If all of those players make good blocks, each play has the potential to go all the way for a touchdown. The Triple Option features a combination of deception, quickness, power and finesse. The defensive tackles, and outside linebackers or defensive ends will be chasing air all day."

"Wow," said Willie. "This is sounding better all the time. The only concern I have is that three of our top players, who are receivers, will not be in the ballgame."

Dan replied, "I understand why you're saying that, but in reality, Wall, Lynx, and Gassman could easily substitute for Boardman and Rice at the end positions. They are all effective blockers down field, and have the speed to get there quickly. That would be good to do to keep all our ends fresh. We could also mix in our regular plays on obvious passing situations to be able to utilize their skills."

Willie then said, "Since playing quarterback in this offense, sounds pretty demanding, I'm not sure Reggie will be able to do it since he's a starting cornerback, too."

"I have thought about that, Willie. I think that we ought to move Ted Thigpen to Reggie's cornerback position and let Voshon Rice play safety alongside Johnny Baugh. Ted has the speed and Voshon has already showed what he can do at safety with his size, speed, and leaping ability."

"Brilliant idea Dan!" Willie said. Man, am I glad I have you on our team now rather than seeing you still up at Oakmont."

Dan grinned and said, "Me, too." He proceeded to show Willie how all these options worked by drawing them on the blackboard several times. He demonstrated how it could confuse the defense and how the defense would always be outnumbered by the blockers attacking it. Willie then suggested that Dan draw up a play sheet with the options on it and have it printed to give to the players to study.

After practice that day, Willie called all the coaches aside. He took them into the conference room and had Dan explain it all again and answer any questions. The formerly morose looks on their faces began to turn into smiles. They all had their assignments for working with the players they were responsible for, and installation of the Triple Option Offense would begin the next day.

When Willie got home, Sally immediately noticed the changed look on his face. She said, "Well, just look at you, Willie! I like that big smile. Did you skip practice and go win a bet on the horse races at Charlestown today?"

"No!" replied Willie, "But, we might have come up with a way to get a win after all against Oakmont. I'll tell you about it over dinner, but right now, I want to get a hug and a kiss from my girlfriend. Then I'll have a cold beer and sit down and relax. I hope you can help me with the first two parts of my desires." Sally smiled and gave him what he asked for. After a great meal that night, and after they turned in for the evening, she did even better than that.

38

Before the players took the field Tuesday afternoon, they were all instructed to stay in the locker room and not put on their pads and helmets. Willie congratulated them again on their win and began to tell them about their plan to overcome the loss of their quarterback in the upcoming game against Oakmont. At that point Dan Benson took over and explained what they would be doing. He told them about the Triple Option, just as he had done the day before with Willie and the rest of the coaching staff. Everyone listened intently and, judging by the looks on their faces, they seemed to they like what they were hearing. He told them that each one of them would get a diagram of how the Triple Option worked. They would also get a brief explanation of each player's role in making it successful at the conclusion of practice that day.

Upon reaching the practice field, the players were lined up on offense and defense. First, Coach Benson had them do some slow motion walk throughs. Reggie and his fullbacks were coached on ball security and how to avoid fumbling the ball on the exchange. This was practiced extensively. The backs were instructed to have their hands above and below the ball, but not to grab it firmly until the quarterback pushed it into their stomach and removed his hands. Reggie was then instructed to watch the defensive tackle on the side the play was going. If he saw the tackle's numbers on the front of his uniform, it meant he was going to try to slant down to the inside toward the fullback. If the tackle went the other way to the outside, Reggie would push the ball into the fullback's stomach and let him carry it.

Conversely, If the defensive tackle went for the fullback, Reggie would keep the ball and run down parallel to the line of scrimmage toward the sideline. There, he had to make his next decision. If the defensive end or outside linebacker came toward him, Reggie was taught to quickly pitch the ball to the trailing running back, who would be following the play side running back and running wide. The play side back would become his lead blocker down field. Conversely, if the defensive end, or outside linebacker, tried to string out the play, and flowed wide with the running backs, Reggie was instructed to keep the ball himself, cut sharply, and head down field behind the blocking of his play side guard, tackle, and end.

Not only did the backs get instruction, but the linemen were also given their assignments. Most of them liked the idea of not having to block the big guys in front of them and instead, going down field to knock off the smaller linebackers and defensive backs. They were as happy as the team's skill players were about this new offense.

When the practice ended, everyone got their diagrams and explanations and were told to study them. The next day, and from that time forward, they would run the plays in full pads. First, they ran at half speed, and then later at full speed in both directions. Reggie's decision making was superb. That made Dan Benson smile and made Willie's smile even bigger. Losing Al Nelson had initially seemed like an impossible hurdle to overcome, but this new approach to offense had given a real lift to his spirits and those of the team as well. However, no one knew how this theory would work on the field. They would have to wait until Saturday November 21st to find out.

There were some other changes made that week. In order to beef up the offensive line following the loss of Charlie Giordano to an injury, Baldwin Tucker was moved to guard to give the team some sorely needed depth at that position. Voshon Rice was given additional coaching about playing safety and Ted Thigpen was moved to cornerback to take Reggie's place out there. Rice would also still come in at tight end on special plays.

Not wanting to abandon passing entirely, Willie installed a few safe passing plays that would give Reggie confidence, and give the team the option to catch the Outlaws off guard. All of them were play action passes and designed for situations when the defense was up tight and looking for a run. The Oakmont Outlaws were going to be in for a rude shock when they came to Warrenton. Nothing they had ever seen the Mosby Raiders do in previous games would be displayed on the field on Saturday November 21st. Willie grinned as he envisioned the surprised and angry look on the face of the Outlaws' Head Coach Irv Swindle.

Defensive preparations for the showdown were made as well. The Outlaws had a powerful offense behind a big offensive line. Bart Benoski, their senior quarterback, while not as good as Al Nelson, was still a very capable player. However, Adams, their backup quarterback was average at best. They had an outstanding big receiver coming back named Stretch Schmidt; he seemed to be Benoski's main target. The Outlaws liked to avoid passing if they could and establish their running game. Having the big tandem of Matt Zombo at fullback and their sophomore sensation running back Horsie Dann had enabled them to pound most of their opponents into submission. Jack Johnson, the Raiders defensive coordinator, installed some defensive line twists and some linebacker zone blitzes to try and stop the Outlaws. Whether or not these preparations would work wouldn't be known until game day.

39

On Friday November 13th, Mosby President Robert Howard IV felt good about the planned program to celebrate the new expansion. The fact it was a Friday the 13th didn't bother him one bit. This was an occasion to celebrate, and he wasn't very superstitious anyway. Nothing bad was going to happen at Mosby that day. At 4PM the next afternoon, the Mosby University orchestra was scheduled to play some light classical selections to entertain attending students and honored guests. At the conclusion of the music, he would briefly describe the construction that would be taking place around the *Estate*. Then he would tell the attendees about the value it would add to what was already an outstanding institution of higher learning. Following that, he would invite everyone out to the bronze statue of John Mosby. Finally, he would dig a spade full of earth from the garden area at the base of the statue as a symbolic gesture of breaking ground on the project. It should be an event that everyone would enjoy.

Unbeknownst to President Howard and other people at Mosby University, there was other planning going on that also centered on the beautiful statue of John Mosby. Two Oakmont University students, who were big fans of their school's very successful football program, had been outraged by what had transpired on the Outlaws field the previous year when Mosby came to play. Not only had the game been embarrassing, they felt that some people at Mosby must have had a hand in what happened to the playing field. A huge "M" started to appear in the grass during the first quarter. By the time the game ended, it was clearly visible to everyone in attendance. These two Oakmont students had a plan to give Mosby some much needed payback.

They decided to come to Warrenton for the game, along with about 3,000 other Oakmont fans. However, they also made a reservation at a little motel in Centerville for Friday night November 13th, which was a week before the game. Leaving Oakmont after classes on that Friday, they drove down to Centerville and checked in. Then they grabbed a bite to eat at a local diner. Later, as darkness set in, they drove to Warrenton and parked their car near the center of the campus. It was very quiet at that hour, and they didn't see anyone in the area. Wearing black clothes, they made their way to the illuminated bronze statue of John Mosby on horseback. Both of them had two cans of glossy black spray paint in their pockets. Their plan was to go up to the statue, empty their cans and paint the statue black, which was the color of the Oakmont Outlaws uniforms. One would work on one side of the statue while the other painted the opposite side. They were pretty sure that they could do it and be gone within ten minutes.

When the Oakmont miscreants thought the coast was clear, they got out of their car and headed toward the statue. They could see the statue glowing brightly; the lights at its base made the bronze patina almost sparkle. Once they arrived, they immediately began spraying. They were silent as they did it. Both had to fight off a temptation to laugh loudly. Suddenly, one of them screamed in pain. His buddy on the other side of the statue heard the sound of a dog barking. When he looked around, he saw his friend being attacked by a very large dog. He immediately tried to pry up one of the bricks around the planting area at the base, and use it as a weapon against the dog. Suddenly, someone came up from behind and knocked him to the ground. When he looked up, he saw a big angry looking guy pointing at him who said, "You better just stay right there on the ground and not move, because if you get up, I'm gonna put you down harder." He wisely did as he was told. His friend wasn't so fortunate. The dog had taken a few bites out of him. When he tried to kick the dog, another big fellow came up swiftly, punched him in the mouth and knocked him to the ground. The snarling dog was standing guard under the command of a young man who had some other buddies with him.

Roger Rambeaux had taken Spooky out for a late night walk prior to turning in for the evening. Jack Delaney, George Maizley and Kenny Cade decided to take a stroll along as well. They hadn't gone very far before they spied what was going on at the statue and headed there fast. Roger sicced Spooky on the perpetrators, and he tore into the leg of one. George shoved the other one down and warned him to stay put. When the guy who had been attacked by Spooky tried to kick the dog, Jack Delaney hauled off and smacked him in the mouth. Kenny told his fellow Serps to keep them there while he went to call the sheriff. It didn't take long for a deputy to arrive and place the two vandals under arrest. They were then taken down to the town jail where they were incarcerated. The statue looked like a mess.

Saturday morning, the sheriff put in a call to President Howard and informed him about the vandalism. He asked him if he wanted to press charges. Bob Howard told him that he would get back to him after he had a chance to assess the damages. Upon seeing what they had done to the statue, he wondered how it could be repaired in time for the ceremony that afternoon. He called Professor Albert Bernstein in the Chemistry Department. The professor advised him exactly what kind of chemical solution would remove the paint without harming the statue.

President Howard called the sheriff and told him that the vandals had the choice of either paying a $10,000 fine or being released from jail under the supervision of a deputy. The two of them would have to thoroughly clean the statue until it looked exactly as it did before they vandalized it. They would be responsible for the cost of any materials used in the cleanup as well. If they were successful in totally cleaning the statue up and making it look like it did before they painted it, then all charges would be dropped. After the sheriff explained those two options, the Oakmont vandals readily agreed to do the cleanup. It took them three hours of hard work to remove all vestiges of the paint. Then, they had to wait for President Howard to come by and inspect the statue. After he declared that it had passed his inspection, they were told they would be set free. Both of them apologized before taking off. It was apparent that they had learned their lesson, and they were feeling lucky as they headed back to Oakmont.

Later that afternoon, all those who attended the fabulous concert by the university orchestra enjoyed the program. Among the selections the orchestra played were excerpts from Liszt's *Hungarian Rhapsody No. 2.* , Beethoven's *Moonlight Sonata* , Ravel's *Bolero,* and Tchaikovsky's *Romeo and Juliet Fantasy Overture.* Following the program President Howard told the audience about the plan to expand the curriculum at Mosby University through the addition of a new school of law. He informed everyone that the planned construction would begin almost immediately. The project would not only include the building of the law school facility, but some other buildings around the *Estate,* including a new lodge for members that were currently not being served by the existing lodges. He said, "This new lodge will be named for a very famous American that some of you in the audience may have heard of. It will be called the Washington Lodge." The crowd laughed a little when they heard him say that. He then invited everyone to come outside by the statue of John Mosby and attend the brief ground breaking ceremony. Everyone who went outside to the ceremony noticed how beautiful the statue looked that day. It actually looked like it had just been shined.

A number of the members of the Serpents Den Lodge attended the concert and the ground breaking ceremony. Some of them were curious about how the statue was going to look. They were all pleasantly surprised to see it glistening and beautiful as it had been before. They wondered how that had happened. When they got back to the Den, they were not pleasantly surprised to walk in the front door and be greeted by the horrible smell of rotten eggs. Peter Suntart had not gone to the ceremony, since he was suffering from a bad cold. He had been upstairs in bed when he heard a very loud noise. Apparently, someone had thrown a paper bag, full of old rotten eggs and a cherry bomb inside the main entrance area. When it went off, it blew fragments of the eggs everywhere. The place reeked. The Serps had to open all the windows and scrub down the walls, floor, ceiling and anywhere else where the residue remained. Since everybody pitched in and worked at the job, the place got cleaned up in about an hour.

Some of the members wondered if the vandals from Oakmont, who had painted the statue, had done this. Maybe they had heard that the guys who caught them were members at the Den. They could have hung around and done this before getting out of town. Bill Fryer advised everyone there not to jump to any hasty conclusions. He told them that he would volunteer to investigate and try to identify the culprits, so justice could be served. Since the lodge building was owned by the university, the vandalism was reported to the security office at the *Estate*.

Once the place was cleaned up and things were back to normal, most of the conversation at the Den centered on the big upcoming weekend's game against the Oakmont Outlaws. Mosby had only beaten them only once in the last several years. Since it was the final game of the season, a lot of the members were working hard on getting a date for the game and the party that night. Social Chairman R.T. Mueller had hired another great band to perform at the Serpents Den. ***Jivin'Johnny and his Badd Blues Boyz*** always packed the house where ever they played their fabulous lowdown Southern blues. They were the BEST!

40

On Sunday morning November 15th Willie and Sally picked up Clyde Langston, Reggie King and Ted Thigpen at the dorms, and the five of them went to church. As usual, little Bobby Hairston spent the time in the church nursery. Following the service, as everyone was visiting in the lobby area, Reggie asked his coach if he could talk to him for a minute in private. Willie told Sally to get Bobby. He and Reggie would meet her and the others out front in a couple of minutes.

Willie looked at Reggie, who had a concerned look on his face, and said, "What's up?"

Reggie replied, "Coach, the more I practice this new offense, the more I realize that a lot of the responsibility for its success will be on my shoulders. You and Coach Benson have been awfully good to me, and I'm worried that I might let you down."

Willie patted him on the back and said, "Both of us appreciate that you feel that way, but both of us have 100% confidence in you as being the best person to get the job done. Don't worry about it Reggie. Dan Benson and I think you're going to do great."

Reggie looked relieved. "Thanks Coach, I promise you I'll make a 100% effort and try to justify your 100% confidence in me."

Willie told him that he couldn't ask for any more than that. No matter how the game ended up, he was sure he could be proud of Reggie's efforts on the field. Reggie was smiling when Sally and the guys came out the front door of the church. They all then headed to the car to go back to the dorms.

On Monday morning, November 16th, President Howard's secretary informed him that the Palmers would be arriving in the Warrenton area on Friday afternoon. She went on to tell him that she had made reservations for Mr. Palmer and his wife to join the Howards as their guests at the Huntsman Club that evening. Ralph Palmer was the president of Oakmont University. Both he and his wife would be the Howard's guests in the presidential box at Mosby Memorial Stadium during the game. Hosting the visiting president had always been a tradition between the two schools. The winner of the game would be awarded the Piedmont Pinnacle Trophy. Bob Howard liked seeing it in the Mosby University trophy case and hoped they could keep it there, but knew the team would have their hands full against the big and mighty Oakmont Outlaws.

The team's practice on Monday was a non-contact day almost entirely devoted to practicing the new offense. At first, they were a little rusty, but got up to speed in no time and began to look very good. Reggie's ability to see and read what the defensive players were doing was uncanny. No matter what Coach Johnson, the team's defensive coordinator, had the defenders do, Reggie would immediately see it. He would either give the ball to the fullback, keep it himself, or toss it to the trailing running back. For the rest of the week, the team worked on their defensive preparations extensively as well. When Friday's practice concluded, Willie and the other coaches felt the team was ready, but they wouldn't know for sure until the big game the next day. Tane Maaka, who had been the team's defensive standout all season, had come to Willie earlier that week. He had an idea, which first seemed a little crazy. However, after thinking about it, Willie gave Tane the approval to proceed.

President Howard and his wife picked up the Palmers in Middleburg that evening in a limousine. Doing so enabled them have a little chat during the short ride to the Huntsman Club. It also allowed the Howards to be able to enjoy some fine wine that evening with their delicious dinner, without being concerned about being able to drive back to Warrenton safely. The couples enjoyed two bottles of 1947 Romanée-Conti from the Côte de Nuits region in Burgundy. The wine turned out to be an excellent pairing for their wild game dinner selections. Later, after they finished their dinner and departed, the limousine dropped the Palmers off at Happy Hounds Haven, a lovely bed and breakfast in nearby Middleburg. It had been a fabulous evening.

Later the same night, a less than fabulous event happened at Saint Bartholomew's Hall at Mosby University. The crash of a broken window on the street side of their lodge heralded the arrival of an unpleasant surprise. Apparently, Bill Fryer had been closely watching some St. B's laughing in the hallway at one of the main classroom buildings at Mosby University earlier that week. Unbeknownst to them, he read their lips and discovered that they were laughing about the rotten egg bomb that Troy Barksdale and Tom Throckmorton had thrown into the Serpent's Den. Troy had said "That serves those Serpents right for snaking Rebecca and Buffy from us during the party at the Stallion Stable." Bill thought, "Really?"

After he told his lodge members about what he discovered, Kenny Cade went to Roger Rambeaux's room. Kenny said, "Get your pick-up truck ready, Roger. We need to load up the catapult and do some practicing." The Serps brilliant engineering students, Kenny and Dick deVille, had designed and constructed a spring loaded catapult the previous fall. They had used it to retaliate against the St. B's for a stunt they had pulled on the Serps that previous year. One would think they would have learned their lesson, but apparently not. They would soon learn the painful lesson once again that paybacks can be a bitch.

After loading several little plastic bags with exactly one pound of dirt, a group of four Serps took the catapult in Roger's truck out of town. They went to an old, abandoned barn that they had discovered the previous fall. Kenny had made the calculations and had even measured the location of the large window on the side of the St. B.'s Hall. Upon arriving at the barn, he had drawn an outline on the side of the barn with chalk. Once he determined the exact distance the catapult had to be away from the barn to hit the target, he wrote the number down. He later went to the local market bought two packages of Limburger cheese and had them packaged so that they were slightly less than one pound each. That enabled him to compensate for the cherry bombs, which would be inserted with modified longer fuses and make the delivery packages exactly one pound each.

At midnight on Friday before the big game against Oakmont, a group of black clothed young men went for a ride in the back of Roger's pick-up truck. When they reached their destination, they unloaded the catapult and positioned it in the little park across the street from the Hall. After Kenny made sure it was lined up exactly as he had previously measured it, the catapult was cranked down. Then, a one pound package of mud in a small plastic bag, which had been taped to make it more aerodynamic, was launched. It smashed through the targeted window; a perfect strike. The device was quickly cranked back down and a Limburger cheese bomb was inserted into the shallow box at the end of the catapult. The fuse was lit, and the projectile was launched for another perfect strike. After the bomb went through the broken window, there was a flash of light and a loud noise as the bomb went off. The guys all piled into the pickup truck and made a clean getaway. After they returned, they put the other Limburger cheese package in the lodge refrigerator, thinking they might need it again in the future. The St. B's were going to be forced to have their postgame party the following night out on their front porch. Maybe it wouldn't be too cold for their dates. If it was, some of the girls might want to leave and go over to lodges like the Den to do some dancing.

The *Fauquier Times-Democrat* and the student *Ghostly Vision* newspapers were predicting a sellout for the big game. The weather forecast was looking good, with temperatures estimated to be in the high 40's, with partially cloudy, but mostly sunny skies. Oddsmakers, upon hearing the news of Mosby's star quarterback Al Nelson's season ending injury, had installed Oakmont as a 17 point favorite, despite both teams sporting identical 9-0 records. Many people were probably thinking that the spread might have been higher if the game was not being played in Warrenton. The Oakmont team not only had over twice the number of players, all of its victories that season had been by big margins. They had literally crushed their opponents in winning all their games. However, regardless of the outcome of the game, if Mosby were to lose and end up 9-1, it still would have been a more than respectable season.

41

Warrenton was bustling with excitement on Saturday November 21st, as many people showed up early and were wandering around town. In the parking lot at John Singleton Mosby Memorial Stadium, lots of people were tailgating, and the smell of barbeque was in the air. The game was sold out; numerous folks were walking around pleading for someone to sell them a ticket. Oakmont had requested 5,000 tickets for its fans, but due to the local demand, Mosby's ticket office could only grant them 3,000 seats. The Raiders were going to need all the home field advantage they could muster. The Oakmont team had arrived the night before, but had stayed at a hotel in suburban Virginia across the river from Washington, D.C. They planned to arrive in their busses a couple of hours before the scheduled 1PM kickoff. It was a crisp autumn day; the temperature was in the 40's as predicted. It was also a great day for football.

President Bob Howard had invited the Palmers to come to his box at noon and enjoy a catered lunch and some libations before the game. He had given them some written directions and a pass to his reserved parking spot near the stadium the previous evening. Before noon, there was a surprisingly large crowd of people already in the stands. The fans were excited, but little did they expect what they were soon about to see and what was about to unfold.

Oakmont Head Coach Irv Swindle brought his 80-man Oakmont Outlaw team out onto the field early. They went to one end of the field to begin their warm up drills. He then left the team under the direction of his assistants and made his way to the 50 yard line. He always liked to stand there facing his opponents and watching them throughout their warm ups. As usual, he was dressed in all black from head to foot and already had a scowl on his face to greet his opponents once they arrived. He liked to glare at them, as if to warn them that they were in for a long day.

When the Mosby team emerged from the locker room, some cheers erupted from the stands. Strangely, all of the players walked out in a very compact and tight group as they followed Tane Maaka out onto the field. He proceeded straight toward Swindle, who probably was wondering what the hell was going on. When Tane got about three yards away from Swindle, he stopped as did the pack of players behind him. They spread out, forming a group two deep. Tane and the rest of the team suddenly flexed their knees and crouched down as Tane rolled his eyes, stuck out his tongue, and let out a loud shout. The team responded in unison with a shout as well. Then, they began beating on their thighs and slapping their arms making a series of loud shouts and grunts that were directed at the astonished Swindle. They chanted "KA MATE…KA MATE…KA ORA…KA ORA" several times, making the same kind of angry faces and stuck out their tongues as Tane had done. It didn't take long for Swindle to beat a hasty retreat away from this band of lunatics. He joined his players, who were standing at their end of the field and watching this strange display, too.

Swindle turned to one of his assistants and said, "What the hell was that stuff? Are those guys a football team or a bunch of damn crazy people?" He was going to find the answer out soon enough. As the Mosby players left midfield and headed toward the other end, many of them were laughing. They also looked very relaxed.

Roger Rambeaux and the cheerleaders began to fire up the crowd with several cheers of "Here we go Mosby Men, here we go!" Bruce, Percy, Horace and Lance were doing back flips and cartwheels. Spooky was on the sideline decked out in his coat with a big "M" on one side and a snake on the other, barking excitedly. Bill Fryer, who hadn't been able to use his unique skill and help very much so far during the season, was on the sideline, too, for the final game. Willie and his assistants had the players do some stretching and a few drills as the kickers practiced a bit. Reggie threw a few passes to warm up his arm, but they didn't run through any plays.

Swindle was still watching, although from a safe distance. He said to an assistant, "Look at that pathetic bunch of losers down there. Their stupid coach doesn't even have them working on any plays. And did you see that King kid throwing those wobbly passes? He is obviously as bad a quarterback as he was as a basketball player. We're going to kill these guys today and make all their noisy fans pretty unhappy. I see they have than damn dog over there on the sideline again. They better keep him over there and away from me after what happened last year."

After the *Fabulous Flugelhorns* appeared and played the school song, Kevin Kahana rode out as the Gray Ghost. The National Anthem was played, and the team captains met with the officials at midfield for the coin toss. Reggie King had been named as the Raiders offensive captain for the game, and Tane Maaka was given the honor for their defense. The Oakmont Outlaws won and deferred to the second half so they would be kicking off to the Mosby Raiders. That brought forth a big roar of approval from the crowd.

Ralph Palmer and his wife settled into their seats in the President's Box. He said to his host, "Well Bob, it looks like your team has the first chance to show everybody what they've got on offense today. Care to make a little side bet on the outcome of the game today?"

Bob Howard smiled and said, "Sure Ralph, but the oddsmakers have us as a 17 point underdog. Will you give me those points? I hear your team has won all of its games by big margins this year. I'm afraid 17 points might not even be enough."

President Palmer nodded his head and said, "Sure why not. I'll give you the 17 points. Do you want to bet a hundred on the game?"

Bob Howard replied, "That's fine, but after last night's dinner, if I lose that bet today, I may have to call my banker on Monday and take out a loan."

Ralph Palmer laughed and said, "Yeah, right Bob! Everyone knows about your net worth, so I don't think you'll need to make that call anytime soon." They both turned their eyes to the field as the Oakmont kicker approached the ball. It went soaring deep and out of the end zone. The Raiders would be starting on their own 20 yard line.

Reggie King huddled with the team. When they broke the huddle they had two tight ends, Boardman and Rice, and three backs, Maizley, Ferrous and Lammhandler, behind their quarterback. At the snap, King turned and started to give the ball to Maizley on a fullback dive play, but the exchange between him and his fullback was not clean and the ball was fumbled. A lot of scrambling and fighting for the ball went on before Clyde Langston recovered the ball for the Raiders on the 18 yard line. Swindle looked angry on the sideline as he yelled at his team, "Get the damn ball when it's loose and on the ground."

On second down, it looked like the Raiders were trying the same play again. Reggie turned to give the ball to Maizley once again as he headed toward his right guard's vacated position. The defensive tackle, who was opposite Henry Frumzeist, Mosby's right offensive tackle, surged quickly to his right. He was going to meet Maizley in the hole. When he got to Maizley and hit him, he discovered that the Raiders fullback didn't have the ball. Reggie had pulled it out and continued down the line. Lammhandler and Ferrous were running hard to the right at the same time, so the outside linebacker suspected that a toss to one of them might be coming. The linebacker angled into the backfield toward Lammhandler and Ferrous to maintain contain around the end. Reggie saw him do it and immediately planted his right foot and went swiftly downfield. His guard Jack Delaney had already fired off the line downfield and blocked the middle linebacker out in front of him. Big Henry Frumzeist leveled the safety out in front of him, who was coming up for run support. Mosby's tight end Parker Boardman, who had lined up on the right side, had ignored the outside linebacker to his right and had raced downfield toward the cornerback near the sideline and knocked him out of bounds. Once Reggie made the cut downfield, he followed those blocks. He used his blazing speed to outrun the Outlaws far side safety and cornerback as he rambled 82 yards for a Raider touchdown. Swindle went ballistic. He was screaming on the sideline, but no one heard him, since the fans in the stands were jumping up and down and screaming with excitement. After Morales' successful extra point conversion, the score was 7-0 in Mosby's favor.

Ralph Palmer looked over at Bob Howard and said, "Hey Bob, you aren't really going to take those 17 points are you?" Bob just grinned at him and said, "Of course I am Ralph. We had a deal, and only one minute's gone. There is lot more football to play out there today."

Following Morales kickoff to Oakmont, the Outlaws began playing their brand of smash mouth football. Their quarterback, Bart Benoski kept handing the ball off to either his fullback Matt Zombo or his big running back Horsie Dann. Their big offensive line, which outweighed everybody on the Raiders except Tane Maaka, was able to open enough holes to enable Oakmont to move steadily down the field. The drive took seven minutes off the clock and resulted in an Outlaw touchdown when Dann punched the ball into the end zone from the 4 yard line. The score became tied at seven all following the extra point midway through the first quarter. President Palmer looked more relaxed in the Presidential Box, and the red color of Irv Swindle's face even became a somewhat paler hue.

On the home team's sideline, Willie was concerned about how dominant Oakmont had looked during their successful scoring drive. He said to Jack Johnson, his defensive coordinator, "I hope we can answer that Oakmont drive when we go back on offense. I also hope that maybe we can do a little better on defense when they get the ball back next time."

Johnson replied, "Take it easy Willie, we will shake things up a bit the next time the Outlaws have the ball. It's still early in the game and too early to be worrying." Willie grinned, gave him a thumbs up and said, "Gotcha, Jack!"

The Oakmont kickoff following their score was returned to the 26 yard line by Ironhead Ferrous. On first down, Reggie turned to give the ball to his fullback George Maizley, as like he had done earlier in the game. The defensive tackle remembered how he had been fooled the last time so he went wide around the Raider's Henry Frumzeist to cut Willie off when he came down the line. Unfortunately for him, Reggie actually did give the ball to George who ran right up the gut behind Delaney and Frumzeist's blocks and picked up 9 yards. On second down and a yard to go, Reggie faked a handoff to Maizley, as the Outlaws middle linebacker Dann was coming hard to meet him. Reggie raised up and hit his tight end Boardman right over the middle on a quick look-in pass which went for 7 yards and a first down at the 42 yard line.

From there Reggie turned to his left and stuck the ball into Johnny Baugh's stomach. Johnny was running behind Clyde Langston, who had fired out toward the middle linebacker out in front of him. The Outlaw's tackle opposite CC Rider Snyder made a quick move to get Baugh, but discovered that Baugh no longer had the ball. Reggie still had the ball and was moving toward the sideline. The outside linebacker, who had not been blocked by Mosby's tight end Voshon Rice, immediately turned inward to intercept him. Just before he got to the Raiders quarterback, Reggie pitched the ball out to a streaking Shakur Wade, who was following Freddie Lammhandler. As Shakur went downfield, he had Rice and Snyder out in front of him as well as Lammhandler and he ran untouched for a 58 yard touchdown. It had only taken two minutes for the Raiders to answer as they went back in front 14-7 after Morales' extra point.

Swindle was furious and screaming at his defensive coordinator on the sideline. Bill Fryer watched him, laughing. He told Willie that Swindle was threatening to fire his defensive coach right there on the field if Mosby made another long touchdown run. Willie just smiled and replied, "I hope that assistant coach has his resume all filled out and ready to go, because as far as I'm concerned, we ain't done yet."

When the Outlaws got the ball back following Morales's kickoff, they attempted to pound away at Mosby as they did the first time they had the ball. This time, things were different as Coach Johnson had Tane Maaka doing some stunts with his middle linebackers Lammhandler and Maizley. After a couple of runs it was third down and still 5 to go. Swindle was so fired up on the sideline, he forgot to put up his play sheet in front of his face when he sent in a passing play. Bill Fryer intercepted it as he read Swindle's lips. He tipped off Coach Johnson, who put up his cornerbacks up pretty close to jam the Oakmont receivers. The ball was snapped and Stretch Schmidt, the Outlaws tall, fast receiver exploded off the line and ran a ten yard post pattern. Benoski, the Outlaw's quarterback, dropped to look for Schmidt. Instead, he saw a blitzing Garrett Gassman coming hard at him around the left side of his line. It forced him to throw a little early and a little high towards Schmidt over the middle. There, the ball was picked off by a leaping Voshon Rice and brought back to the Oakmont 9 yard line before he was run out of bounds. Willie looked over at Bill Fryer and said, "About time you earned your sideline pass." Bill just grinned and said, "Who knows, maybe there's more to come, Coach."

After Reggie huddled with his team, he ran right again, but this time he saw that the Outlaws defensive tackle over there hesitated to move toward his fullback Johnny Baugh, who alternated with Maizley. Baugh took the ball and ran right by the Outlaws' Horsie Dann who was blitzing from his linebacker position for a four yard gain. Although Reggie had already handed the ball off, Dann unloaded on him and knocked him down pretty hard. Willie was worried for a second, as Reggie was slow to get up. When he did get up, he signaled to his coach that he was okay. He figured that the Outlaws would gamble that they would run to the wide side of the field again on second down, so Reggie called the Triple Option to the right once again. This time the defensive tackle closed down on his fullback. Reggie kept the ball and, seeing the outside linebacker was a little slow to react, he planted his right foot, kept the ball and broke a tackle at the goal line to score.

That score turned out to be secondary to another event that occurred on the field. Mosby's right guard, Jack Delaney, had fired off the ball at the snap. His assignment was to block the play side middle linebacker. Rather than try and block the 235 pound Horsie Dann high, Jack went low for Dann's legs and chopped him down. Right after Reggie scored, Dann got off the ground and kicked Jack in the head. Delaney jumped up and pulled his helmet off, and so did Dann. Both threw a couple of punches. Dann's wild swings only were glancing blows, but Jack landed a good one on the side of Dann's head that dropped him to his knees. The officials broke it up and threw offsetting penalty flags against both of them. Then they threw BOTH players out of the game. Swindle went ballistic on the sideline and ran onto the field, screaming at the officials. They told him to go back to the sideline. When he didn't do it right away and continued to rail at them, they threw another flag. The game was getting out of hand in a hurry. Finally, order was restored. Morales made the extra point conversion and the score became Mosby 21-Oakmont 7.

Spectators in the stands had no idea how dramatically the tide had shifted in favor of the Raiders. Bill Fryer was still watching the Outlaw coaches. He came over to Willie and said, "I think we've got 'em now Coach! I just saw Swindle screaming at his defensive coordinator. He wanted to know what the hell we were doing on offense. The defensive coach told him that he couldn't figure it out. He said he had never seen an offense do the kind of stuff we were doing." Willie laughed.

Without Horsie Dann in the offensive backfield, Oakmont's running attack lost its effectiveness. Benoski was forced to throw, and he was sacked several times by blitzing Mosby linebackers. Tane Maaka even got a sack, too, despite being triple teamed all day long and making things easier for Fincie and Vorache. When the Raiders had the ball, Reggie never had to throw another pass all day as he ran the Triple Option to perfection. Without Horsie Dann at linebacker, the Outlaws had not only lost their leading rusher, they lost their leading tackler, too.

It got pretty ugly for the few Outlaw fans, who had come all the way to Warrenton in the hopes of a big win and seeing the team take the Piedmont Pinnacle Trophy back to Oakmont. However, they weren't as unhappy as Irv Swindle, who was beet red and almost foaming at the mouth in rage. He even screamed and rudely shoved a player, who got faked out and missed tackling Raider running back, Ironhead Ferrous as he ran for a touchdown.

The final score was 56-7 as the Raiders scored every time they had the ball that day. Reggie King ran for over two hundred yards and scored three touchdowns. George Maizley had over a hundred yards and a touchdown, and Johnny Baugh, George's replacement at fullback also had a score. Each of the team's three running backs, Shakur Wade, Freddie Lammhandler, and Ironhead Ferrous scored a touchdown as well. Although Mosby only had seven yards passing on Reggie's singular attempted pass that day, its rushing total was an amazing 535 yards. No one in the stadium had ever seen an offensive display like that before. Neither had Irv Swindle. That was for sure. The

Mosby Raiders, led by Reggie's superb quarterbacking, had moved the ball up and down the field all day with amazing precision. The ease in which they cut through the Outlaw's defense reminded one of the fans of a hot knife going through room temperature butter. The team's performance obviously delighted Mosby's fans, who sang the school song with exultation after each touchdown. Many were still on their feet and ecstatically cheering when the game finally ended.

When Willie went out to shake Swindle's hand following for the game, Swindle had already left. A couple of his assistants were seen steering him back to the locker room while he was yelling at the top of his lungs at people in the stands and also at his players on the sideline who were heading to the locker room. Swindle's face was bright red and salivating so it looked like he was foaming around his mouth. Many in the stadium thought he had gone crazy and Mosby fans were laughing at him.

Willie returned to his sideline where Reggie had huddled his team on their knees for a post-game prayer. At the end of the game, Reggie had shaken hands with some members of the Outlaws and invited them to come join the Raiders for the post-game prayer. A number of the Oakmont players took him up on his offer and knelt beside their Raider opponents. Reggie offered a prayer of thanks for the brotherhood being demonstrated and the fact that no serious injuries had occurred. Meanwhile, Willie saw Dan Benson and told him, "When I went out there to shake hands with your former boss, I saw him leaving the field. I guess he doesn't like playing against fancy schmancy offenses."

Dan broke up in laughter. "Well, I think old Irv ought to be happy. At least Spooky didn't go over and pee on him this year." Willie cracked up laughing when he remembered that event.

Once the team was in the locker room, Willie singled out Reggie King for doing an outstanding job of running the Triple Option offense. Then he congratulated Tane Maaka for intimidating the Outlaws before the game by leading the team in the Haka and playing a great defensive game. Jack Delaney was mentioned, too, for getting kicked out of the game and taking the Outlaws leading rusher and tackler with him. Finally, he recognized assistant coach Dan Benson for suggesting and teaching them how to run the Triple Option offense. When he was finished with those words of individual praise, he made another announcement. "Men, since it takes a team effort, with everyone doing his part to make the Triple Option work effectively, EVERYONE on the team will get a game ball for their efforts out there today." Dan Kojak jumped up and said, "Be sure you and your coaches get one, too. You guys are the BEST!" As everyone applauded, Dan led them once again in a "Here we go Mosby Men…here we go," cheer.

In the Presidential Box, a gracious Ralph Palmer pulled out a $100 bill and handed it to Bob Howard. He said, "It looks like you get to keep that pretty trophy for another year, Bob. But, seriously, aren't you embarrassed that you asked me for points? You can forget about that next year when your team comes back to Oakmont."

Bob Howard nodded. "I guess the oddsmakers don't understand that this is a real rivalry. The players and coaches don't care about the records and the stats when they get out on the field."

President Palmer asked, "What in the world was all that yelling and chanting out there at midfield before the game? I think it might have been voodoo or something like that, because it obviously scared our coaches and our Oakmont Outlaws team."

Bob Howard shook his head and said, "Your guess is as good as mine Ralph. I've never seen it before either. I'll have to ask my coach about it. If it was voodoo, it sure worked. Other than the game, I hope you enjoyed your visit with us down here."

Ralph replied, "We did and thanks again for the excellent meal last night."

As they left the suite, Bob Howard said, "It was certainly my pleasure Ralph, and I look forward to seeing you again next year up in Oakmont."

42

By the time the game ended, even Marshall Holcome was excitedly cheering the victory along with most of the other fans in the stadium. Most of the 3,000 Oakmont supporters didn't have much to cheer about and had left the game midway through the third quarter. Marshall tapped Troy Barksdale II on the shoulder and asked him if Tidewater National Bank was going to renew their block of season's tickets next year. Barksdale replied, "In view of what is going on at Mosby University these days, I seriously doubt that the bank will want to renew their subscription. However, I will send out an announcement to everyone who had seats this year and see how many are interested in returning. If enough want to keep their seats, and are willing to appoint someone else to be the custodian, I will consider making a transfer the season ticket rights to that new custodian."

Marshall then replied, "Troy, I really enjoyed being here this year, and I would be happy to take on the responsibility of being the custodian. I've also decided that I don't care what color the players are either. As far as I'm concerned, they are our players and they are Mosby men just like you and me."

Barksdale looked shocked by what he had heard his friend say. As he was getting ready to leave, he responded, "You can be the custodian, Marshall, but you should know in advance, that I won't be returning. Some of those players may be wearing the school uniforms, but they will never be true Mosby men as far as I am concerned. Did you see them out there kneeling on the ground with those nasty Outlaw players after the game? That's outrageous! Oakmont University and their players are our enemies. They have always been our rivals and we shouldn't be kneeling with them."

The *Estate* was overflowing with happy students and fans after the game. Some were heading home or to their dorms or lodges, but others were already thinking about the big parties that night. Most of the members at the Serpents Den had made dates for the evening. However, Cadillac deVille was on the Den's pay phone after he got back to the lodge following the game. He was trying desperately to convince some girls at Mary Washington to come to the party. Johnny Baugh overheard him making a pitch to the second one he called, after the first one had turned him down. Cadillac said, "Hey! You gotta come here and be with me tonight. ***Jivin'Johnny and his Badd Blues Boyz*** are playing at our lodge and it's going to be fabulous. Hey, what do you mean that I should have called earlier? Every time I tried during the last couple of weeks, you've been out. Didn't anyone tell you that I called? No? Hey, they promised they me would. Nice buddies you have there. Hey, don't hang up. I'm sure they are nice. You could even bring one with you if you came. No, not for me. I'm sure there are some guys here at the lodge who don't have dates, so they could meet them, do some dancin' to the ***Boyz,*** and maybe meet a Prince Charming. Maybe? Some other time? Hey, Hey, that would be great! Bye-bye!"

Johnny said, "No luck Cadillac?"

"Not yet, but I've got a couple more to call before I give up," Cadillac replied as he pulled out some more coins and prepared to dial. "Quitters never win and winners never quit."

Meanwhile, at the Stallion Stable, Kevin Kahana was still wearing his Gray Ghost outfit and was in great spirits. He spotted Joey Galatta and said, "How bout those Raiders today? They kicked a whole bunch of Outlaw butts out there."

Joey laughed and said, "Be careful about talking about kicking any Outlaw's butts around here. I think Mike Marino's uncle Tony works for the family. You wouldn't want him coming by to see you with his baseball bat, would you?"

Kevin grinned and shook his head side to side as he said, "Who do you have coming tonight Joey?"

Joey said," I assume you mean the band and not my girlfriend, huh? I've got the **Harmonic Hosemen** coming down from D.C. These guys sound almost as good as Smokey Robinson and the *Miracles*. The Stable is going to be really jumping tonight.

Kevin laughed, "I'd have to hear it to believe it. How did they get that name?"

Joey said, "From what I understand, they are all D.C. firefighters, so it's logical."

Kevin was still chuckling as he replied, "Oh, I was thinking their name meant something a little more obscene."

It was a little less festive over at the St. B. Hall. They had reported the damage to their lodge to the security office at the *Estate* and told the officer there that they suspected that members at the Serpents Den Lodge might be the culprits. The security officer dismissed that assertion, since he knew that the Den had been the victims of a similar attack recently. He told the St. B.'s that it was probably someone from Oakmont University. He told them that a couple of students from there had already been caught vandalizing at the *Estate*.

The smell of Limburger cheese in the Hall's main entrance area was still overwhelming. As a result, most of the members were hanging out on their front porch that evening. Many of their dates started to complain that it was getting cold. That was probably going to put a damper on any romantic ideas the guys might have had. Several of their dates demanded to either go where there was a combo playing, or be taken back to where they were staying. Troy Barksdale and Tom Throckmorton didn't have any dates. They were having a hard time finding any girl worthy of their attention after those tramps, Buffy and Rebecca, had abandoned them for a pair of cretins.

Later that night, after ***Jivin'Johnny and his Badd Blues Boyz*** started playing, the Serpents Den Lodge was jumping. Al Nelson, despite a broken collar bone, had been on the sidelines with the team during the game. He had made a point to invite all the new guys on the team to come to the lodge that night. When he saw Reggie King, Shakur Wade, Reggie Langston, and Ted Thigpen show up at the party, he immediately went over, and welcomed them and introduced them to his date Sandi. It wasn't long before LeRoyce Forsett, Voshon Rice came in the door, too. Later, Tane Maaka came over from the Stallion Stable and brought his buddy Kevin Kahana. All of the guys loved the music, but none of their buddies on the team ever invited them to dance with their dates except Johnny Baugh. He tried to talk Reggie into getting out there with his date, Lilly Dahlen.

Reggie declined. "Hey Johnny, I may be able to run a Triple Option, but I don't think I can do that fancy swirl around move I saw you performing out there. Thanks, but I think I'll just hang out and enjoy the music. Those ***Badd Blues Boyz*** are great and Jivn' Johnny can really sing. His dance moves might even be almost as good as yours. Maybe next year, some of us guys might be living in our own lodge and will have a group play there. I will invite you and hope you will come. The coach told me that the school is going to build a new lodge that will be especially for the colored students here at Mosby."

Johnny Baugh said, "I think that's great. That must be what President Howard was talking about at the groundbreaking ceremony last week. I wonder where they are going to build it. He told the audience that it would be called Washington Lodge."

Bill Fryer came over and introduced the guys to his date, Dovie Eckstrah. He said, "It's been great watching from the sideline this year, but I'm sorry I wasn't more help to the team."

Johnny Baugh laughed. "I don't know about that, but I do know your abilities sure weren't much help to the St. B's. I walked by the Hall earlier tonight. It looked like all of them were hanging outside on their front porch. I think your intelligence gathering abilities might have had something to do with that. Brrrrrr, I'd rather be in here myself, listening and dancin' to the **Badd Blues Boyz***.*" Reggie didn't understand what Johnny was talking about, but he laughed along with Bill, Johnny and Jack Delaney, who had come over to say hello.

Social chairman R.T. Mueller came by. Everyone congratulated him on hiring such a great group. When asked if he had a date that night, R.T. told them no. He mumbled something about his last one. He said that she didn't have a sense of humor, and he was a little worried that she might turn him into a frog.

Parker Boardman had brought his hometown sweetheart Marie Jeanette back down for the weekend and was having a ball on the dance floor. Garrett Gassman was dancing with the date that some of the guys called the "Polish Princess." Actually, she wasn't from Poland. She was a real *ghost* who went to Averett College down in Danville named Letta Kowalski.

43

As a follow up to his announcement of the big expansion project at Mosby University, President Robert Howard IV issued an official news release on the Monday before Thanksgiving. It went out to all the major newspapers and TV networks as well as the local *Fauquier Time-Democrat* newspaper and the student *Ghostly Vision*. It mentioned the planned construction of a school of law to honor the memory of John Mosby, who practiced law for many years following the Civil War. The news release also spoke of the university's efforts to integrate the University. It mentioned how successful those efforts had been. It went on to tell about the recent enrollment of a number of Negro students for the first time in the school's history and mentioned that they were proving to be excellent scholars. In order to provide these students with an equal opportunity to enjoy their experience at Mosby University, the announcement said that a new student lodge would be constructed on the vacant lawn area adjacent to the existing Saint Bartholomew's Hall Lodge. This lodge would be specifically designated for students of color. The name of the lodge would be the Booker T. Washington Lodge, named in honor of the esteemed Negro educator. Mr. Washington had been an author, orator, and advisor to Republican presidents Theodore Roosevelt and William Howard

Taft and had also served as the first president of the highly respected Tuskegee Institute in Tuskegee, Alabama.

It didn't take long for some people to react to this announcement. The colored students at Mosby, having seen the nice lodges around the *Estate,* were excited about the opportunity to have a lodge at Mosby University especially designated for them. Some other people were not as excited. Troy Barksdale II was sitting in his office at Tidewater National Bank when his secretary brought him an issue of the *Richmond Times-Dispatch.* It was opened to the page where she had circled the news release. As he read the article, Barksdale became furious. He didn't like this recent effort at desegregation at his alma mater and felt that it had been a big mistake. However, the idea of building these people their own lodge, and putting it next to his beloved Saint Bartholomew's Hall was outrageous. The Hall was the place where he had been a member when he attended Mosby University, and now his son was a St. B. as well. The members there were the truly elite students at Mosby and deserved more respect.

Barksdale had his secretary put in a call to President Howard immediately. He was pleased when she reported that he was available to take his call. Of course, he was available, Barksdale thought. Why wouldn't he drop what he was doing, and be available for someone as important as me?

When Bob Howard came on the line, he said, "Good morning Troy, what can I do for you today?"

Barksdale's voice sounded agitated. "I just read the news release you issued. I wanted to tell you that I don't like what you are doing one bit."

President Howard calmly said, "So, you don't feel that we should build a law school to honor the memory of Colonel Mosby, who was a lawyer himself?"

Barksdale quickly said, "That's not what I'm talking about and you damn well know it. I don't like that you have not only allowed colored students to matriculate at our alma mater. You are also encouraging more of them to come by building them their own damn lodge."

"Well Troy, I'm sorry that you feel that way, but I happen to think that it is the right thing to do, and that is why we are going to do it. I don't understand why anyone would feel that it is objectionable if they have any sense of fairness."

Barksdale said, "Well, I do object and to put the damn thing right next to the St. B. Hall, where I was a member, and now my son is, really upsets me."

Bob Howard replied, "I'm sorry you're upset Troy, but that space was available and since the university owns the land, we felt it made sense to put it there. That planned construction site is in the general area at the *Estate* where all of the lodges are located. You might have been able to have had some input in this matter if your bank was financing the project. However, since your bank isn't handling the financing, you really don't have a say. I respect your opinion Troy, but we are going to proceed with the planned construction on the selected site. I sincerely hope that this little disagreement will not deter you from continuing to support your alma mater. I also want you to know that I appreciate Tidewater National buying the big block of seats for the home football games this year. I thank you for your support."

Barksdale then said, "Well, right now, I'm not so sure we will be renewing those seats next year."

Howard replied, "I'm sorry to hear that, but after the successful season we just had, I wouldn't be a bit surprised if there weren't a bunch of individuals or companies that would love to have those prime seats next year. In fact, I wouldn't be a bit surprised if the nice folks at Franklin National might be interested."

Barksdale quickly responded, "Now Bob, don't you go jumping to conclusions. If our bank doesn't renew them, Marshall Holcome has told me that he would be happy for me to transfer the tickets to him. He will find people to fill the seats."

Bob said, "Well that's fine Troy, but be sure to do that before the payment is due on February 15th. Season tickets that aren't renewed by that day are automatically available to others. It was nice talking to you today. I have to run and attend a meeting regarding the construction project. Stop by anytime and see how things are progressing."

Barksdale was still fuming when the call ended. The biggest cause for his frustration was the realization that there was nothing he could do about what he had heard. He was used to telling other people what to do, not the other way around.

44

Meanwhile at Oakmont University, President Ralph Palmer had his secretary put in a call to Head Football Coach Irv Swindle. Coach Swindle had previously called a meeting that morning. All of his assistant coaches were there. Just as the meeting was about to begin, his secretary came to the door of the athletic facility's conference room and informed him that President Palmer's secretary was on the line, and the president wanted to talk to him.

Swindle, whose red face and squinty eyes gave evidence that he was not in a good mood, snapped at her and said, "Tell his secretary that I'm in a meeting and will get back to him later." She nodded her head and hurriedly left the room.

Swindle turned back to his assistants and said, "In all my years of coaching, I've never experienced such embarrassing losses as we have had for two consecutive years against that rinky dink Mosby University. Frankly, I'm sick of it, and if any of you people out there aren't also, you might as well hand in your resignation and leave right now." There was a lot of nervous shuffling going on by all the assistants in the room.

He went on and got louder as he spoke, "Our offense stunk last Saturday, but the defense was worse. We gave up 56 stinkin' points for crying out loud. That was outrageous! That was almost as many as points as we had given up all season. Mosby's lousy quarterback didn't even have to throw but one pass the whole damn day. How pathetic is that?"

Harry Grotski, the Outlaws' Defensive Coordinator spoke up. "We scouted both of Mosby's last two games prior to our playing them, and they never did anything in those games like they did against us."

Swindle replied, "Well Boo hoo! Please pass me a tissue! So what if they did something different. You get paid a lot of money to be a defensive coach, and you're supposed to be able to make an adjustment to any offense you come up against and stop them. You failed! They ran the ball just as good in the second half as they did in the first half. Nothing changed out there. The scored every time they had the ball. Your defense stunk! I think that turncoat Dan Benson might have had something to do with the things they did out there on offense. He told me a little about some kind of fancy schmancy offense that some high school coach had taught him. The little that he told me sounded kind of like the stuff they were doing out there. That's really pathetic if our defense couldn't handle some stupid high school offense if that was what it was. "

Grotski pleaded, "We tried Irv. It seemed like every time we tried to tackle the runner, that damn quarterback would fool our players and give the ball to someone else. I've never seen anything like that before in all my years of coaching. "

Swindle looked angrier. He interrupted Grotski and said, "Well, unless you figure out an answer and prove to me you have a good answer that will work, all your years of coaching around here are going to be over." Grotski sat looking chastised and shocked. The other coaches kept their mouths shut and didn't dare to try and defend their actions during the game.

Swindle ranted and raved for five more minutes before he ended the meeting. He told all of them that he would be evaluating the performance of his entire staff and that some changes were going to be made. Then he told them to get out the conference room. They got up and left with grim looks on their faces.

Swindle returned to his office. On the way, he asked his secretary what the president wanted. She told him that she didn't know, but he was supposed to call President Palmer as soon as possible.

He grumbled and then made the call. After the president's secretary put him through he said, "I heard you wanted to talk to me. What can I do for you today?"

President Palmer told him that he was in the middle of something right then, but he would like for him to some to his office that morning at 11AM. Swindle confirmed that he would be there and then wondered what in the hell the president wanted.

Upon Swindle's arrival at the appointed time, President Palmer remained sitting behind his desk. He calmly said, "When I spoke to you on the phone earlier this morning, you asked me what you could do for me today. Actually, Oakmont University and I needed you to do something for us on Saturday. I was the guest of Mosby's president in his suite there and saw the debacle that occurred first hand. That's two straight years of embarrassing losses, and since we pay you a lot of money to serve as our Head Football Coach, I would think that you should be embarrassed too."

Swindle quickly replied, "I am not only embarrassed, I am disgusted that my assistants did such a lousy job. I just finished telling them that earlier this morning. I may be making some changes to my staff very soon. I want to bring in some new coaches who can get the job done around here if these bums can't do it."

Ralph Palmer then said, "I recall that President Harry Truman once said, "The buck stops here." If your assistant coaches fail at their jobs, part of the responsibility for that failure ultimately falls upon the person who wears the title of Head Coach."

Swindle angrily responded. "My won/loss record ought to tell you that I am a damn good coach, and my team's ending up at 9-1 this year is certainly no disgrace. There are tons of schools around the country that would love to have me as their football coach with my record of success."

The president said, "You are quite right about that Coach. Your won/loss record has been outstanding and would look good on your resume. However, the main thing I wanted to talk to you about today was not about your record. It was about your behavior. Not only did you not have the good sportsmanship to go out and shake hands with the Mosby coach after the game, I observed that you were abusive to any and all people around you on the field. Everyone there at the game could easily see it. On many occasions in the past I have witnessed your temper tantrums on the sidelines. They have been directed against the officials, your assistants and your players. Last Saturday, I even saw you shove one of your players on the sideline. That is totally unacceptable behavior and not reflective of the kind of fine institution that Oakmont prides itself as being.

Swindle blurted out, "That kid blew an assignment, and it gave them a touchdown."

Mr. Palmer replied, "Sorry Coach, that didn't justify your actions. Since Mosby made so many scores the other day, did it really matter, or affect the outcome of the game? As I mentioned earlier, with respect to the success of the football program here at Oakmont, the buck stops on your desk. Conversely, with respect to the reputation and overall success of this university as a respected institution, the buck stops on mine. Because of that, and in consideration of the disgraceful way you have conducted yourself in public, I have decided that I would like to ask for your resignation today."

Swindle sputtered, "You can't do that, I have another year left on my contract."

President Palmer nodded. "I am well aware of that fact. Oakmont University will honor that contract and pay you next year not to coach. However, as part of that agreement you signed, if you resign and accept the money, you are prohibited from coaching elsewhere else during that period of time in which you are still receiving compensation."

A flustered Swindle said, "That's not fair! There would be a lot of teams that would love to have me as their coach next year. What if I refuse to resign?"

Ralph Palmer calmly told him, "Then I would have to fire you. If you have ever taken the time to read your contract, it clearly says that if you are fired for any infraction of the rules set forth in the agreement, you would not be entitled to any future compensation. One of the listed infractions, are any actions on your part that bring disgrace to the school. You might argue that you didn't do that, even though I think you did. However, another specifically states that physically abusing any player on your team is a clear cut violation. As far as I am concerned, you have done both things. I am think I am being more than fair by giving you the chance to resign and walk away with a year's salary. If you truly believe there are a number of teams that would like to hire you, then clearly, you might not want to resign. You might want to forgo getting the money we would have paid you and just take the chance that you are correct. The choice is yours. I will give you until 4PM to make it. Good bye, Mr. Swindle. I will await your decision." With those words, the president told the coach that he needed to go to a meeting. It ended the conversation. A thoroughly shocked Irv Swindle got up and left the office.

Irv Swindle couldn't believe what he had heard. He knew he was a damn good coach and plenty of teams would want to hire him. However, he was making pretty good money at Oakmont and he hated to lose out on that salary. He could get that money by doing what the president had suggested if he just submitted his resignation. The more he thought about it, the madder he got. He started throwing some books and other objects around his office in an obvious temper tantrum. His secretary, upon hearing the racket, got up from her desk in the adjacent room and came to his door. Upon seeing her, Swindle yelled out, "What the hell do you want? Get out of here and leave me alone." He picked up a book and threw it in her direction. It hit the wall right beside the door with a loud bang. His secretary closed the door, made a quick retreat and went out of the athletic office building. She made her way to the office of Oakmont University's Human Resources Department. Upon her arrival, she told one of the executives about what she had just seen and experienced. He was shocked and advised her to not return to her desk and to take the rest of the day off. When she left, he picked up the phone and called the office of President Palmer.

After Ralph Palmer heard the story, he immediately called campus security. He instructed the officer in charge to send two of his men over to Irv Swindle's office and escort him to his office right away. When they arrived at the coach's office, Swindle was still fuming. Upon being told that the president wanted to see him right away, he told the security people that he didn't have to go back there until 4PM. One of the security officers replied, "President Palmer has just given us instructions that he wants you back at his office right now."

A reluctant Swindle went with them to the president's office. Once they arrived, the president's secretary called her boss to let him know they were there. She told them, "He will see all three of your now."

Swindle wondered why in the hell these guys would be invited into the president's office if the president wanted to see him. As he entered Ralph Palmer's office, the coach said, "You told me I had until 4PM today before I had to get back to you. Why are you having these guys drag me over here now?"

President Palmer sat calmly at his desk with a serious look on his face. "That time of 4PM was your deadline for having the opportunity to resign and be paid for an additional year. In view of your conduct this morning, I am taking that option off the table. You're FIRED!"

An irate Swindle angrily blurted out, "You can't do that. You told me I could give you a resignation letter and not be fired."

Ralph Palmer looked at this blustering person with the angry look on his red face. He replied, "That choice went off the table when you threatened your secretary this morning. If you need further clarification I will say it once more. You're FIRED!" He then addressed the two large security officers and said, "Please escort Mr. Swindle back to his former office and arrange for some boxes to be sent over there. After he has gotten all his personal items together, have him turn in his keys and all other property belonging to the university before you help him load his vehicle. When you are at his vehicle, also be sure to remove his university parking pass before he leaves the campus." Following those directions, the three men left the president's office. One of them left it for the last time.

45

The following morning, all of the Oakmont assistant coaches were notified that Coach Swindle had been terminated and that the school would immediately start looking for a replacement. They were told that all of them would continue to be paid until the replacement was found. The new head coach would decide if he wanted to retain members of the coaching staff or not. They were also advised that if any of them wanted to apply for the job, the school would be happy to consider their application. Some were stunned by the notice, while others were overjoyed to be out from under the foot of a tyrant. A couple of them were even overheard humming the song, *Ding Dong the Witch's Dead*, from the classic movie, *The Wizard of Oz*.

Ralph Palmer put his administrative assistants to work on coming up with a list of potential candidates to replace Swindle. However, in the back of his mind, he had an idea about one already. He picked up the phone and made a call to another university and asked for the office of the head football coach. When President Palmer was put through, he heard the phone ring. When it was picked up, a voice said, "Hello, this is Coach Hairston."

President Palmer introduced himself and told Willie that he had been at the game the previous Saturday. He congratulated Hairston on coaching his team to a stunning victory.

Willie responded, "Thank you President Palmer. That is real nice of you to call and say that. I have to tell you that it is the first time I have ever had a congratulatory call from the president of a school that we played and beat. I know Oakmont doesn't lose very often, but when they do, is this something you usually do?"

Palmer laughed, "No! But today, I must confess that had an additional purpose in calling. I wanted to inform you that Coach Irv Swindle has been terminated. While he had an outstanding won/loss record, his personal conduct as a representative of Oakmont University was totally unacceptable. We are now beginning the process of searching for a replacement. Knowing the fabulous job that you have done, I wanted to see if you might be interested in interviewing for the job. Oakmont is a much bigger school and unlike Mosby, we can afford to offer athletic scholarships to outstanding athletes."

Willie said, "I am flattered that you would consider me after I've only had a couple of years of coaching experience. However, I have to tell you that I signed a five year agreement with Mosby and I have four more years to go on it. I recall that one of the conditions in the agreement was that, if I elected to leave to go elsewhere, I would have to pay Mosby University back for any money that had been paid to me under the contract. That means that I would have to pay back the salary they paid me for this season, and I can't afford to do that."

President Palmer said, "Do you mind telling me what you are receiving in compensation? I can assure you that whatever you tell me will be kept in complete confidence." Willie hesitated, but maybe out of curiosity about where this conversation, was heading, he told Oakmont president what he was making.

President Palmer then said, "If we were to hire you, we would not only give you the money to reimburse Mosby University, we would give you a five year contract at double the money you are now making. How does that sound to you?"

Willie took a moment to think about what he just heard and said, "I'm very flattered that you would consider me for the position. I am even more flattered by the generosity of your offer. However, I feel an obligation to President Howard because he not only made it possible for me to attend Mosby University and become the first Negro to graduate from there, he had the confidence to give me a five year contract to be the coach there. I feel a real responsibility to respect and appreciate all that he has done for me. To do otherwise would be a breach of honor as far as I am concerned."

Ralph Palmer replied, "Coach, I want you to know that I really respect you for what you have told me. You are precisely the kind of man that I want to be our coach here, because I think our coach should be an inspiration to our young men. I wonder, could I ask you for a favor today Willie?"

"Of course," Willie said.

"Could you please not tell Bob Howard that I called?" Palmer asked. "I consider him to be a good friend as well as a fine gentleman. I was trying to do what I thought was the best for my university, just as I know he tries to do the best thing for his. I wouldn't want him to be angry at me for calling you. It could possibly ruin our friendship."

Willie said, "I understand sir. I appreciate your offer and also appreciate your understanding the reason I declined it. I won't mention it to President Howard if you promise to do the same. I sure would hate for him to come to me and ask me why I didn't tell him about this, or maybe wonder if I contacted you and applied for the job."

A relieved Ralph Palmer said, "We've got a deal Willie. Good luck next year." Then he laughingly said, "You wouldn't happen to know where I could find a good coach do you?"

Willie thought about it for a moment and then said, "Actually, I might have a lead for you. When we played Cedaredge this year, they gave us a real battle. I talked to their coach, Dick Myers, after the game. He mentioned that his contract was expiring. The school seemed to be dragging their feet on renewing it and paying him at the level most of the other coaches around here were making. He's not only a quality coach, he's a quality person. Hey, wait a minute. I guess I must be stupid. If you hired him, he would still be my rival, but at a school with greater resources."

President Palmer laughed and said, "If that happened, in appreciation for your recommendation, maybe I could instruct him to throw the game against you the first year you played each other. After that, you would be on your own. Fair enough?

Willie was laughing too as he said, "Yeah, right! I'm sure that would happen. I wish both you and him the best, and I'm not afraid of competition. Hope to see you next year."

With that exchange, the call ended. Willie sat quietly for a moment and then put in a call to his president. Once he got President Howard on the line he said, "I wanted to run something by you today if you have a moment."

Bob Howard said, "Sure Willie, go ahead."

Willie went on with what he wanted to say. "I think my staff did a great job this year and that all of them deserve a 10% pay increase."

Bob Howard didn't hesitate for a second as he said, "I agree. You can inform them that their pay will be increased starting on January 1st."

Willie continued, "One of the two new assistants that came to us from Oakmont this year did a particularly outstanding job. I would like to elevate Dan Benson to the position of Offensive Coordinator and give him a 20% pay increase. I'd also like to have him sign a four year contract to coincide with the length of time I have remaining on my contract. I would hate to lose him or have Oakmont try to get him back. Frankly, I don't think he is interested in ever working for Coach Swindle again. However, if you could have your lawyers put a very expensive penalty in his contract for leaving before his four years are up and then make the penalty double if he went back to Oakmont, that would make me very happy."

Bob Howard laughed and said, "Willie! Are you sure you aren't a lawyer instead of a football coach? If you feel he is worth it and want these things to be done, I'll take care of it for you. How soon would you like to be able to have that contract for him to sign?"

Willie replied, "Yesterday. " Bob Howard told him that they would get right on it and that he would notify him when the contract was ready. Before the president got off the phone, he jokingly asked, "Anything more you need from me today, Willie?"

"Actually, yes, I do have one more request today. I'd like the money to have a buffet dinner and awards party for the team and the coaches before we break for Christmas."

Bob Howard replied, "You got it. The team and the coaches did a great job, and I will agree to that request, if you promise to invite me to the celebration."

"You deserve to be there, too, Mr. President. I would have invited you without your having to ask. Your support for me and the program has been tremendous. Thanks!"

After he hung up, Willie thought to himself about what he had requested for Dan Benson, "I already gave President Palmer the name of one good prospect today that I might have to coach against next year. I sure don't want him to have that one, too."

46

Later that same Monday afternoon, Willie told all his coaches that, since Thanksgiving was that Thursday, he'd like them all to come in on Wednesday morning for a quick meeting before taking off for the four day weekend. The next morning he got a call from the head of the school's legal department, who told him that he would have a few copies of a contract for Dan Benson by midday. He told Willie that could have his secretary run over to him to him as soon as they were ready. Willie thanked and then planned his strategy for presenting the contract.

At about 1PM, the legal secretary arrived with a sealed manila envelope for Willie.

He opened it and read it carefully. After he was convinced that it contained what he was looking for, he went down to Dan Benson's office to ask him to join him in his office. Dan was busy finishing his notes on the various games during the season and figuring out some things they need to improve upon the following year.

Willie said, "Dan, could you come down to my office for a couple of minutes?" Dan nodded his head. As he got up he said, "What's up Coach?"

"You'll find out soon enough Dan, replied Willie. Once they were in Willie's office, Willie shut the door and said, "I think that your joining my staff this year was a key factor in our successful season. You came up with that Triple Option Offense after we lost Al Nelson. It was just the shot in the arm we needed when we were in deep trouble. In appreciation, I would like to relieve you of your responsibilities with our offensive line and promote you to the position of our Offensive Coordinator. I think the Triple Option is going to become our offense from this time forward, and since you are the man who knows it better than any of us, I want you to be our Offensive Coordinator. You should get off to a great start with it next season, since we have Reggie King coming back for his senior year to run it. It seems all we have to do is to find and groom his successor and back up for next season."

Dan said, "Thanks, Willie, I can't begin to tell you how excited this makes me feel. Coming down here, from being an assistant at Oakmont under that ogre, Swindle, is one of the best things that ever happened to me. I really appreciate this opportunity, Willie,"

Willie smiled at him and said, "Do you appreciate it enough to agree to a 20% pay increase and get a contract to coach for four more years here at Mosby?" Dan was stunned.

He said, "Are you kidding me Willie? You told me this spring that you had a five year contract, so that means we will be together the whole time. Thanksgiving is supposed to be this Thursday, but you've made me it happen for me today."

Willie told him, "You've earned it, Dan. I talked to President Howard and told him that I would like this promotion for you. He agreed to what I wanted and had his legal staff prepare an agreement. Here it is, and all it needs is your signature on the document, and we have a deal." Dan was almost in tears as he signed.

Willie gave him his copy and kept the other one to return to the legal department. He shook hands with Dan and said, "It's great having you aboard Coach."

The next day, Willie met with all the coaches and congratulated them on a great season and told them that, effective January 1st, they would be getting a 10% pay increase. He also announced that Dan Benson would become the new Offensive Coordinator. A number of the other coaches cheered and gave Dan a pat on the back. Then he said, "I know all of you are looking forward to a four day vacation starting tomorrow on Thanksgiving. I'm sorry, but there's been a change. I want you to take all of next week off as well, and we will get together a week from next Monday to begin planning for next year. And there is one last bit of news to announce. President Howard has given us the okay to have a season-ending buffet banquet and awards celebration for the team and the coaches. It will be sometime after Thanksgiving and before Christmas. Once we get the date nailed down, I will put the word out to everyone."

Jack Johnson said, "How about a Mosby cheer for the best Head Coach around." All the assistants jumped up and joined in a round of "Here we go Mosby Men…here we go."

The meeting broke up and everyone wished their friends and associates the best for Thanksgiving. It had been a great season, and now it had been a great day for all the coaches at Mosby.

There was some activity and excitement going on that day at the *Estate*. The big D.C. area construction company that had been hired to do the work for the expansion project had arrived with a number of trucks. They were delivering materials and unloading machinery at the locations where the construction would take place. Preston Wickersham and Tom Throckmorton returned to Saint Bartholomew's Hall after classes. They were preparing to pack up and head home to Richmond for Thanksgiving when they ran into Troy Barksdale III coming out the front door. He directed their attention to the big bulldozer and front end loader sitting on the grass right next to the Hall.

He said, "Can you believe they are going to build a lodge for the coloreds right next to us? When I first heard about this proposed Booker T. Washington Lodge, I thought they would put it off somewhere by itself. Instead, they have had the audacity to stick the damn thing practically on top of us. I'm sure my father is going to have something to say about this when I get home. He might even call up President Howard and tell him to move it somewhere else. He's a very important guy and you can bet that President Howard will listen to him."

Willie was the last to leave the athletic offices that day, since all the other coaches had taken off. He had told his secretary to go home before he had his meeting. He went to his car, started it up, and began his short drive home. The Fleetwoods were singing **Come Softly to Me** on the car radio, and he was looking forward to having a few days off. It would be wonderful to spend some time with Sally and little Bobby, who was getting bigger and cuter every day. It had been a long, tough and sometimes stressful season, but his home was like a port in the storm, and Sally had been a wonderful wife and mother. He felt very blessed and thankful for all the good things that had been happening to him over the last couple of years.

Sally was waiting and holding little Bobby in her arms when he came in the door. He gave both of them a kiss and a hug. Then he kicked off his shoes, flopped on the sofa and let out a big sigh of relief. Sally had started a fire in the family room fireplace and the two of them enjoyed a glass of wine before having a tasty light dinner. Later, when they sat down at the table, Sally said, "I didn't want to feed you too much tonight, because I plan to stuff you tomorrow."

Willie laughed and said, "That's fine with me. I'm looking forward to your usual Thanksgiving feast, and I know my mama is, too. I'll head over to Alexandria tomorrow morning and get her so that we will be back here way before we have supper around 4. I know she is going to want to try and spoil Bobby rotten, but hopefully he will be re-trainable after I take her back home on Sunday afternoon."

Sally smiled and said, "I hope so too, since I'm the one who has to deal with him most of the time. I plan on putting you to work on some of that dealing while you're here on vacation. Don't you go thinking that you're going to just lie around and watch TV every day."

The next morning, Willie ate breakfast, then jumped in his car and drove up to Alexandria. He had the car radio set to his favorite station; he heard some great songs along the way. They ranged from upbeat tunes like Lloyd Price's **Personality** and **Stagger Lee** and Freddie Cannon blasting out **Tallahassee Lassie** to some easy listening songs like Frankie Avalon's **Venus** and the Platters playing **Smoke Gets in Your Eyes**. Upon arriving at his mama's apartment, Velma had her little suitcase all packed and was all ready to go. She gave her boy a big hug and kiss and told him how proud she was of him. He told her that the reason he had done pretty well so far was because he had the best mama in the world.

Upon arriving back in Warrenton, Velma was anxious to see her grandson and get a tour of Willie and Sally's new home. She hadn't seen it since they moved in that past summer since Willie was so busy coaching. Sally had driven up to Alexandria a couple of times to let her see Bobby, but as far as Velma was concerned, she hadn't seen enough of him and she planned on doing just what Willie was afraid of…spoiling him rotten.

That afternoon, Willie was watching the game between the Green Bay Packers and the mighty Detroit Lions on TV. Green Bay, under their rookie head coach Vince Lombardi, won the game in an upset 24-17. Green Bay had been pretty pathetic for a number of years and Willie wondered if they were going to do any better under this unproven newcomer. He told Sally, "This win by Green Bay was probably just a fluke. Their coach is just a rookie head coach. It will probably take him years to turn the team around."

Sally replied, "Willie, you were just a rookie coach yourself last year. You have been pretty successful haven't you? I wouldn't be too quick to judge Coach Lombardi if I were you. He might just turn out to be a good coach someday."

Willie thought about what Sally had said and, as usual, she was right. All he had needed was a chance. Who knows? Maybe that's all Coach Lombardi needs too.

Sally's meal was delicious. They enjoyed a big turkey with a tasty sausage stuffing and gravy that they would probably be eating for days to come. She also had turnip greens, sweet potatoes, roasted carrots and cornbread. Willie thought he'd died and gone to heaven. That was before she served the warm pecan pie with vanilla ice cream on top for dessert. Once he took a bite of it, he was sure he was at the Pearly Gates. His wife was not only sweet and good looking; she was also a fabulous cook. Yes, he sure did have a lot to be thankful for.

The Hairston family enjoyed the rest of the holiday weekend. On that Sunday, he took Sally and Bobby and his mama to church. Following the service, a lot of the members at the Second Baptist Church were delighted to meet her. Once she heard all their praise for Willie, it made her a very proud mama, not that she wasn't already.

47

The big construction project at Mosby University was in full swing on the Monday after Thanksgiving. Huge holes were being dug in the ground and foundations being poured in a rush before it got too cold. There were lots of workers and equipment all around the *Estate*. The roar of bulldozer engines and flying dust was going to be very annoying to the most of the members of Saint Bartholomew's Hall. Preston Wickersham was afraid it was going to trigger a reoccurrence of his childhood asthma, while Troy Barksdale was just furious about what was happening in general. He was glad that he would be graduating in June and returning to Richmond, where he had a job waiting for him at Tidewater National Bank. However, he felt sorry for all the other members who would have to put up with this change in the formerly tranquil environment they had always enjoyed. A lot of the changes going on at Mosby were disgraceful as far as he was concerned.

President Bob Howard didn't share the opinions of either the senior Mr. Barksdale or his son. As he sat in his office, he felt that the changes he had instituted at the university had been positive, and that the school was making a bold move forward. He was proud of the success of his desegregation effort and the fact that the beautiful Piedmont Pinnacle Trophy had been retained for another year. As he thought about all of these things, he realized that his making it possible for Willie Hairston to become the first Negro student in the school's history had been the catalyst for many positive things that had occurred since. He was also proud of the fact that, when so many people in Virginia were clinging to the past, he was moving forward and so was his university. He was smiling as these thoughts flashed through his mind.

Two weeks later, in mid-December, the team held its season ending banquet and awards dinner. President Robert Howard IV was the honored guest. He congratulated the team and the coaches on their undefeated year. He told them how happy he was that the school had retained the coveted Piedmont Pinnacle Trophy. Winning it the previous season had been the first time in many years. He also mentioned that they had broken all previous home game attendance records this season. He said that he fully expected that season ticket sales would increase the next year, even if some ticket holders might not renew their seats. Other special guests included Billy Fryer and David Seligman. Their contributions to the team's success were recognized by Willie. Al Nelson and Reggie King were named as the co-winners of the Offensive Players of the Year, and Tane Maaka was named the Defensive Player of the Year.

Reggie modestly said he didn't feel he deserved it, since he really played only one whole game on offense that year. Willie laughed and said, "Yeah, that true. However, the one you played and won was the most important game of the year." The players applauded. Each member of the team was then called up to the podium and recognized for their contributions. Willie expressed his opinion that it had taken a tremendous effort by everyone to make the season successful. The festive evening came to an end as graduating senior center Dan Kojak led the entire room in a round of the school cheer, "*Here we go Mosby Men…here we go!*"

Epilogue

Oakmont University's President Ralph Palmer was busy interviewing a number of possible candidates following the firing of Irv Swindle as the school's Athletic Director and Head Football Coach. He would have loved to have persuaded Willie Hairston to take the job. However, he understood and respected Willie's loyalty to Mosby University and his counterpart there in the person of President Bob Howard. After talking with numerous qualified men, who expressed an interest in the position, he selected Cedaredge Coach Dick Myers to fill the position. He was very thankful that Willie Hairston had recommended Coach Myers, who had just completed the final year in his contract at Cedaredge and had led them to a 7-3 record. He thought that Cedaredge had been very foolish not to renew his contract before the season ended. As a result, they had let an excellent coach get away. It was their loss and Oakmont's gain as far as he was concerned.

Another positive was that Coach Myers came with a reputation for being a true gentleman, respectful to everyone he dealt with. That was a sharp contrast to the embarrassment of having a person like Irv Swindle out in public view as a representative of the university. President Palmer didn't know if Coach Myers would enjoy the same level of success on the field as Swindle had enjoyed, but he felt that he had the potential for doing so. He was pleased that Coach Myers made a point to meet with each one of Swindle's former assistants once he arrived. Myers decided to retain most of them, and they seemed delighted to be rid of their tyrannical former boss. A couple of them expressed their disappointment that Swindle had been fired. They were probably hoping to join Swindle where ever he ended up, so Myers didn't offer them positions on his staff.

It didn't take long for Swindle to hire a fairly notorious lawyer from Philadelphia named Sammy Schlickovitz to represent him and then file a wrongful termination suit against Oakmont University. In response, Oakmont hired Howard Duncan, the famed gentlemanly trial attorney from the D.C. area to represent them. Both sides waived having a jury and were content to have a judge make a decision in the case.

When they came before esteemed Judge Thomas Brooke, Swindle's lawyer presented the outstanding won/loss record during his tenure as Oakmont's Head Football Coach as evidence of his outstanding ability. He argued that his premature firing, prior to the end of his contract, had not only cost Coach Swindle the money he was to receive for his final year, but had damaged his ability to find work elsewhere. He asked for a declarative judgment in favor of his client and that he be awarded the amount of a full year's salary. He also asked that triple that amount be paid as a punitive judgment for the damages Swindle had suffered to his previously impeccable reputation. Following that, Schlickovitz sat down.

The impeccably attired Howard Duncan approached the bench after his counterpart Schlickovitz had argued his case. He presented a copy of Swindle's employment contract to the judge and entered it into evidence. He told the judge that he would like to defer talking about it right then. Instead he'd like to call a witness. The judge allowed him to proceed.

Mr. Duncan said, "Your honor, I'd like to call Miss Janice Phillips at this time as a witness." After she was sworn in, Oakmont's attorney asked her a few questions.

"Miss Phillips, what is your relationship, to the plaintiff Mr. Swindle?

She responded and said, "I was his former secretary at Oakmont University."

"Can you please describe the events that took place at your office on Monday November 23rd following Mr. Swindle's returning there after his meeting with the president of Oakmont University? I realize that you already provided the answer to this question during discovery testimony, but I would like the judge to hear you describe what happened in your own words."

She said, "He began thrown things around the office and even threw something at me too. He looked very angry. I was scared, so I ran out of the building." Mr. Duncan thanked her and she stepped down after the plaintiff's lawyer said that he didn't have any questions.

Attorney Duncan then called Jimmy Wilson to the stand. After he was sworn in he was asked to tell the judge what his relationship to Mr. Swindle was. He said, "I have been a player on Oakmont University's football team for the last two years."

"What position did you play?"

He responded and said, "Defensive back."

"Did anything unusual happen to you during the game against Mosby University on Saturday November 21st, 1959?"

Wilson said, "After one of Mosby's touchdowns in the second half, I had missed a tackle. When I came off the field, Coach Swindle shoved me pretty hard and called me a few names."

Swindle stood up and yelled out, "He's lying. He wasn't worth a damn as a player, and he's in here trying to cover his ass."

The judge looked at Swindle and said, "Sit down and be quiet, Mr. Swindle. I will not tolerate that kind of outburst in my courtroom. If you do that again or use any more profanity in here, I will find you in contempt of court."

A chastened Swindle sat down, but his face was bright red and his eyes were squinty. It was obvious to everyone that he was furious.

Attorney Duncan then said to the judge, "I have filmed evidence to support Mr. Wilson's assertions, which were entered into discovery, and I will be happy to have it played at this time if you would like to see it or have any questions as to what happened that day."

Sam Schlickovitz, the attorney for Swindle, quickly said, "We won't be questioning Mr. Wilson's testimony today so showing the film will not be required at this time."

Swindle looked at him and said loudly, "What the hell are you doing? Don't let that Duncan guy get away with this. The judge glared at him sternly and advised Mr. Schlickovitz that he should control his client.

After that exchange, Oakmont's attorney called Jim Rockmont to the stand. After he was sworn in, he was asked what his relationship to Mr. Swindle was. He revealed that he had been an assistant football coach at Oakmont and worked under Irv Swindle.

When asked about what happened at the end of the game against Mosby University, Mr. Rockmont replied, "I asked him if he was going to go out on the field for the customary hand shake after the game with Mosby's coach. He yelled at me and said he wasn't going to do that, and then he began yelling at the officials who worked the game. He also yelled at some of the coaches and players. Then he started making threats against some of the fans in the stands. At that point in time, Walter Quimby, another Oakmont assistant coach, and I escorted him off the field to the locker room before he got into more trouble."

Swindle was looking daggers at Coach Rockmont and started to get up, but his attorney grabbed him and kept him in his seat. Mr. Duncan then told the judge that he could have Walter Quimby, who was in the audience, come up and verify what Mr. Rockmont had just said under oath. However, he would waive doing that unless the plaintiff's attorney would like the opportunity to cross examine him. Swindle's lawyer, Mr. Schlickovitz agreed to waive that testimony which had already been recorded during the discovery process.

Then Howard Duncan asked the judge if he might call Irv Swindle to the stand. Swindle grinned and said in a low voice to his attorney, "Now I can straighten that wise ass lawyer out."

After being sworn in, Mr. Duncan addressed the judge and told him that the paper he was holding in his hand was Coach Swindle's contract with Oakmont University. It had already been entered into evidence during discovery. He said that he would like to ask Mr. Swindle to read a certain portion of the provisions that the contract contained. He then handed it to Irv Swindle and asked him to read the highlighted part.

Swindle picked it up and read the following, "If you are fired for any infraction of the rules set forth in the agreement, you will not be entitled to any future compensation."

Mr. Duncan continued, "Here is a list of violations and unacceptable actions that would bring disgrace to the school. I see that one of them includes any abuse of officials, players, and team personnel. Could you please read this section, Mr. Swindle?"

Swindle looked at it and said, "Any physical abuse or threatening the players or the team personnel shall be considered a major violation and grounds for immediate termination. If such a termination is a made under this provision, no further compensation shall be made by Oakmont University, and none shall be expected by the guilty party."

Howard Duncan then said, "It seems very clear to me, and I hope Judge Brooke as well, that you clearly violated your contract with Oakmont and not the other way around. I would ask the judge today to rule in favor of the defendant Oakmont University and that you be awarded no damages in this case."

Swindle stood up, sweating profusely, and said in a loud voice, "Oakmont owes me for all the games I won for them. Just because they hired some smart-ass lawyer to represent them doesn't mean that they don't."

Judge Brooke banged his gavel down hard and said, "I find in favor of the defendant in this case and rule that no money or damages are due to the plaintiff. I also sentence the plaintive, Mr. Swindle to 30 days in jail for his actions in the courtroom today, because I hereby find him in contempt of court. Bailiff, please take Mr. Swindle into custody and remove him from this courtroom. All of us here have had our fill of him today."

The following year, in early 1960, a big group of members from the Serpents Den Lodge, at the suggestion of Roger Rambeaux, made the decision to go down to New Orleans during Mardi Gras. They agreed it might be fun and a change from returning to Fort Lauderdale during Spring Break. In addition to a number of individual cars, they took the Snakemobile and Roger's pick-up truck, which had the lodge catapult bolted onto the truck bed. Upon arriving in New Orleans, they joined all the other people in the celebrations on Bourbon Street and had a ball. Roger's uncle bought a lot of colorful beads from a buddy of his that was a wholesaler. The Serps had a great time using the catapult to shooting beads into the crowd. They marveled at the obvious appreciation that some of the young ladies demonstrated after they caught the beads.

All of the Serps managed to have a good time during Mardi Gras and do some pretty wild things. It was pretty amazing that most of them avoided being arrested for disturbing the peace and various other acts of unruly behavior. In reality, the New Orleans police let a lot of conduct go during Mardi Gras. However, Garrett Gassman was the exception to that rule. He was arrested by the police shortly after he was caught shooting off a big cache of cherry bombs. The explosion was responsible an accident involving one of the floats which was being pulled by a team of horses. The exploding cherry bombs apparently spooked them. They took off out of control and raced down the street. The float they were pulling eventually overturned when the horses crashed into the float in front of it. Fortunately no one was injured. Gassman was incarcerated and later sentenced to 30 days in jail. Because of that, he had to be left there by his lodge mates. Cadillac deVille drove Garrett's car back. The other Serps couldn't wait for him to serve out his sentence, because they all had to return to school.

Prior to Garrett's release from jail and his return to Warrenton, Cadillac took the car on a raid to Mary Washington. It was an unusually mild day for February when he arrived. He discovered that, if he put the top down and turned up the radio, he could attract a whole lot of *ghosts*. He was amazed that he didn't even have to perform a coin trick to get their attention. He took three of them with him to the nearby little juke box joint for some beers and dancing. It was like magic!

Due to his absence, and missing so many classes, Garrett failed the second semester of his senior year. However, he vowed to come back and finish school that fall. The good news was that he still had a year of eligibility since he had quit the team his sophomore year under the previous old coach before playing any games. Garrett told his coach that he wanted to play one more year. Willie was sorry for the trouble he had experienced as a result of his being too mischievous. However, he also was more than a little happy about the prospects of having him back. Willie had previously thought that he would be losing both Garrett Gassman and Ronnie Wall to graduation and was wondering if he would be able to find some good replacement receivers. Despite the new offense not emphasizing passing the ball, Willie figured Garrett would still be valuable in his role as an outside linebacker. Sometimes you get lucky, and while that luck can be either bad or good, Willie knew that he had been blessed to have more than his share of the good variety.

Reggie King was invited to become a youth assistant counselor at the Second Baptist Church in Warrenton, and he was happy to accept the offer. He began to serve the congregation in that capacity once the New Year arrived. Reggie enjoyed it so much that he told the pastor he might even want to go to a seminary after he got his BA degree and someday maybe even have a congregation of his own.

February 15th, 1960 came and went, but Troy Barksdale II had apparently been too busy to notice. An unopened letter from Mosby University had been lying on his desk for over a month. It was the ticket renewal notice for the Mosby Raiders football team's 1960 season. Mr. Barksdale was a busy man. Everyone knew that. He had more important issues to attend to including the upcoming Board meeting. It was at that meeting that he was going to have to explain how the bank had lost the Mosby University account.

There had been numerous requests for tickets arrive at the university ticket office following the successful 1959 season. Most of the people and organizations had to wait to learn if any would be available. Existing seat holders at John Singleton Mosby Memorial Stadium had the first right to renew, and nearly everyone understood that this policy was very fair.

Justin Webb, who managed the stadium ticket office at Mosby University, sent President Howard a memo on February 16th, 1960. It was a compilation of the season ticket sales. It listed the total sales as well as the number of tickets that had not been renewed. Upon receiving the report, Bob Howard noticed that Tidewater National Bank had not renewed their tickets. That didn't come as a surprise to him. However, he was a little amazed that the block hadn't been transferred to Marshall Holcome, based upon the conversation he had previously had with Troy Barksdale. He picked up the phone and put in a call to Ralph Mitchell at Franklin National Bank.

When Ralph came on the line, President Howard told about the block of 100 season tickets that were the best seats in the stadium. He also told Ralph that he would like to offer them to the nice people at

Franklin National, if they wanted them. Ralph Mitchell was delighted, but wondered if it would be possible to reserve about 70 instead. Bob Howard informed him that it would be no problem and that they could have ten seats beside each other for seven rows up right on the 50 yard line.

Mosby President Bob Howard had been approached with another idea by Head Football Coach Willie Hairston following the team's season ending banquet. Willie had told him how so many members of the Second Baptist Church were very loyal and enthusiastic fans of the team. It was a shame they couldn't afford to have better seats at the games. The ones in the north end zone bleachers weren't very comfortable. Willie asked if the university might consider making some better seats in the west stands available on a reduced cost basis, if the church was willing to commit to buying a good sized block of seats. Bob Howard reflected back on that conversation, thought about it, and agreed. He called Willie and asked him to get in touch with the pastor at the Second Baptist Church. He wanted to see if they would like to have 30 of the best seats in the stadium for half their regular cost.

It didn't take long for Willie to report back to him. He told the president that the church would love to have them, but didn't have the funds to buy them. Upon hearing that, Bob Howard came up with a better idea. He would personally make a donation to the church in the amount of the cost of the seats. That contribution would enable them to buy the seats. He would get a tax deduction. As far as he was concerned, it was a Win-Win Deal.

Bob Howard's kindness endeared him and Mosby University to many members of Warrenton's colored community. The pastor told Willie that he would even be willing to talk to any future prospective applicants and assure them that they would be very welcome at the university. The word began to spread, and from that time forward, many of the top black scholar athletes in the country began to want to enroll at the formerly 100% white school. That made both Bob Howard and Willie Hairston very pleased. The admission standards remained high, but the increased opportunities at Mosby University became a beacon of hope for many young men of color, whose educational aspirations had been held down by many politicians and others, for way too many years.

Marshall Holcome was very disappointed when he learned that Troy Barksdale II had let the deadline pass and the bank lost their block of seats. This was the final straw as far as Holcome was concerned. He had finally grown tired of Barksdale's arrogant attitude. He felt that it had caused the bank to lose the Mosby University account. As a member of Tidewater National Bank's Board of Directors, he was only one of many on the board who were considering replacing Barksdale as president. They saw the need to have someone more forward looking as their president and Barksdale was stuck in the past.

The End

Author's Notes

MOSBY'S RAIDERS RETURN is a work of fiction, and any resemblance of the characters in the book to actual persons living or dead is purely coincidental. However, there are a number of things in the book that are indeed a fact. I will attempt to describe them below.

Obviously, many of the geographical places in the book actually exist. The idyllic town of Warrenton, Virginia, is located in the beautiful horse county in Northern, Virginia just south of Middleburg. Not only does it exist, but it was the place John Mosby called his home. Following his death, he was put to rest in Warrenton, and his remains are buried there today. However, there is no fine men's university there which bears his name. It seemed like the logical town in which to place this fictional school. With respect to schools, none of the schools that were Mosby University's opponents in the story actually exist, even though most of them proved to be worthy foes on the gridiron.

Other things referred to in the book that had a basis in history are noted below:

The **TUSKEGEE AIRMEN** were the first African –American military air group in the history of the United States armed forces. The US military, as well as most of the federal government, was racially segregated during World War II. A pilot training program for African-Americans began in June of 1941 at the Tuskegee Institute in Alabama. The unit was called the 99th Pursuit Squadron. The squadron eventually became part of the all black 332nd Fighter Group. When the pilots were finally given the chance to prove themselves, they flew bomber escort missions over Sicily, Normandy, Italy and Germany. They painted the tails of their P-47's and later their P-51 Mustangs, red. This practice led to their nickname, the Red-Tails. However, the bomber crews they escorted called them the Red Tail Angels. The 332nd Fighter Group received a Distinguished Unit Citation and individual pilots of the unit earned at total of 96 Distinguished Flying Crosses during the war. They were the subject of the 2012 movie **Red Tails**.

J.R. EASON is widely recognized as one of the most talented female sculptors in America. Her works have been collected throughout the USA and Canada and are represented in top art galleries around the world. Originally from Idaho, she now makes Scottsdale, Arizona her home. The author is the proud owner of some of her fabulous works.

The **MOSQUE** Theater in Richmond, Virginia described in the book is an actual place. In fact, it is one of the best known buildings in the city and is located next to historic Monroe Park. It was built in the mid 1920's and used as temple shrine by the Shriners organization there. It featured a couple of tall minarets and extensive gold plating. It was later bought by the city of Richmond in the mid 1940's and turned into a theater that had 4,600 seats. It was later refurbished. Over the years, it was a very popular venue for visiting artists, and it has hosted many events. Many of the most famous entertainers in America have performed there. The name was later changed to the Landmark Theater.

RACIAL DESCRIMINATION in the late 50's in Virginia most certainly existed. Everyone knows that Richmond had been the capital of the Confederacy during the Civil War. That war had been over for many years, yet many of the old prejudices and attitudes remained. After the U.S. Supreme Court ruled against the "separate but equal doctrine" in the landmark case, *Brown v. Board of Education*, the governor of Virginia and the State Board of Education refused to integrate the schools in defiance of that ruling. Virginia voters and their representatives then made the decision to fund private schools in order to maintain segregation. After Virginia U.S. Senator Harry Byrd, Sr. advocated a policy of Massive Resistance to the Supreme Court's ruling in 1956, the state legislature passed a resolution that the Supreme Court's decision had been an illegal encroachment against their state's rights.

Later in 1958, Virginia's Governor Lindsay Almond threatened to shut down any school that was forced to integrate. He actually did force some schools to close, but they were later reopened after rulings were made in the Federal Courts. These policies had a negative impact on both public education and race relations in the state for many years. Finally, in 1971, in response to the protests by parents against the school closings, a revision to the Constitution of Virginia was made that included some of the strongest provisions on public education of any state in the entire country.

Readers of either the original **LEGACY of the GRAY GHOST** or its sequel **MOSBY'S RAIDERS RETURN** might find it hard to believe these days that some of the decisions made by Mosby President Bob Howard would be a cause for concern. When he, as the president of the elite all-white Mosby University, allowed a black man to attend and become its first graduate, it was guaranteed to upset some of his alumni. Then, to hire an all-black coaching staff for their all-white football team seemed preposterous. Finally, allowing qualified young African-American men to matriculate and play on their team was the last straw for some people who were clinging to their old Jim Crow beliefs. However, that didn't deter President Howard from moving forward. Readers who have finished these two tales will probably come to their own conclusions as to whether or not he was right.

BOOKER T. WASHINGTON was born into slavery in 1856. He later became the dominant leader of blacks in the United States from 1890 until his death in 1915. He was an educator, orator, author, and advisor to some presidents and spoke out in behalf of Southern blacks who had been denied the ability to vote by the local legislatures. He was also named the first president of the Tuskegee Institute in Alabama in 1881. Over the years, he associated with some of the richest and most powerful businessmen and politicians in America, and because of those contacts, many educational opportunities became available for blacks that previously weren't available. Later in his life he was criticized by the NAACP and called the "Great Accommodator" for his belief that cooperation with supportive whites was the best way to overcome racism in America.

DR. HOMER RICE was a native of Kentucky and went to Fort Thomas Highlands High School in the northern part of the state, just south of Cincinnati, Ohio. After high school, he went on to Centre College where he played quarterback. He later returned to Fort Thomas Highland High School as their football coach. While there, he compiled an amazing record of 101-9-7 by using formations and plays that allowed his outmanned players to use quickness and deception to defeat bigger and stronger opponents. He revolutionized football by developing the **Triple Option Offense** which had never been seen by anyone prior to him using it. He later coached at Kentucky, Oklahoma, Cincinnati, and Rice Universities as well as coaching the Cincinnati Bengals in the NFL. Later, he became the Athletic Director at the University of North Carolina, Rice University, and was the Director of Athletics at Georgia Tech in Atlanta from 1980 to 1997. Each year, the NCAA Division IA Athletic Directors Association presents the prestigious HOMER RICE AWARD to the worthy Athletic Director recipients in his honor.

The HAKA is a traditional war cry or challenge of the native Maori people of New Zealand. It was usually performed by warriors prior to a battle to proclaim their strength and to intimidate their opposition. The New Zealand rugby team's practice of performing a HAKA before their matches has given it international fame. The HAKA always employs facial contortions, sticking out the tongue, rolling the eyes, slapping of the hands against the body and stamping of the feet. Guttural grunts, cries and chants are part of it as well. Ka Mate means –It is Death and Ka Ora means – It is Life.

REP DREATH – A term used in the late 50's to describe someone who was the essence of preppy tweediness.

TRIPLE Option 1- Playside Defensive Tackle Rushes **Outside** Shoulder of Offensive Tackle
To the right   Quarterback gives ball to Fullback on Dive Play up the middle

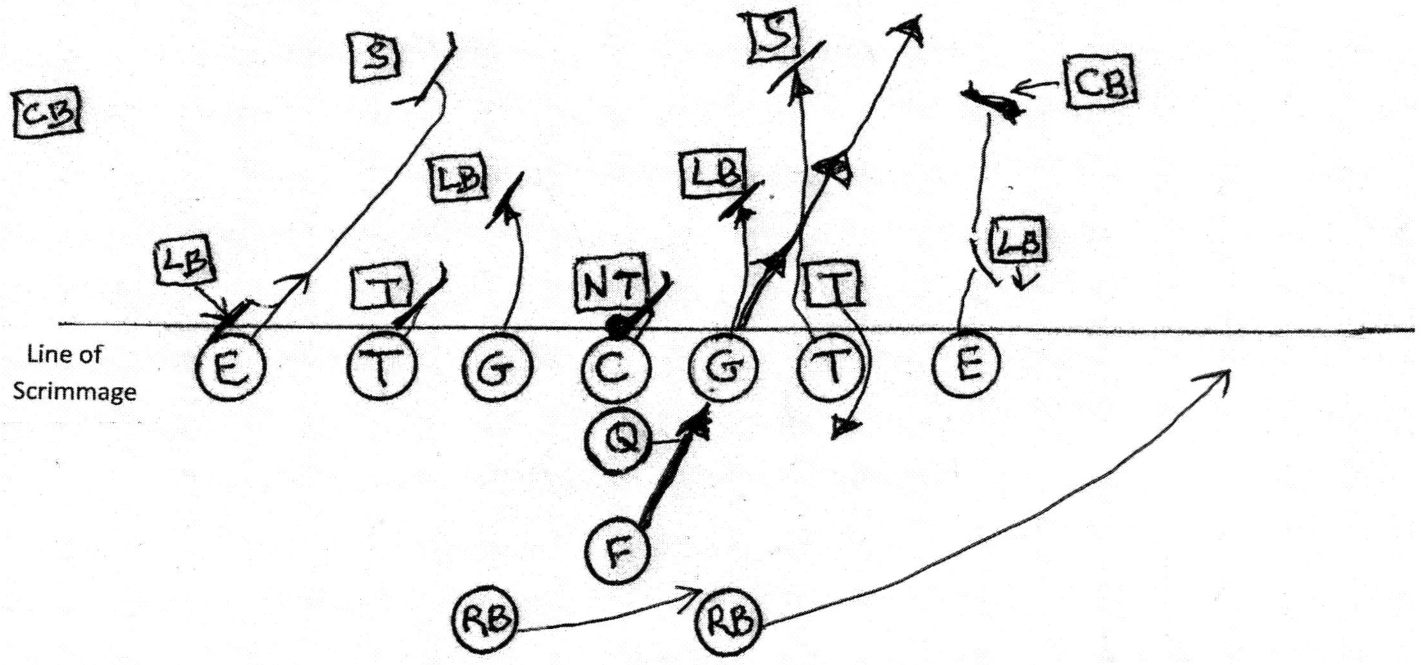

GERRY A. ZIMMERMAN 307

TRIPLE Option 2- Playside Defensive Tackle Rushes **Inside** Shoulder of Offensive Tackle
To the right Quarterback pulls out ball and continues to the sideline to the right
QB sees that Defensive End/linebacker has penetrated backfield and
his shoulders are not square to the QB. QB plants foot, keeps the ball,
and heads down field behind blocking of his tackle and end

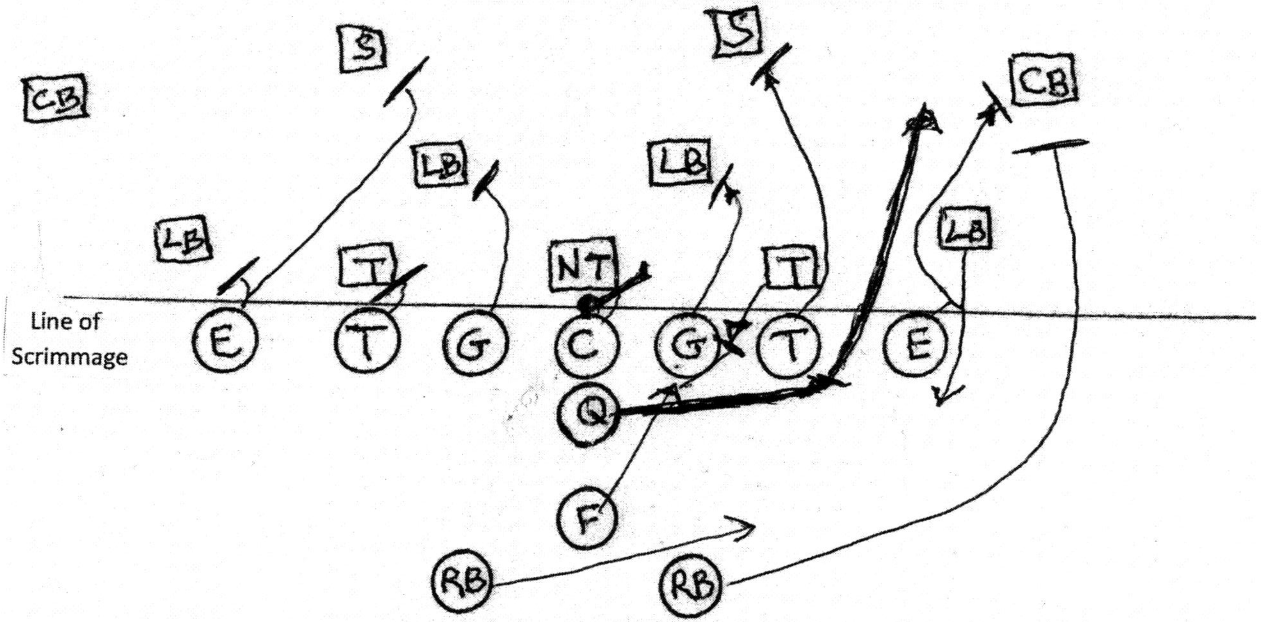

TRIPLE Option 3 - Playside Defensive Tackle Rushes **Inside** Shoulder of Offensive Tackle
To the right Quarterback pulls ball out and continues to the sideline to the right QB sees that Defensive End/linebacker has turned his shoulders toward him. QB pitches ball to trailing Running Back who follows the blocking of the playside running back and goes down field by the sideline

About the Author

Gerry A. Zimmerman is a graduate of the University of Virginia, where he received a B.A. degree in History while pursuing a Pre-Med course of instruction. Upon leaving college he served as a U.S. Naval Intelligence Officer for four years on active duty and then sixteen years in the reserves. After his active duty naval service, he enjoyed success in sales and management while in the Insurance and Investment business and coaching football. He later went into the Cable TV Industry as an investment banker and a broker and was successful in that business as he personally handled over $1,000,000,000 of Cable TV transactions and eventually became president of his own company. Originally hailing from the Washington, D.C. area and Alexandria, Virginia, the author lived in Colorado for many years prior to his moving from Vail to his current residence in Scottsdale, AZ in 2004. His book, **Legacy of the Gray Ghost** was named as the Best Southern Fiction Novel of 2011 and also honored as the Best Historical Fiction book of that year. He enjoys golf, tennis, skiing, traveling, photography, playing the piano, fine wine, gourmet food, surfing the Web and most of all, the company of good friends and interesting people.

QUICK ORDER FORM

MOSBY'S RAIDERS RETURN

and/or

LEGACY of the GRAY GHOST

For **postal orders – Send to**:

Gerry A. Zimmerman.com

39081 N. 102nd Way

Scottsdale, AZ 85262

Name: _____

Address: _____

City:_____ State:_____ Zip:_____

Check which book ordered:

    Mosby's Raiders Return   _____

    Legacy of the Gray Ghost   _____

Price for each book: $14.99 USA   _____

    $24.99 Canada   _____

Note: Orders for both books at once will be discounted @ only $24.99 + S&H

Shipping &   Media Mail $8.01   _____

Handling: 1st Class Priority Mail $10.01   _____

Sales Tax: Please add 8.95% for AZ residents   _____

TOTAL ENCLOSED   _____

Or go to www.GerryAZimmerman.com to order using credit cards or PayPal